Black Mafia

Black Mafia

Mikell Davis

The Secret Society

Stepping Stone Publishing
A division of Donaldson&Davis Publishing

Third Printing

This book is a work of fiction. Names, characters, places and incidents are products of the author's imagination or are used fictitiously. Any resemblance to actual events or locales or persons, living or dead is entirely coincidental.

Editors | **Crystal Frager and Mikell Davis**
Creative Director | **Anthony Van Dunk**, AVD Graphics
Design | **bill butt** for AVD Graphics
Photography | **Edward B. Lea**
Typesetting | **AVD Graphics**
Proofreader | **Shanene Pinder**
Illustration | Mo' Funky Fresh • **David Sagorski 1993**
Type design | Flange • **Les Usherwood 1981**
| Calvert • **Margaret Calvert 1980**
| CapGun Slab • **Wilson Capellan 2001**

Printed in Canada
ISBN 0-9714883-2-0

Stepping Stone Publishing
A division of Donaldson&Davis Publishing

***THIS BOOK IS DEDICATED TO MY MENTOR* LLOYD ANDRE MILLER**

"NEED CASH TO LIVE WITH, the beat goes on. Everyday is a hustle the heat goes on. Funny things happen when the years chasing money unfolds and the only thing worse than getting old is not getting old. Niggas stay low like 64's with shitting gold's and watch for hoes with form fitting clothes and I hope you shine, see many wrinkles and enough memories to last you two lifetimes but you can't knock the hustle."

Infamous Jay-Z

Contents

Contents more

Chapter One Atlantic City, New Jersey

Making a Small Fortune

Christopher walked into the grocery store. He was wearing a long dirty overcoat, a raggedy blue skullcap, and some old worn- down military combat boots. All of this to conceal his appearance and help him perform his shoplifting task. It was January the second and it had been snowing heavily for the last two days. Christopher brushed his overcoat off, shook his head in order to shake snow off of it, but he didn't remove his hat.

Christopher was brown-skinned, 5'11" with a nice looking face and square chin. He had dark brown serious looking eyes and black shiny hair.

Christopher walked up the first aisle directly past the security booth. As soon as he passed the security booth he caught the attention of the guard. Christopher cut a right into the aisle that carried the spices and placed a couple of items in the small cart he was carrying. He glanced around and discreetly placed a couple of items in his pockets. Then he entered another aisle and repeated this practice. When he was done he decided to head for the register.

As Christopher started walking towards the cash register, one of the security guards popped up. Christopher paused and acted like he was reading the ingredients on the back of one of his items.

The guard just laughed and chuckled to himself. He had been through this scene a million times before. Every time a shoplifter got caught shoplifting, he did something stupid to give himself away or make himself look suspicious.

Christopher and the security guard met in the middle of the aisle. The store was due to close at 9:30 and the security guard wasn't in the mood for any unnecessary bullshit.

"Excuse me sir," the security guard said. He was medium height, and dark-skinned. Christopher would easily be able to take him if he had too.

"Yes," Christopher answered.

"Do you want to pay for those items you have in your pockets?" The guard smiled because he had been through this a thousand times, the part where the shoplifter plays dumb was coming up next.

"I don't have anything on me," Christopher responded but the guard could tell by the expression on his face that he was lying.

The guard just shook his head. Thieves never learn. The guard lifted his walkie- talkie. "John to base. Please send Lester to aisle two." The guard released the talk button on the transmitter.

"See what you made me do? Now if I find something on you I have to call the police and I don't feel like going downtown to press charges. Shit." The guard was pissed off. Maybe he'd let Christopher go.

"Okay," Christopher said surrendering. "Take this nasty shit." Christopher reached in his pocket and pulled out a couple of items. He threw them to the ground like he was being robbed.

The security guard shook his head. "You took more shit than that." He felt a little more comfortable now. At least the thief was returning some of the items.

"John, what's up?" said a young guy appearing out of nowhere. He was young and dark- skinned with a sloppy shaped body. He probably never worked out. He was about the same age as Christopher, in his last year of college.

"Everything's cool. He's leaving." John looked at Christopher waiting for him to pull the rest of the items out that he had hidden in his pants.

"What you got in your pants?" John continued.

"Nothing." Christopher looked towards Lester, the young security guard and he could tell he was getting pissed off. He was itching to hurt somebody or probably pissed off because he had a fucked-up name.

"Nah, fuck that. I'm tired of these motherfuckers.' Lester said and Christopher smiled. "Yo, let's take him to the back and strip search him."

Lester grabbed Christopher by the arm and Christopher didn't pull away. He must have been scared shitless the security guard thought to himself. Lester had been through this plenty of times before but it had been a couple of days since he took somebody to the back and fucked them up.

"I gave y'all everything," Christopher said in desperation.

"Shut the fuck up before I knock you the fuck out," Lester said grabbing one of Christopher's arms and leading him to the back. John didn't really want to but he grabbed Christopher's other arm and pulled him to the back where they cut the meat. The "Beating Room," as security called it.

Christopher didn't put up a fight. "Alright man. I'll give you what's in my pants."

"Shut the fuck up." Lester was pissed and ready to hurt somebody. As soon as they got to the freezers double door, Lester pushed Christopher through the door and Christopher slid across the floor on his hands. He was soaking wet and he was going to be sick in the morning. It was freezing in the back where they cut the meat.

Before Christopher could get to his feet Lester kicked Christopher in the ass. The blow made Christopher slide into one of the meat cutters where he hit his head against one of the machines.

"Hey, calm down. You're gonna kill him," John said. He didn't have the youth or the strength to fight and he didn't feel like wrestling with anybody.

Lester walked over to Christopher and swung his leg to kick him again. This time when he did, Christopher turned around and grabbed his foot while it was in the air.

Lester lost his footing and crashed to the floor. He was soaking wet too. It took him a second, but he jumped to his feet. Now Christopher and Lester were facing each other.

Christopher reached in his waistband and removed his gun. He pointed his gun at Lester's face. Lester's mouth dropped to the floor.

John stood there frozen.

"Oh shit," Lester said shocked.

"Shut the fuck up." Christopher smacked Lester across the face with his gun.

"Oh my God. Jesus help me." Lester crashed to his knees from the blow and clasped his hands in prayer.

"Shut the fuck up." Christopher reached in his pocket and removed a role of duct tape. It wasn't until that moment did either of them notice that Christopher was wearing gloves or that his hat was pulled down so far on his face that it concealed his identity.

Christopher threw John the duct tape. "You, tie this fat nasty looking mother fucker up." Lester was still on his knees trying to stop the blood dripping from his mouth.

Christopher stepped back while John the other security guard tied his friend up.

"And you better tie him up good." Christopher placed the gun to the back of John's head.

John jumped. "Oh God, please don't hurt us."

Christopher hit him in the back of his head. "Shut up cry baby." John screamed loudly. He was terrified. He started crying.

"Come on let's go to the front and don't try anything stupid or I will kill you."

Christopher grabbed John's arm and walked him back to the shopping area. They walked directly past the cashiers who were busy counting their registers down. None of them even looked up from what they were doing.

The manager was in the manager's office doing paper work for closing.

Christopher and John turned the corner to the entrance. When they got to the door, four men were standing outside of the door wearing black scull caps.

John unlocked the door and the others rushed inside pulling their scull caps down over their faces to conceal their identities. They were all carrying guns.

"A." One of the guys stopped dead in his tracks. "I want you to hit the manager's desk with me. Bee and Cee, you guys hit the registers. I want this shit done fast. We only have a couple of minutes. You heard me?" Christopher said and then he continued. "Dee, tie everybody up. John will help you."

Corey paused for a second, puzzled. "Who in the fuck is John?" "He is." Christopher pointed towards the security guard.

Corey placed his gun in his waistband and shook John's hand. "It's nice to meet you," Corey said after shaking the terrified security guards hands.

The manager's booth was a small booth that separated the entrance and the exit to the supermarket. Christopher walked up to the cage. The manager was in a chair working on the machine that looked like an enormous calculator, punching buttons and writing on pieces of papers that looked like receipts.

The manager didn't look up from his work until Christopher was directly in front of the cage with his gun sticking through the bars. Christopher pressed his gun against the manager's face.

It took a second before the manager realized what was happening.

"Listen, I know you got some kind of button back there that can alert the police and you probably got your feet on it right now, so this is the deal. If the police come, I'm blaming you and you'll be leaving out of here in a body bag. Do you understand me?"

The manager swallowed and shook his head yes.

"I understand," he replied.

"This is a stick up," Christopher announced.

The manager looked across the store and saw that the cashiers had disappeared. They were lying on the ground being tied up.

Two of the guys wearing masks were talking between themselves. "Should we take these food stamps?" one asked.

"Hell yeah, take everything."

Christopher and Corty were standing next to the door. "Hit the door," Christopher commanded.

Corty raised his gun and aimed at the doorknob. He pulled the trigger and the doorknob to the manager's office exploded.

The manager ducked like the gun was aimed at him. He was terrified.

Christopher walked to the door and kicked it open. The manager was still in the chair, but he had pushed himself to the corner. His eyes were as big as saucer pans.

Christopher grabbed him by the collar and lifted him to his feet. "Lay down."

"Please don't kill me. I've got a wife and kids." The manager dropped to his knees with tears in his eyes.

Christopher kicked him in the stomach and he fell over. "Tie this mother fucker up," Christopher said. When he walked into the office, the safe was open and full of money.

"Go get two paper bags and tell everybody it's time to get the fuck out of here." Corty disappeared and returned a couple of seconds later with the bags.

Christopher filled one of the bags immediately.

After Christopher filled the last bag he glanced at the surveillance camera system in the office and shot it. The manager jumped. He thought they were shooting at him. When he realized they weren't he started crying that he was quitting in the morning.

Christopher saw the light switch panel and turned the buttons in the opposite direction. The lights on the inside turned off and the one's on the outside came on. Christopher placed his gun in his waistband and exited the manager's office. He saw the cashiers lying on the floor hog-tied. He smiled because he was proud of his people.

Christopher exited the store and when he got outside. Frank was standing outside of the store pretending to be using the phone. He had an old '75 Caprice classic parked next to the phone booth. He was being paid as a look out.

As soon as Christopher walked out, Frank hung the telephone up.

Christopher smiled at him pulled his mask off and jumped in the car, they pulled off.

"You alright?" Franklin asked. He was light-skinned with beautiful black curly hair smooth skin and clean-shaven, a very nice looking man.

"I'm alright." Christopher was carrying two paper bags full of money. "How long have those cars been outside?" Christopher asked. They were blocks away from the grocery store now and headed to the getaway spot.

"A couple of minutes. Probably dudes coming to pick up their wives or something. There's nothing to worry about. I had my eyes wide open." He smiled after he said it. If those bags were full of money, then he had just made a small fortune.

Christopher and Franklin were best friends. Christopher was engaged to Franklin's cousin Tahwan. They had been dating since the 11th grade.

Christopher and Franklin sped off. Just then, the police rode pass with flashing sirens. Automatically Christopher and Franklin reached for their guns. Christopher slid down in his seat until they drove pass.

Chapter Two Atlantic City, New Jersey

This is Only The Beginning

Frank and Christopher pulled up to David's Bar and Strip Club. It was on Rhode Island and Arctic Avenue way up in the Inlet, a dilapidated section of Atlantic City. David and Mr. Gaston were partners. They controlled all the numbers in the Atlantic City Inlet section before the casinos came. After the casinos came their gambling empire was destroyed.

David's used to be a small casino but after Resorts, the first casino, was completed he went out of business. David placed his energy into making money by selling heroin and speed. Legally the bar was very profitable. Resorts International Casino Hotel had only been completed a month and already David and his associates recognized the potential. The city was in the process of building two more casinos by the time 1980 rolled around and they knew Atlantic City would never be the same. David and Mr. Gaston also owned a small construction company. The Italian Mafia was making a fortune from construction in the city. They were buying up all the valuable property before the casinos bought it. Then reselling it to the casinos for exorbitant amounts.

Christopher and Frank knocked on the side door of the bar that led to the apartments. David the owner of the Bar and

Strip club opened the door.

"Yeah?"

"Hey," Christopher greeted him.

"Yeah, what's going on?" David asked blocking the door and preventing them from entering."Tiffany's throwing Mark a surprise birthday party. You gonna let us in?"

David twisted his face. "Tiffany's throwing Mark a surprise birthday party. What kind of shit is this? I've got a business to run, and you guys are fucking it up."

Frank was about to push his way through. David's Bar was hot and he didn't feel like standing outside. When the police saw people standing outside of that bar they were bound to search them.

"Look I got a gun on me I can't stand outside." Frank said.

David stepped aside and let them in. Christopher and Frank knocked on Tiffany's door and she opened it. Tiffany had lost it. Christopher could remember just a couple of years earlier when she was a beauty queen. Now she was fat and washed up. Her skin was bruised from years of the fast life. Her body was bent out of shape from her five kids and numerous abortions.

Tiffany opened the door and she was irritated. She didn't know her brother invited this many people to his party. "I knew I shouldn't have let you mother fuckers have your get together here." She walked to the back of her apartment to her bedroom and slammed her bedroom door closed. As soon as Christopher walked into the living room the room burst into pandemonium. Everyone started embracing and hugging him screaming at the tops of their lungs.

Corey popped a bottle of Moet, spilled it on Christopher and then gave him a kiss on the cheeks.

"We did it mother fuckers. We did it." They were excited and screaming. They didn't stop until Tiffany came bursting through her bedroom door.

"What and the fuck is wrong with you, nigger? My kids are in here sleeping. Quiet the fuck down or get out."

After that they calmed down. They had business to conduct.

Christopher grabbed the bags and dumped them on the table. Tiffany's entire kitchen table was covered with money.

"Anybody want a beer?" Corey was carrying two six packs

in his hand. He had put them in the freezer earlier that morning so they could celebrate. He was the wild, exciting one. He was dark-skinned with a nice grade of curly hair. He was a lady's man and a life of the party type of guy. If Christopher hadn't devised this plan, he would've been the leader. Everyone listened to whatever he said. He was Mr. Gaston's biggest heroin distributor. The other's either worked for him, or under him.

Mark turned the television on. The crew popped beers and watched television while Christopher counted the money.

Lindsey, their other friend, was sitting in the corner rolling joints. He was the quiet one. Six three, two hundred fifty pounds, gigantic hands and gigantic feet. He was very handsome also.

It took about thirty minutes but Christopher had the money rubber banded and counted. "One hundred and thirteen thousand." As soon as the words came out of his mouth the room exploded into pandemonium again.

"Shhh. Shh." Christopher placed his finger to his mouth. "Shut up. We don't want Tiffany coming out and seeing this money."

Christopher was right. They immediately calmed down.

Mark jumped to his feet and walked to the back. If his sister came out he was going to block her vision and as soon as he entered the hallway Tiffany cracked her door open.

"Sorry." Mark said.

"I don't wanna hear that shit. Y'all got one more fucking time and then I'm putting y'all out." She slammed the door shut.

He returned to the living room.

"Mark did you buy that calculator like I said?" Christopher asked.

"Yeah."

"So where did you put it? Go get it."

Mark walked into the kitchen and turned on the lights. When he did, hundreds of roaches were walking on the counters. Some we're eating off of crumbles of food that Tiffany or the children had left on the kitchen counter, neglecting to clean up after themselves. There were all kinds of different food stains on the table where the children had played with their food and never ate it. Mark wanted to throw up and when he took a step further he heard a crunch.

One of the kids had dropped cereal on the floor and Tiffany had forgotten to clean it up.

"Shit." Mark reached in the silverware draw and pulled the calculator out. He returned to the living room and passed Christopher the calculator.

"I'm buying this bitch a roach bomb when I get out of here." They all laughed.

Christopher picked up the calculator and started punching buttons. He spoke out loud. "One hundred and thirteen thousand divided by five is.... Twenty two thousand six hundred dollars."

Corey jumped off the couch several feet into the air. "Yeah!"

Everyone else jumped up to quiet him. If Tiffany saw this money she would go crazy.

"Sorry." Corey said. He walked over to Christopher and kissed him right in the mouth. He was crazy like that.

"Hold up, don't go crazy. We have to give up two fifty a piece for the guns." Thanks to Little Aaron, "And the look out gets five hundred from each of us."

Lynn sucked his teeth. He wasn't greedy but Franklin didn't do anything.

"What you sucking your fucking teeth for?" Franklin asked. He didn't get along with any of them except Christopher, his cousin's boyfriend. "Nothing don't worry about it." Lynn said calming down.

"I thought so," Franklin snickered.

"What?" Lynn jumped up and the others jumped between them.

"Calm down gentlemen. Let's not destroy a beautiful thing. This is only the beginning."

Christopher counted out five stacks and passed them to Franklin. He had provided them with two of the get away cars and had posed as a look out. Whether the others agreed or not he deserved a share of the money.

Franklin picked up the stacks and smiled.

That was the easiest sting he had made in his life, a couple thousand dollars, for twenty minute's worth of work. Directly after leaving Tiffany's house Christopher and his crew walked outside to talk and have a quick smoke.

Christopher reached in his coat pocket and pulled out a

pack of Newport cigarettes. The only time that he smoked was when he was nervous or had just finished smoking marijuana.

"Where are we headed?" Franklin asked curiously. He was the partying type and he liked to party all night, especially after making a big score. "I've got to go home and put this money up first," Christopher said pulling on his cigarette. "But if y'all want to get together later and celebrate we can."

"Okay." Lynn responded. "Call me at the house. I'll be waiting."

They broke off, Christopher and Franklin walked up the block to where Franklin had parked his car and just as they were getting in the car a police car pulled up.

"Freeze." The officer yelled and they both looked at each other. Franklin was waiting for Christopher to give the signal. He would shoot it out or run if he had too.

The officer jumped out of the car and started walking over to them. Just then a call came over the radio.

"McClusky we got a call," His partner said and the other cop stopped dead in his tracks. He turned around and jumped right back in the car. They quickly sped away.

Christopher was sweating bullets. He had warned them about meeting at David's Bar and Grill. Too much drug traffic and too much police surveillance.

"Dirty fucking cops." Franklin breathed under his breath. They jumped in the car and sped away. The cops were going to search them for nothing.

Christopher went to his mother's house and placed the money in a safe place. His mother and girlfriend were sitting in the living room talking. Tahwan was two months pregnant and Christopher had promised her he wasn't going to do anything but he needed some emergency money. They were going to need their own apartment and money for the baby. It was a promise that he intended to keep. In a couple of days he had an interview for a job at Resort's International Casino Hotel and he wasn't going to blow that opportunity. People were just dying to get jobs in the casino. Supposedly the casinos were going to change Atlantic City for the better.

After chatting with his family, Christopher took a quick shower and called Franklin who was dressed and waiting. Fifteen minutes later, Franklin and the others were at his door.

"Christopher, where are you going?" Tahwan asked. It was eleven o'clock at night.

"I told you I have important business to take care of baby." He kissed Tahwan on the cheek and exited.

When he jumped in the car, they sped away and drove thirty or forty miles to Cape May, New Jersey to Caroline's, a small little whorehouse that had been in operation since the forties.

Mrs. Caroline still owned the business but one of the girls had taken over the day to day operations. Caroline's was one of South Jersey's best kept secrets. Most of their clientele were politicians and successful businessmen. They dealt with an established clientele of criminals.

Caroline's was the kind of place that if a client got drunk and acted up, they could call the local police and have him removed with no problem. Of course Mrs. Caroline would never press charges; she wanted her customers to come back and visit but under better circumstances. Usually, the police would pick the customer up and roll him for money depending on the customer's status. Then leave the customer right at his front door with a quick five-minute lecture.

Franklin's first time at Caroline's was with Mr. Gaston. Up until the late seventies, Mrs. Caroline paid Mr. Gaston protection money but he had fallen in love with one of the girls and he stopped charging her. It helped that she never charged Mr. Gaston when he came for her services even if he wanted more then one girl. Caroline herself had joined in when she was in her hey-day.

Christopher and the others walked in the front door. They were greeted by a beautiful woman dressed in lingerie. Mrs. Caroline had kidney problems and retired in the early seventies, but she lived in the house connected to the whorehouse and let her most trusted girl run everything.

"Hey baby." The lady walked over to Franklin and planted a kiss right on his lips. They loved him. He was a regular who loved to spend money and tip properly.

"I wanted to bring a couple of my friends by here to celebrate a big score."

Christopher was pissed but he didn't say anything. He would chastise him later in privacy.

"Oh, you won big at the casino." The lady said not

understanding exactly what Franklin meant. "Yeah, we hit the jackpot," Christopher said and they all laughed.

"Well, it's slow tonight maybe we can give you guys a two for one." The madam of the house was young and very good looking. "A two for one? What and the fucks a two for one?" Corty asked. He looked barely old enough to be there.

"Two ladies for the price of one." The madam explained licking her lips in the process. "Ladies." Out of nowhere, ten beautiful women of different ethnic backgrounds appeared. They were so good looking, they could have easily passed for models.

"Oh shit." Christopher said. A pretty light skin one with gray eyes grabbed his hand.

"You want to come with me?" She asked in a seductive voice.

"No problem." The group disappeared upstairs.

The gray-eyed beauty walked Christopher to the top of the stairs into one of the bedrooms, closed the door, rammed her tongue into his mouth and started passionately kissing him like they were married. Christopher pushed her away. "What the fuck is your problem? The only woman I kiss in the mouth is my wife."

Instead of getting offended she said. "Ah, I'm sorry daddy. What you want Mommy to do for you?" That turned him on.

"Take all of your clothes off and play with yourself."

Chandelle removed her lingerie in seconds. Her body was beautiful and tight. Nice medium size breasts and light creamy skin with nice shapely legs. She jumped from the bed and started undressing Christopher. "Do you mind if I take off your clothes?" She asked. She could tell Christopher was shy. "Go right ahead suit yourself."

Chandelle removed his outer garments. When she removed his underwear his penis was rock hard. She placed his dick in her mouth. "Umm I love it. Daddy watch Mommy suck on it."

Christopher placed his hand on her head and watched her perform oral sex. He loved it.

"Daddy are you gonna cum in Mommy's mouth?" She asked. All this talk excited Christopher. "Or are you gonna fuck me?" She asked in an innocent voice that was driving him crazy. He loved it when women talked in bed, it was a definite turn on.

She pulled away from him and laid on the bed. She had a

pack of rubbers on the nightstand.

Christopher admired her body in the dim light. It was beautiful. She reached her hand out for him and opened her legs.

Christopher placed a rubber on and entered her. Surprisingly, she was tight and a little hard entering but when he did they rocked the night away. After his first orgasm she got up, sat in one of the chairs in the room and finger fucked herself, while she let him watch. Then she started playing with her breast, finger fucked herself again and licked her own fingers. Christopher loved it. They went through three rubbers that night, and each time she came. She had a good time. If she could meet a guy like him to settle down with, she wouldn't have to do this. She could continue her studies at college without trying to raise money. Did he have a girlfriend or a wife? She didn't see a ring, she wanted to ask him but Mrs. Caroline forbid any questioning of customers. She wanted her men to come, have a good time with no interruptions, whether that good time last five minutes or ten hours.

Chapter Three *Atlantic City, New Jersey*

A Measly Two Thousand Dollars

It would be three weeks after the robbery before Christopher received any of the robberies rippling affects. Three weeks after the robbery Little Aaron called Christopher's house and told him that his father wanted to see him, it was very important.

Little Aaron picked Christopher up in his brand new 1980 BMW. Christopher loved it. He thought about buying one but decided against it. He vowed to get one the next time as a treat to himself. Instead of buying a car with his money he gave Tahwan a thousand dollars and told her to find an apartment. Christopher and Little Aaron got in the car. Little Aaron was a quiet guy when you had him cornered but if he had back up he could be a loud mouth. Most people in the city hated him but everybody knew that he was a future star in the Atlantic City drug game. His father was Black Mafia, official Black Mafia.

Little Aaron's father Big Aaron was into all kinds of illegal rackets. He controlled a majority of speed, heroin and marijuana distributed in Atlantic City and the South Jersey area.

In many ways, he controlled everything because if you

weren't working for him you had to pay him a street tax in order to operate safely. Nobody in Atlantic City made money without somehow sharing with him. In the early seventies before the casino's came he completely controlled the numbers business and he operated several successful gambling houses. In Atlantic City he was a street legend and multi-millionaire.

Big Aaron's advantage over other drug dealers was that he still had police officers on the payroll from when he ran gambling houses and number spots. Plus, he had an invisible crew of soldiers from Philadelphia at his beck and call. Mr. Gaston got heavily involved in drugs after the Casinos came because his gambling operations were completely destroyed. Why would someone risk gambling at one of his places when they could go to the Casino and not have to worry about getting arrested or the place getting raided?

Little Aaron pulled up in front of his father's Bar and Grill located a couple of stores from the corner of Kentucky and Arctic Avenue. They jumped out of the car and entered the bar.

Christopher was surprised when he walked in the bar. He found Mark and Lynn sitting at one of the tables having drinks. The bar was closed and wouldn't be opening until twelve o'clock in the afternoon.

An old man dressed in black slacks and a white shirt was busy mopping the floor and placing chairs upside down on tables.

Christopher sat with Mark and Lynn at the table. He started whispering and asking questions. Little Aaron disappeared into the back of the bar. When he returned he came back with his father, Big Aaron and Crazy Moe, Big Aaron's right-hand man.

Big Aaron was short, only a couple of inches over five feet tall, he was thin but he dressed immaculately. His son, Little Aaron, looked like his identical twin just thirty years younger.

Big Aaron was brown-skinned with reddish brown hair. If he didn't dye it, it would have been salt and pepper. Both vanity and the desire to hide his age made him dye his hair. It was red the same color that it was in his youth.

He was still handsome in an elegant kind of way. His height made him appear meek, which was deceiving. He looked like he wouldn't step on a roach if it crossed his path, but he was a terror with an uncontrollable temper. Lately, he had been calming down. Maybe with old age he was losing his touch. The rumor on the street was that he suffered from the Napoleon complex.

Mr. Gaston snatched a chair from one of the tables. He sat the chair next to Christopher and the others. "Charlie, can you give us a minute?" Big Aaron said to the bartender cleaning the place and without even a response the bartender disappeared. Charlie had been tending the bar for almost twenty years and had been introduced to some of the most powerful men in organized crime. He knew when a meeting was being held.

Big Aaron picked his chair up again and moved right beside Christopher.

Christopher glanced down to show humility. For some reason, a reason that he couldn't comprehend, he wasn't afraid. Just like the robbery. His mind raced a million miles a second. He was already thinking of other deals.

"Did my son tell you I wanted to talk to you?" Big Aaron picked up the bottle of liquor that was sitting at the table and poured everybody drinks.

Crazy Moe was sitting at the table making everyone uncomfortable with his silence. He was a serious looking man with dark features and a stocky body. Christopher believed the rumors circulating that he was a murderer "Yes," Christopher said and Little Aaron let out a little sigh. He had been arguing with his father all day about selling those guns to Christopher and his crew.

"He said you had to see me. It was important but if you're busy I can leave and come back. I could always talk to you another time."

Big Aaron smiled. "No, I wanted to talk to you now. Christopher you know me right? You know who I am don't you?"

Christopher didn't say anything, but he understood.

Big Aaron continued. "You know what I do right?" He asked again.

"Yes."

"Well listen and get this straight. I don't fuck with kids. Do you hear me?"

Christopher looked at him but didn't say anything.

"You're nothing but a baby to me. My son sold you some guns right?"

Christopher didn't respond. He let Mr. Gaston continue.

"He sold you some guns that didn't even belong to him." Mr. Gaston was pissed and Christopher could tell. He looked like he might blow his top at any minute. "He didn't have my fucking permission."

Mr. Gaston looked over at his son who was bending his head like a coward and looking at the table.

"I'm going to tell you this one time and one time only. People are talking about that robbery. If my name comes up in this shit I'm going to kill you." He pointed at Christopher. "And you three." He pointed at his son, Lynn and Mark.

"Don't think I'm fucking kidding." He took a sip out of his drink and placed it back on the table. "I don't do business with children. If any of you get picked up my name better not come up in this bullshit. Do you understand?"

They all nodded yes. They knew that he wanted some kind of response.

Christopher was embarrassed. He had never felt so uneasy in his life. If Mr. Gaston wanted to, he could have killed them all. Christopher promised himself that he would never do business again with out carrying a weapon, friend or not.

"Where's the money for the guns?" Mr. Gaston asked.

Christopher reached in his pocket. Crazy Moe jumped and shoved his hand in his jacket. He was about to pull out his gun until Christopher pulled out the envelope.

Mr. Gaston smiled. He loved it. Moe was on point.

Christopher placed the envelope on the table.

Mr. Gaston picked it up and counted the money. "Seventeen hundred dollars. How much money did you take from the supermarket?"

Christopher was about to lie but decided against it. "One hundred grand."

Mr. Gaston and Crazy Moe were shocked. "That's a lot of fucking money. The next time you come to me, Junior doesn't own any fucking guns." Mr. Gaston finished his liquor and poured himself another drink.

"Junior, if some of the punks that did this shit implicate you, do you think your lawyer is gonna cost you Seventeen hundred dollars?"

Mr. Gaston looked at his son who was too embarrassed to respond. He continued. "If my son's implicated in this bullshit I want twenty thousand dollars cash. You understand?"

Christopher looked at him and nodded his head yes.

"This time I'm going to let you slide because I believe that you didn't know anything but the next time my son assists you, I'm a silent partner. Do you understand?"

"Yes."

Mr. Gaston smiled. He liked Christopher, plus the money they made impressed him. "Christopher, you're a good kid with a lot of potential. You need to stick with me. I can help you get rich if this robbery shit doesn't send you straight to jail. Your partners are running around bragging, buying new cars and shit. Just giving themselves away." In the years to come, Christopher would realize that this small business meeting would be a blessing in disguise. He would need Mr. Gaston's assistance on a lot of things and this meeting would actually be the start of their business relationship. Christopher was about to become very rich and extremely powerful.

"Now where's the money?" Big Aaron asked, pissed the fuck off. Somebody had picked the envelope up off of the table while he was talking.

Crazy Moe reached in his pocket and passed it to him.

Big Aaron grabbed the money and smacked his son in the face with it. "Here pussy, thanks for risking my life for a measly two thousand dollars. I should kick your ass." Mr. Gaston walked towards the bar and returned with another bottle. He was an alcoholic but didn't realize it.

"The next job that you do I'm in. I want half of everything you make. We're forming a partnership right now, today. You talk to me and not this piece of shit." Mr. Gaston slapped Little Aaron on the back of the head so hard it sounded like something snapped.

The others jumped. Christopher glanced over at Lynn. He was snickering. Lynn was crazy like that. He would laugh at anything.

Christopher had started working at the casino and already several angry gamblers had spit in his face. It took every bone in his body not to jump over the craps table and slap the shit out of the customers. After the third time, Christopher realized that either he was going to have to get his education or own his own business. There was no way in the world Christopher was going to take physical abuse on the job and only be paid five hundred dollars a week before taxes. In the early eighties, five hundred dollars a week was excellent money but no amount of money was worth the pressure of the job and the physical abuse from the gamblers. In Vegas, they said the gamblers were worse because the stakes were higher.

Christopher, Little Aaron, Mr. Gaston and Crazy Moe were sitting in the bar having their first official business meeting as partners. "You know Nicolos Scarfino?" Mr. Gaston asked. As usual he was drinking.

"He's the head of the Italian Mafia in South Jersey and Philly isn't he?" Christopher asked.

"Yes, he is and were personal friends. His son runs the weed trade here in the city. I'm gonna put in a call to him so that maybe you and Little Aaron can go partners on a couple of pounds. I'll front half the money, you guys sell it and make me a partner. We split everything down the middle." Mr. Gaston looked at Christopher for his approval. He liked Christopher because he saw seriousness and honesty in him. "Is that all right with you Christopher?"

"That's perfect with me. I'm gonna form a little crew. I think we'll set up shop in Moses' bar on the Westside. It's nice and quiet over there."

Mr. Gaston smiled he was impressed. He had finally found a person who could watch Little Aaron's back when he took over.

"We set up the weed and then the next thing you know it we can put some speed and heroin over there."

In the early eighties Speed and Heroin were the drugs of choice in the Tri-state areas. People sold powdered cocaine but it was hard to get and too expensive. Sometimes you could snort or shoot speed and be up for days. It took a couple of weeks but the marijuana business exploded because nobody hardly ever had it and before they knew it people were coming to the bar to buy large quantities at wholesale prices so they could resell it from houses or other bars.

The only problem with the young Italians was they couldn't keep it, they were always running out.

Chapter Four Atlantic City, New Jersey

The Better Idea

Several weeks after Christopher had the meeting with Mr. Gaston. Little Aaron called Christopher again to arrange another meeting.

Christopher and Franklin walked into the bar. Franklin was Christopher's bodyguard. As they walked into the bar they saw the same guy cleaning up again. Mr. Gaston and Little Aaron were obviously discussing important business because they were sitting at a table near the back of the bar talking quietly by themselves.

Christopher and Franklin pulled two chairs down from one of the tables. As soon as they sat Crazy Moe appeared from nowhere. He was carrying a bottle of Hennessy and several glasses. He sat the bottle on the table.

"What you drinking?" His voice was deep and powerful. It matched his reputation and his appearance.

Franklin glanced at the bottle of Hennessy. "I'm drinking what you're drinking." Franklin sometimes drank too much and couldn't control his temper. Christopher had warned him about drinking but he never listened to advice. It was too damaging for his ego.

"And you?"

Christopher just looked at him for a second before he answered, he felt a little leery.

"Chris."

"Yeah."

"What you drinking?" Franklin asked. "The same thing."

Crazy Moe poured them all a drink then walked away and stood behind the bar like he was nursing a shot gun.

A few minutes after the drinks were poured Mr. Gaston walked over. As usual he was dressed in dress slacks and a dress shirt with no tie. He dressed like a businessman. "Christopher." Mr. Gaston extended his hand. Christopher stood up and they embraced.

"Mr. Gaston this is..."

Mr. Gaston interrupted him. "I know Frank. Frank how you doing?" Franklin sold heroin for Mr. Gaston but nobody knew it, not even Christopher. He was one of Mr. Gaston's secret weapons. Just like nobody knew that Christopher and Mr. Gaston were marijuana partners. You never let your left hand know what your right hand is doing in the drug business, in any illegal business for that matter.

"Excellent." Franklin lifted his drink and gulped it. He grabbed the bottle and poured himself another drink.

"Christopher can we talk in private?"

Christopher looked at Franklin and he stood up without saying a word. Franklin grabbed the Hennessy bottle and took it with him to the back of the bar where Mr. Gaston and Little Aaron had been previously sitting.

"Aaron said you've been killing them with the weed. How's business going?" Mr. Gaston asked.

"Business is going good. I'm just trying to reestablish everything."

"Christopher there's no real money in weed?" Mr. Gaston said.

"It's good enough for me." Christopher smiled. "So now that you're fucking with weed you think you can leave the robbery business alone?"

Christopher looked at him and smiled. "Maybe."

"Maybe." Mr. Gaston was surprised, he thought that

Christopher was smarter than that. "Christopher you're too talented for the robbery business. I want you to come and start working directly for me. You can run my heroin and speed ring with Little Aaron."

Christopher smiled because he was impressed with the fact that an Atlantic City street legend wanted to work with him.

Mr. Gaston continued. "In a couple of weeks I'm gonna have some guys come down from Philly." He paused after he said it because he was thinking while he talked. A business habit. "And I want you to work with them."

"Work with them doing what?" Christopher asked.

"Extortion."

"Extortion!" Christopher raised his voice and Mr. Gaston immediately put his finger to his own lips signaling Christopher to be quiet.

"Calm down son. Calm down. Not anybody just people that owe me."

"I've got a better idea." Christopher said.

"Shoot," Mr. Gaston replied. Little Aaron came out of the bathroom and sat at the table.

Christopher told him his plans and Mr. Gaston smiled because he knew that it could work.

"And how can I help?"

Christopher and Little Aaron laughed. "Just get me two vans, a get away car and storage space."

"And what's my cut for this?" Big Aaron asked.

"Partner. Were dividing everything down the middle."

Big Aaron smiled. "Lets make a toast then." Mr. Gaston ran to the bar and pulled out his most expensive bottle of champagne and popped the cork. He poured his son and Christopher a glass.

"Christopher I still want you to think about this street tax were gonna start enforcing." A street tax was where other dealers paid a percentage of their proceeds for protection.

"When my son takes over this drug shit I want you to be his right-hand man. I want you running every thing with him. You're his only friend that really impresses me." Like magic the bottle of wine was finished and Morris came over with another bottle of Hennessy.

Franklin sat quietly in the corner soaking everything in. Even thought they were talking low he heard everything that was said.

Christopher and Mr. Gaston discussed a couple of other things and then Mr. Gaston excused himself.

"The bar's about to open in a couple of hours I have to make it to my office before it gets crazy in here. The more motherfuckers see me the more begging." Mr. Gaston lifted the bottle of Hennessy off the table. "If you need anything before the robbery you contact me you hear?"

Christopher looked up at him and smiled. "I hear you."

The meeting was over.

Christopher and Little Aaron were generating about three to six thousand dollars a day from the bar selling marijuana. The major problem was that the guys selling heroin and speed bought a lot of heat from the police. Moses' bar went from a small bar on the Westside to a drug haven. The narcotic task force was constantly there now that the heroin and speed popped up.

Mr. Gaston wanted Christopher and Little Aaron to oversee his heroin operations at the other bars and organize it like they had done the marijuana. He warned his son. "Keep Christopher next to you. I've seen his kind before. He's gonna make this family millions. Mark my words and I'm gonna make sure that the both of you rise to the top."

They clashed wineglasses and made a toast on it.

Chapter Five *Pleasantville, New Jersey*

A Young Criminal Genius

Christopher's marijuana business had exploded and financially, for the first time in months, his income was steady. Chris was selling about twenty-five pounds of marijuana a week and the business seemed to be constantly growing.

Christopher made Corty head of the marijuana operation. Corty and Corey were fraternal twin brothers who looked nothing alike. Corty was the youngest and sometimes the others treated him like he was a baby.

Christopher and Lynn pulled their cargo van to the wooded entrance of Charleston Beverages. Charleston Beverages was the biggest liquor and beer distributor in the Atlantic County, South Jersey area. Not only did they service hundreds of bars and restaurants in the area, but they had just received a million dollar contract with Resorts International and were in negotiation with the other two casinos that were presently being constructed. Before the arrival of Resorts International Casino Charleston Beverages was just a small liquor distributor working out of a small factory in Atlantic City. Now they were major with an enormous facility in Pleasantville.

Angelo Tuno, the man that controlled the Italian Mafia in the early seventies, secretly owned it and left it to his family when he died.

The other major distributors were Harrison Beverages and Krammer's but they were newly open and nowhere near as profitable as Charleston's.

Christopher and Lynn were sitting in the cargo van at four o'clock in the morning. Lynn had a small but profitable heroin outlet going on at the bar but he had made so much money at the grocery store robbery that he refused to miss out on this one.

Lynn pulled the truck a couple of yards away from the entrance and turned slightly into the woods. Charleston Beverages was buried at least a quarter of a mile into the woods. In the early eighties most of the Pleasantville area was still undeveloped and a lot of companies started building facilities in the area. Resorts International Casino Hotel had a facility for employees there and the other two casinos began constructing facilities there also.

After Lynn pulled the cargo van up to the security gate and parked in the wooded area he hit the lights. They didn't want any security guards to see them because they would definitely call the police.

"Turn the engine off," Christopher commanded.

"It's gonna get cold in here," Lynn said. Then he reached in his pocket and pulled out a joint. He pulled his lighter out and lit the joint. Lynn took a deep pull and passed the marijuana to Christopher.

"You like this shit?" Christopher asked with his mouth full of smoke.

"I'm impressed. Big Aaron got the connections for everything." Lynn was still holding smoke in his mouth. When he released it from his lungs it filled the entire van.

Christopher released his smoke and started coughing.

Christopher and Lynn waited in the woods freezing for a half-hour and then a liquor truck pulled up to the gate. A security guard wearing a uniform came out of the building.

There was a little booth but it was empty, probably because it was to cold for somebody to be standing outside. The security guard walked to the cab of the truck. He had a hot cup of coffee in one hand and his clipboard in the other. He sipped on the coffee as he walked trying to keep warm in the freezing weather. When he got to the front of the truck, he stepped up and passed the driver the clipboard.

The driver signed it and passed it back. Then the security guard walked into the booth and punched a couple of buttons. A couple of seconds after that the gate slid open.

Christopher glanced at his watch. It was four thirty in the morning. The sun wouldn't be coming up for at least an hour. Everything was moving right on schedule.

It took about two minutes before the gate was open enough for the truck to drive through. When it opened enough the driver hit his lights and started down the quarter mile road.

Christopher and Lynn ducked near the dashboard letting the truck drive pass. As soon as the truck passed Lynn reached for the ignition and Christopher grabbed his hand, preventing him from putting the keys in the ignition.

"Wait one second. We know where they're going." Christopher glanced over at the security booth. He wanted to make sure that the security guard had returned to the inside. They waited a couple more seconds and then they pulled off following the truck without their lights on. They weren't going to turn them on until they hit a main road in Pleasantville or some other traffic.

The truck drove straight down Main Street until it hit the major highway that lead from Pleasantville to Atlantic City. Christopher and Lynn quietly tailed it.

Pleasantville and Atlantic City are only six miles apart it took them fifteen minutes to get to the city. That was because it had snowed a couple of days earlier and the highways were not completely cleared, especially of ice.

The truck drove down the highway until it turned into Absecon Boulevard. Once it hit the boulevard it made a left at the Armory and turned into the Liquory House. The Liquory House was the only liquor store and bar that sat in the area besides Jack and Jill's, which had been closed due to renovations. Most businesses were just beginning to reap the benefits of having legalized Casino gambling in Atlantic City and they eagerly waited for the other two casinos to finish construction.

When the truck pulled into the bar's property, two cargo vans were already there. The vans were snow white with company advertisements on the side of them. The snow partially camouflaged them.

One of the vans sat next to the gas pumps, which hadn't been used for a couple of years now. The owner of the bar, Mrs. Donaldson, was contemplating having them turned back on. When they first got them they had made a fortune but after the seventies oil crisis, they had decided to turn them off. The gas station was two small and not conveniently located. It would be too costly to continue to operate it. The only people that bought gas there were usually bar patrons, which weren't many until the casino's arrival. Now many of the casino employees that lived on the Westside came there to relax after work.

When the truck pulled up on the property, both of the drivers in the cab jumped out and so did the occupants of the vans. The truck drivers didn't notice the two cargo vans discreetly parked near the gas station and if they noticed them they obviously paid no attention to them. Christopher and Lynn had pulled up behind the truck. Christopher's crew wore white clothes and white scull caps. They exited the vans as soon as the liquor truck arrived.

Their guns were the only things visible. It took a couple of seconds for the drivers to realize what was happening and one of them raised his hands.

The other one, the one with a nice body size just kept walking like he didn't see them.

"Put your hands up big man." Lynn said he was six three and damned near three hundred pounds himself.

"Fuck you," Rocco responded. He was Italian and connected to the mob. How dare these niggers try to rob him? They would have to kill him first.

Lynn flipped the sawed-off shotgun he was carrying and smacked Rocco in the mouth with it. The impact from the gun made a crack sound, Rocco immediately threw his hands to his face.

Rocco dropped to his knees and tried to spit but he could hardly open his mouth. When he did get his mouth opened he yelled in pain and spit out a mouthful of blood and teeth. A couple of seconds later, he fainted.

"You to the doo," Christopher commanded the other driver. The other driver walked to the door. The delivery guy knocked on the door and an intoxicated voice answered it. "Who is it?" The voice was slurring.

"It's Charleston," the driver responded.

The door opened and Christopher pushed the driver through the door. "Ouch," the driver moaned.

"Shut up." Christopher raised his gun and his partners rushed in behind him. Without being told, Corey ran to the back of the bar where there was a business office. He grew up on the Westside and he knew the interior of the bar like the back of his hands. That's how many times he had been there.

Corey and Corty walked into the business office with their weapons drawn and their white ski masks covering their faces.

Mrs. Donaldson was sitting behind the desk terrified. She had heard the driver scream and was picking up the phone to dial the police when Corey and Corty burst through the door.

"Put the fucking phone down," they said pointing their guns towards her face, something they didn't want to do. Everybody respected Mrs. Donaldson she was a pillar in the community. She helped a lot of people.

She raised her hands. "Please, don't hurt me."

"Shut up." Corey walked over to her and grabbed her. He didn't want to but he had, too. They walked her to the front of the bar and tied her up. Then they returned to the business office and started searching.

Christopher looked at his watch and glanced over at the cash register. He punched a couple of buttons and it opened.

Then he heard it, something had gone wrong in the office. Corey and Corty had let off six shots. Christopher dropped what he was doing and ran to the back. When he got there Corey and Corty were stuffing a bag with money they had retrieved from a safe.

"It's time to exit. We've been here for damn near fifteen minutes."

Corey looked up. "Okay, just give us a few minutes." He stuffed the bag and jumped up running out of the bar followed by Christopher and Corty.

When they left the bar all the cargo vans were gone except one and Rocco, the big driver, was lying in the snow on his back tied up.

Christopher patted his pocket. "Lynn left with the keys. That stupid mother fucker."

They were standing outside with weapons drawn and a beer truck completely empty of its contents except a few boxes.

"Check the van." Corey's mind was racing and when they walked over to it the keys were sitting on the floor of the van near the gas pedal.

Christopher and the rest of them jumped in the van and sped away. They were gonna make a nice piece of money off of this robbery.

Later that night Christopher and his crew had a meeting.

Christopher didn't tell everybody that one of the reasons why he did the liquor store robbery was because he was going to enter the heroin business, but he didn't want to enter it without Corey and Franklin's assistance. He didn't even tell Mr. Gaston his plans. Mr. Gaston was co-signing for Christopher's first loan so that he could buy the small grocery store on Indiana and Grant Avenue on the Westside.

The store was going to be in his mother's and wife's name. This way, if anything ever happened to him, they would own property and be able to support themselves financially. They knew that Christopher was doing something illegal but he never exposed them to the business and they liked it that way.

Things were changing. Christopher was no longer that young man he had been a couple of months earlier. Now he was focused and full of ambition. He had finally found his calling. He hated to admit it, but like Frank Matthews, Carlo Gambino and Pablo Escobar he was a young criminal genius.

Chapter Six *Venice Park, Atlantic City, New Jersey*

You Gotta Problem With That

Christopher threw Tahwan a surprise birthday party two days after the liquor store robbery. He invited all of their friends.

The apartments in Venice Park were small, especially for the crowd of twenty-five people. Many of the people attending the party were Tahwan's family from Lancaster, Pennsylvania.

Christopher sat around entertaining everyone. They brought presents, envelopes and cards filled with cash. Tahwan would probably make a good two to three thousand this birthday.

Frank walked over with his girlfriend. Some pretty looking Spanish chick that he had brought down from the Bronx, New York. His parents still lived there.

"What's going on partner?" Everyone was anxious. This was the first time they had seen each other since the robbery.

"I'm ready to get out of here," Christopher said and Tahwan had over heard him. She was in the refrigerator removing some kind of dish that she was going to feed the guests with.

"Chris, you're leaving." She gave him that sad face look. It didn't match with her dark complexion and pretty brown eyes. She was wearing a one-piece printed bodysuit with a big collar and some boots. She looked cute in it. "Yeah. I've got business to handle. It's only gonna take a minute. I have to pick up your birthday present." That put a smile on her face. She was tired of everyone approaching her and asking her what he got for her birthday.

Christopher's crew went outside and jumped into Corey's brand new Pontiac Bonneville. The car was white with a powder blue leather interior.

"You like it?" Corey asked. He stood beside it with his black skin sporting a black turtleneck and black slacks to model for the crew.

"All you need is a bottle of beer and you'll look like one of those guys modeling for a liquor company." Everyone burst into laughter.

"Let's get out of here. I have to get back before my baby starts bitching." They jumped in the car and sped away. They had work to do.

They drove straight to the storage houses that were built in Hammonton, New Jersey a couple of miles outside of Pleasantville.

The ride took a little over fifteen minutes. They could have gotten there faster but it had rained for two days and the snow had turned to slush and ice. The weather would get better as soon as March rolled around.

Christopher and Mr. Gaston were the only ones with keys to the storage room. After the robbery, Christopher and his crew had parked the cargo vans inside of the storage house. Christopher didn't know how much it cost but the place was enormous.

Once they got inside of the storage house Christopher dug in his pocket and pulled out a thick envelope. He held the envelope in the air. "We got twenty-five thousand in cash from the safe."

Franklin could do nothing but smile. He was impressed. He already knew how much was in the safe. He had gone to Christopher's house after the robbery and witnessed him count the money.

Franklin tried to get Christopher to lie and say that there

was only ten thousand in the safe so they could keep more money for themselves, but Christopher wouldn't do it.

Christopher divided the money by seven people that left them with twenty-eight hundred and some change.

Christopher had taken the money to Resorts International and dropped it on the craps table. After gambling a couple of hands, he cashed the money in and the cashier gave him hundreds.

"Corty found this ordering sheet in the back of the truck. It has the prices of the liquor, the name brands and the count. Wholesale from the distributor this shit's worth about four hundred grand. I say we half price it and make a clean two hundred thousand."

"How and the fuck are we gonna get somebody to buy two hundred thousand dollars worth of liquor? Don't nobody have that kind of money except restaurants or casinos and they're not spending that money with somebody off of the streets." Franklin had a valid point and the others waited for the answer.

"This is what we're gonna do. We'll sell the liquor to little honky tonk bars in the area then we'll hit Philly and New York City. The out-of-towners don't give a fuck. They'll buy the liquor as long as they're getting a deal. I'll handle everything and we'll divide the money as I sell it. Is that alright with everybody?" Christopher asked.

"I don't give a fuck what we got to do as long as I get a piece of the money. You know I trust you," Corey said. The twenty eight hundred dollars was enough for him. His heroin business was growing constantly. He didn't need to make another dollar. But he did have another question.

"Chris did you say we could make two hundred grand wholesaling this shit?" He wanted to clarify and make sure he understood what was said.

"We sure can."

"Do we divide the money after that?" He asked again.

"No, we divide it as we go."

"So your saying we're gonna see another..." He paused and calculated in his head. "Twenty-five to thirty thousand apiece?"

"Easy." They were amazed.

"You got any more jobs we can do?" Everyone laughed.

"Maybe we should just divided it and go for self." Franklin was selfish and that was why the others didn't care for him much. Christopher was the only one that trusted him.

"No, let Christopher handle everything he's the mastermind of this shit."

"Help me check the vans before we leave." Christopher didn't tell them but he had purchased his own storage space and he was moving the liquor in a couple of days.

They went to the vans and checked them. "Some boxes are missing from the van." Lynn said.

Christopher walked over and checked the van for himself. "Mr. Gaston's been here." He just shook his head.

"I told you I don't trust that greedy mother fucker. There goes our money," Corey said and the others shook their heads in agreement.

"Don't worry, it's coming out of his share," Christopher said.

"You better do it, I'm tired of that skinny motherfucker getting over. He doesn't do anything and he always wants to get a cut." After checking the vans they returned to the house to finish partying.

The week after the party when things quieted down Christopher rented a brand spanking new 1980 Lincoln Continental from the airport in Pomona and drove to New York City. They were about to have their first meeting with Franklin's heroin connection.

In the early eighties, Pedro Hector Gonzales was one of the largest heroin distributors in the entire New York City area. With the arrest of Nicholas Barnes and the council, the Puerto Ricans regained complete control of heroin distribution in the city. Mr. Gonzales had major distribution outlets in every borough except Staten Island. Staten Island and Long Island were predominately residential and drug trafficking there remained in bars. Years later it would eventually creep into housing projects.

Franklin pulled up to an apartment complex on 163rd and Edgecombe Avenue. They met a guy who drove them over to the Bronx on the Cross Bronx expressway. The Bronx was predominately Hispanic.

The driver of the first car led them to the Morris Soundview section. Pedro had just purchased a building on 172nd Street and Manor Avenue where he sold wholesale heroin. Only customers spending large amounts of money were taken there. Pedro ran the whole operation from several apartment buildings in the Bronx. Pedro's other retail outlets were located in different boroughs; his lieutenants ran them.

Franklin stepped out of the car first. He was light-skinned. Most of the people that lived in New York thought he was Puerto Rican. He was wearing a shiny silver sharkskin suit. The other's laughed at him because of the color but it fit him nice and matched his flamboyant personality.

Christopher stepped out. He was wearing a quiet navy blue pinstriped suit with the white chalk lines running through it, and a light powdered blue colored shirt that Tahwan had picked out for him. He topped that off with dress shoes, a nice Cartier watch and a simple gold wedding band announcing his engagement.

Corey jumped out, he was wearing a nice gray suit with a matching Grey turtleneck sweater. Against his dark skin and jet black curly hair it looked gorgeous. A couple of the young ladies sitting on the stoop outside of the building immediately noticed them.

John-Martin was sporting a black suit with a white shirt and printed tie. He was the only one wearing a tie and Christopher was the only one carrying a bag. He had the money.

The bodyguard walked them to an apartment and used a key to open the door. He escorted them in and the first thing that hit them was the smell of food cooking.

They walked past the kitchen where five beautiful Spanish women were cooking and dancing to Spanish music on the radio.

The bodyguard escorted them to the living room and Senor Pedro stood up. He was a handsome guy. Six two,maybe six three, thin with a nice build. Black salt and pepper hair that he had combed back, with a thin mustache and no beard.

He extended his hand to Franklin first. "Poppy."

"Pedro, what's up Poppy?" Franklin replied. Pedro still thought that Franklin was Hispanic and he was careful what he said around him.

Pedro spoke with a light Puerto Rican accent. He was dressed in a pinstriped suit and a dress shirt, which was opened almost to his navel revealing a thin gold chain with several religious charms. "Which one is Christopher?"

"I am." Christopher said and Pedro extended his hand.

"It's nice to meet you. I've heard beautiful things about you." Just as he said it, a gorgeous Spanish chick walked into the room and sat a plate in front of Pedro.

"Mommy, what's wrong with you? Feed my friends."

The lady looked at him terrified. "I'm sorry, Poppy. I have their plates I wanted to feed you first." He was the man of the house.

Pedro shook his head in anger. "You can never teach these women. Feed my friends first."

She looked at Christopher and the others, then apologized. "Forgive me Poppy, I sorry."

She rushed out of the living room into the kitchen. The young lady was gorgeous. She was wearing a tight dress shirt with dress slacks that clung to her behind. She was one of those light skin Puerto Rican chicks with long black shinny hair. She returned two minutes later with several plates.

"So, what kind of business we talking about?" Pedro asked. Franklin had told him that Christopher wanted to buy a kilogram of heroin.

"We want to get a kilo of heroin." Christopher said.

"Two hundred and fifty grand cash," Pedro said without budging or twitching an eyelid.

"I want to see it and test it first."

"No problem." Pedro picked up a napkin, and wiped his hands. "I have to count the money first," Pedro said.

"How much you gonna charge me if I get four?"

"When?" Pedro asked.

"Now."

"You got a million dollars cash on you right now?"

"Yeah."

Pedro was pleased. His biggest customer spent five hundred thousand dollars a week and he lived in Newark, New Jersey. His second biggest customer was from Baltimore, Philadelphia and Boston respectively.

"You let me count the money on my money machine for two and I'll go get them. Then I count the rest of the money and get the rest."

"That's no problem but what kind of deal you gonna give me?" Christopher asked.

"If you spend the million dollars then I'm gonna charge you two hundred thousand a brick which is a fifty thousand dollar discount on each kilo. I was going to give Franklin twenty-five thousand for bringing you I can't give him twenty-five thousand if I give you the discount."

"Don't worry about Franklin I'll take care of him."

Pedro looked at Franklin. "Is that alright with you Frank?"

"Of course, these are my brothers." Franklin said. When he came to talk to Pedro earlier that week, he told him to over charge Christopher. That way he could give Franklin the extra. Pedro realized this might be another one of those customers he could do serious business with in case he ever wanted to distribute wholesale only and leave the retail business to his little cousin and brother.

Pedro jumped up and began speaking in Spanish. When he returned, he returned with three men. They took stacks of the money and counted it in the money machines. It took a half an hour to count the first five hundred thousand then two of the men disappeared and came back with three kilograms of pure heroin. By the time they came back the other monies were counted and the deal was finished.

This was Christopher's first power move where he didn't inform the others on the details. Mr. Johnson in Philadelphia would get two kilograms. Mr. Gaston was getting one and Christopher was buying one. Now that they had extra Christopher was getting two.

When they left the apartment Christopher pulled Franklin aside. "Let's catch a cab."

"Okay." Franklin was excited. This was his big break.

They walked to Westchester Avenue and caught a cab. "Frank you said you've got a lot of people in New York that you wanted to set up. Well I'm giving you the extra kilogram for three hundred grand. You got a problem with it?"

Frank tried to contain his excitement. The most cash he ever saw was one hundred thousand dollars. This move was going to set him straight.

"Christopher I love you." He grabbed Christopher's face and kissed him on his cheeks.

They drove to Manhattan later that night where they were

meeting Pedro to celebrate. There was not a single beautiful Dominican or Puerto Rican that Pedro hadn't slept with. He dated at least five different women a week and most of them slept with him.

Between the five boroughs he had about fifteen different kids, not counting the five he had with his wife.

Chapter Seven Atlantic City, New Jersey

The Next Legend

Christopher and Mark drove over to the bar in Chris's brand new Lincoln Continental. The only time he drove it was when he was conducting legal business. The car was more Tahwan's than his. He drove her Caprice Classic more than he drove his own car. The Caprice Classic was more discreet and didn't draw attention.

Christopher and Mark walked straight to the back of the bar where Mr. Gaston's business office was located.

Mr. Gaston conducted most of his legal business in his office at the bar.

Christopher knocked on the door.

"Come in," a voice from the inside said.

Christopher walked in and Mr. Gaston was sitting at his desk reviewing rental agreements for one of his apartment buildings.

A nice looking lady was sitting on the opposite side of the desk; she was his accountant and mistress. She looked like one of the young girls that worked at Caroline's. Christopher could tell by how far her blouse was unbuttoned that something had went down or that something was about to go down. The woman was in the process of fixing her clothing when Christopher entered.

When Christopher entered the office the woman stood up and extended her hand to Mr. Gaston. They shook hands and the lady walked past Christopher smiling as she left the office.

Christopher smiled back.

"What's up?" Mr. Gaston asked.

"Nothing." Christopher replied. "We got twenty something thousand from the bar," Christopher said reaching in his pocket and passing Mr. Gaston his share of the money.

Mr. Gaston opened the envelope and smiled. He loved it; Christopher was a talented businessman. Men like this came by maybe every twenty years if you were lucky. It was Mr. Gaston's responsibility to recognize this talent, get Christopher's loyalty and utilize his skills before something ruined his potential. Mr. Gaston had seen it. It happened to Nicky Barnes.

"How much is the liquor worth?" Mr. Gaston asked.

"About four hundred thousand wholesale." Christopher said.

Mr. Gaston released a whistle. "I'm proud of you Christopher. The sky's the limit for you. I wish you were my son." He smiled after he said it and Christopher felt pride build up in him. If Mr. Gaston said you were talented, then you were talented.

"If you have any connections with bars or people that want it let me know. I'll be giving you your share of the money as we make it." Christopher said.

"I already have a couple of bars in Philly that have placed in orders. Don't worry; that liquor will be sold in a couple of days. Leave those vans in place. I'll take care of them." He returned to his rental agreements. "These fucking tenants are killing me. It cost more money to throw them out then it does to keep them." He balled one of the papers up. "This shit is crazy."

"Let me know if you need help removing somebody." Christopher said.

"Hell no. You're too talented for that. That's small time. You just keep doing what you're doing. I got the strong arm for that."

Christopher didn't even mention the missing liquor. Why argue he was just going to short Mr. Gaston his share of the money.

Mr. Gaston contacted every bar owner he knew on the streets. It only took four weeks and most of the liquor was gone. Sold for cash. Every bar in Atlantic City bought a couple of cases except the honest businessmen.

Mr. Gaston had a lot of outlets in Philadelphia. Christopher went to Fat Albert's restaurant and the owner, Fat Albert, cornered him outside.

"Come on, this shit is hot and you expect me to pay half price for this bullshit? You must be fucking kidding me."

Christopher just turned and walked away.

The owner tried a different approach. "Do you know who I am?" He asked. "I'm best friends with Mr. Johnson. He's gonna be pissed the fuck off that you charged me this much."

"We're not working with Mr. Johnson; we're working with Mr. Gaston."

"What?" The Fat man said. "That's the same fucking thing. Leave the liquor here and I'll pay you later."

"Sorry. Cash on delivery," Christopher said jumping into a new van that they were renting.

"You're a fucked up businessman. You need to learn who your people are." The man handed over the cash and Christopher handed over the liquor.

Within four weeks the liquor was gone with an overwhelming demand for its return. Christopher's reputation was growing in the streets. He was only in his twenties and they were already labeling him the next street legend. He had a promising future in organized crime and all the older guys were getting more and more anxious to meet this young upstart. It could turn out to be millions of dollars for everybody. Mr. Gaston had him and he wouldn't relinquish Christopher's talents to anyone, except maybe William Johnson but not even to him if he didn't have to.

The liquor store robbery was Christopher's last robbery because his heroin business had exploded to enormous proportions a matter of weeks.

The heroin that Mr. Johnson had supplied them with was so good that Christopher had established major distribution in all the bars in Atlantic City, Pleasantville, and the other hick towns in the South Jersey area.

Mr. Johnson sold his two kilograms in less then a week. His

distribution covered the entire state of Pennsylvania. Not only did he have lieutenants in Philadelphia, he had lieutenants in Pittsburgh, Chester and Lancaster to name a few areas. Through Little Aaron he controlled heroin and speed distribution throughout the entire New Jersey area.

Later that week, he would hold a meeting with the families that controlled Newark and the North Jersey areas. Not since Nicholas Barnes and Frank Matthews had anybody set up heroin distribution to this extent.

The Scarfino family was connected to the five families in New York and they were bringing heroin over by a group of Sicilians through the ports of France and Spain. Once in a while something would happen to a shipment and there would be a drought.

Chapter Eight Atlantic City, New Jersey

In Control of Everthing

Within a couple of months after the liquor store robbery Christopher established heroin distribution over the entire Atlantic City. After establishing distribution he went to Philadelphia where he had a meeting with Mr. Johnson and Mr. Gaston. Mr. Gaston and Mr. Johnson were going to go partners and finance Christopher's operation, and in return he split half of the profits he made with them. It was a hell of an opportunity. For Christopher it was a power move. With Mr. Johnson and Mr. Gaston out of the way as partners the other members in the family were under his command. He could set up the operations any way he wanted to. It only took a couple of months and Christopher had become a multi-millionaire. The chances of him returning to the casino to work as a dealer had completely disappeared.

Christopher did all of his business directly with Mr. Gaston and Mr. Johnson.

It would take a year before Christopher would understand the secrecy of alliances, but he learned quickly. In this business, you could never let other people know who your friends were unless it was absolutely necessary.

Most guys that lived in Atlantic City didn't know that Christopher was connected to the guys that were extorting everybody. He didn't approve of it, but they were his friends.

The only time that extortion came in handy was when somebody at one of the bars didn't want to follow the rules and had to be eliminated. Atlantic City was too small a place for excessive killing. Christopher usually let his crew handle anybody that acted foolishly. The guys from Philadelphia didn't always use their heads.

Mr. Gaston, Crazy Morris, Little Aaron, Christopher and his crew were sitting in Mr. Gaston's bar drinking. Christopher and the family ran a heroin spot in Atlantic City that was generating fifty to seventy-five thousand a day depending on what time of the month it was, the closer to the first and welfare checks the better the money.

Mr. Gaston was a millionaire before Christopher but now he had just made another easy million, in less then six months, dealing with Christopher and his heroin connections. There was no disputing the boy was gifted.

"From now on Christopher and Little Aaron are in control of everything. Nobody is allowed to bother me for anything unless it's an absolute emergency. Anything you have to say or do you deal with Christopher and Little Aaron directly."

"Does anybody have a problem with it?"

The others sat there quietly. They didn't really have anything to say because, unofficially, Christopher had already taken over. If you didn't do business with him you weren't going to make any real money.

Mr. Gaston waited for a response and didn't get any. "Well it's official. Christopher and Little Aaron are in charge now."

Later that night after the meeting, Mr. Gaston and Christopher had another private meeting. It was just them, Crazy Moe and the bartender that cleaned up everyday.

Mr. Gaston placed his hands on Christopher's shoulder as he walked him to the back of the bar that led to the alley. "Christopher, Mr. Johnson's crazy about you. He's gonna make you and Little Aaron soldiers in the family. When I retire, you'll become lieutenants. You guys are gonna control the entire South Jersey area with Michael."

Christopher smiled but he didn't say anything. He didn't care to much for Michael, he was a knucklehead.

A couple of weeks after meeting with the family Christopher and his crew flew over to Puerto Rico for the weekend with their wives to celebrate Pedro's birthday at his estate in Puerto Rico.

Pedro had property all over Puerto Rico but he had a bachelor pad in Arecibo, a small city that sat on one of the shores surrounded by tourist attractions and hotels.

Pedro had a small mansion built in the village area near the woods surrounded by larger houses.

Pedro, several of his lieutenants, Christopher and Mr. Johnson were sitting at the pool surrounded by some of the most beautiful women that lived on the Island of Puerto Rico. There were dark-skinned women with coarse hair, dark-skinned women with silky hair. Light-skinned women with coarse hair, and light-skinned women with silky hair. It was a colorful rainbow of beautiful women, all of the women were wearing bathing suits. Some of them were playing in the pool with Pedro's lieutenants and others were lounging around the pool dancing to salsa music, and drinking liquor.

Christopher was sitting in a chair being fed grapes by Pedro's sister Maria, a pretty creamy-skinned Spanish girl with full lips, and a full nose. She was gorgeous and she laughed at everything Christopher said.

Tahwan and the other wives were with the children shopping for souvenirs. They wouldn't be back until nightfall.

Chapter Nine *Atlantic City, New Jersey*

Since We're Family

Little Aaron called Christopher and informed him that his father had arranged an important emergency meeting. The only thing that alarmed Christopher was that the meeting place was at the bar at twelve o'clock at night. Christopher and Mr. Gaston had been meeting at his house in Bungalow Park for their last couple of meetings and Christopher's warning signals went up.

Christopher and Little Aaron were sitting in Christopher's living room drinking coffee and conversing about the meeting.

"What's up, L.A.?" This was the nickname that Christopher used for Little Aaron.

"I don't know what the fuck's going on. My father said the Italians called him yesterday and said to arrange a meeting with you because they heard some bullshit about that liquor." Little Aaron had concern on his face, but something seemed fake about it. Christopher could sense that something was amiss.

"Do I have to bring my gun?" Christopher asked.

"Hell no. My father would never let anything happen to you. We're making too much fucking money. Just don't fess up to robbing that liquor truck. Somehow they got the word on the street that you did it. They're gonna want a cut."

"What did your father say?" Christopher asked, and for the first time in his life he felt a major distrust for his business partners.

"My father said 'Fuck them'. We're not giving them shit. All's fair in love and war."

"I'm bringing my gun. Fuck that shit."

"Nah, don't bring your gun. Mr. Johnson and some of his people are gonna be there, so they're not gonna do anything to you. They just want to talk."

Christopher looked at Aaron to see if he could read anything, but Little Aaron was stupid or naive about the business.

"Alright, I won't do anything."

"Do you have the money you owe my father?" Little Aaron asked.

"Yeah, give me a second." Christopher stood up and walked to his bedroom. He reached under the bed and pulled out a brown paper bag. He returned to the kitchen and dropped the bag on the table.

"Count it; it's all there. One hundred and twenty-five thousand."

Little Aaron opened the bag and glanced inside. "I trust you. I know you would never cheat anybody." Little Aaron lifted the bag and walked outside with it. When they got outside he dropped the bag in the trunk of his car.

"What's up with Corey?" Little Aaron asked.

"He's all right," Chris answered.

"What's up with his case?" Little Aaron asked.

Corey and Lynn had been set up by an informer a couple of weeks earlier. They were both charged with possession of heroin with the intent to distribute.

"The case is bullshit. They're gonna have to throw a lot of that stuff out. He still might have to do a little time, but nothing major. He hired Daniel Kraft and this mother fucker is so bad he made Corey and Lynn attend the indictment hearing." Christopher was proud that his people had the money and common sense to handle the situation like that.

"Okay then. I'll see you tonight at twelve. I've got to get out of here and

handle this business. Bobby Roseland owes my father two hundred grand." It was a lie. Aaron wanted Christopher to think that his father had a string of successful distributors and that Christopher's business wasn't really needed; appreciated but definitely not needed.

Christopher's first and original business partner in all affairs was John Martin. Martin was one of those guys that had been introduced to the business the same time that Christopher was introduced to the business. When Christopher was arrested and went away he left John and Franklin his money. Christopher waited until about six o'clock at night. Then he drove to Ventnor with John Martin to have a light dinner at this Italian restaurant. When they arrived the place was closed, so they drove all the way back to Atlantic City. On Georgia and Arctic Avenue there was a restaurant called "Angelino's II". The place had the best tasting Italian food.

Christopher was wearing a sharp black suit with a dress shirt and an expensive tie. He looked like a lawyer, but his age gave him away. The dark suit brought out his shinny black hair and handsome features.

Martin was wearing a similar suit. They had brought their wives and children. After dinner the wives and children were going home without them. Christopher ordered an Italian seafood dish and John ordered veal. They ate slowly and before they knew it, it was eight o'clock.

"I have to make a call. Excuse me for a minute, John." Christopher disappeared around the corner to the phone booth and made his call.

When he returned he motioned to the waiter, a happy looking Italian guy. "Excuse me, we're trying to blow a little time. Send us our bill, but we're gonna sit and drink."

"No problem," the waiter said. "Maybe this might mean a bigger tip," he thought to himself.

The waiter had remembered Christopher and Mr. Gaston coming in a week before. Their bill was only sixty dollars and they had left him a forty-dollar tip. He loved it and had told the maitre d' to seat them at one of his tables when he saw them walk in.

Christopher and Martin parked their car directly in front of Mr. Gaston's bar and grill. The bar had been closed early because of the meeting. Christopher had never remembered the bar being closed unless it was a holiday or the police had shut it down because of a rowdy fight.

When Christopher and Martin walked in there was an enormous Italian guy guarding the door. He was wearing a blood red silk shirt with tight tailored black slacks, the Italian style for the eighties. The young Italian guy had a gun sticking out of his waistband and he frisked Christopher and Martin as soon as they entered. "They've got guns," the young Italian said.

"Take them," the old Italian man sitting at the table said. He was short and handsome. He looked like he could be the father to the giant standing near the door.

Christopher relinquished his gun even though he didn't feel absolutely safe. Mr. Gaston, Crazy Moe, the infamous Mr. Johnson, the old Italian and a small team of Mr. Johnson's bodyguards were sitting at three tables. The old-timers were sitting at the table by themselves with one chair left and that chair had to be for Christopher. The table was cluttered with dinner plates and half filled wineglasses. They had obviously eaten dinner before this meeting.

"Christopher," Mr. Gaston said. Then motioned Christopher over to the table and Martin followed him.

"Just Christopher, homey."

Surprisingly, Martin didn't budge until Christopher motioned for him to have a seat. The other guys were sitting in the back of the bar laughing and drinking. If they were going to kill him over that liquor they were sloppy because there were a lot of witnesses. This made Christopher feel a little safer because he assumed that they would be a lot smarter than that. Christopher sat at the table and everyone was silent. Christopher could feel the power. Compared to these men, he was a baby in the crime game but that was going to change because he was constantly growing. One day he would be just as powerful or more powerful then all of them put together.

"Christopher, this is Mr. Carfagno."

Christopher reached over and extended his hand. The two men shook hands. Christopher sat and Mr. Gaston poured him a glass of wine from the bottle that was sitting on the table.

Christopher always waited before he drank just in case he was being drugged or poisoned.

"Drink up," Vincent Carfagno said.

"No, thanks. I rarely drink during business meetings."

Christopher smiled his famous smile hoping not to offend the Italian.

"Okay, suit yourself." The Italian grabbed the bottle and poured himself another drink. "This bottle is empty. Bring us another one." He held the bottle up. Morris snatched the bottle and took it back to the bar to throw it in the trashcan. When he returned from the bar he was carrying another bottle.

"Christopher, do you know who I am?" Mr. Carfagno asked. He looked familiar. Like one on the mobsters that Christopher had seen recently in the newspapers. "Well, I'm your family. We're all family." Carfagno looked towards Mr. Johnson.

"This man," Carfagno said looking towards Mr. Johnson. "Is like a brother to me. That's how long we go back. Mr. Gaston Aaron Gee." Christopher had never heard anybody call Mr. Gaston that before.

"He's like a brother to me and he speaks highly of you. He said you're like a son to him, so that means you're like a son to me. We're family. Do you understand me?"

"I understand," Christopher replied, but his expression remained blank and for some reason that appeared to upset Mr. Carfagno.

"Good, because the word on the street is that you hit my beer truck and made off with a shit load of liquor." A smile crossed his face. He had to admit when he heard about it he was impressed. The last time he heard about a nigger high-jacking trucks was in the early seventies, when that fool Dumb Zack was running around North Philadelphia high-jacking soda trucks. They killed him.

He continued, "That beer truck belonged to me and some very important people. We lost a lot of fucking money over that truck." He was shaking his head and singing the words as he explained the incident. "When I first heard about it I said, 'I'm gonna kill the cocksucker that did this to my people', then I got the word on the street it was this young black kid, Christopher Larkin. So I decided to check around and see if he's running with somebody. Somebody we can talk to, and settle this thing without unnecessary bloodshed." He smiled after he said it, but his smile was a warning rattle for danger and Christopher immediately picked it up.

"So, I ask around about you and Mr. Johnson says, 'Hey that's my family. Let me talk to him,' and that's what saved your life. That's why you're still walking around." Mr. Carfagno picked up a piece of bread and ran it over the spaghetti sauce left on his plate. The words made Christopher's heart drop. Christopher kept his cool because he had too, but he had already lost a lot of respect for Mr. Gaston. If this man was saying all of this there had to be a meeting that took place before this one.

"I want my cut of the fucking money. Where's my fucking money." Carfagno's voice was rising now. He was getting a little angrier.

Christopher kept his cool. "Mr. Carfagno, I don't know who told you I stole that liquor but I didn't. I don't have anything that belongs to you and if I can, I'm willing to help you, especially since we're family." The entire table was impressed. He had heart and a straight face when he lied, definitely a plus for the future.

Christopher continued. "The truck that got robbed had to be insured. I'm sure you'll get your money. The police will catch the guys."

Mr. Johnson was so impressed that he almost smiled, but he kept silent. His part was only to arrange the meeting and mind his business. He gave those same instructions to Mr. Gaston and because he was the boss Mr. Gaston had to follow them.

Mr. Carfagno was infuriated. He looked at Mr. Johnson. "Does he understand this shit?" Mr. Carfagno had a puzzled look on his face. "It doesn't matter if the shit was insured or not. When somebody scores big in this town we get our cut. Don't fuck with me. I'll split your fucking nigger head open right now." Mr. Carfagno had lost his cool and used a racial term, something that Mr. Johnson had never seen happen.

Christopher kept his cool. "I told you I didn't have anything to do with it."

Before Christopher could say another word Mr. Carfagno jumped out of his seat and landed on Christopher. They rolled around the floor wrestling for a couple of minutes and for an older man Carfagno was pretty strong, but not strong enough for Christopher.

A couple of seconds later Christopher had the old man pent to the ground. One of the young Italian bodyguards walked up behind Christopher and placed a gun behind his head. Everyone remained seated except Martin. Martin walked over and another bodyguard appeared out of nowhere. He was twice the size of the first one and he pointed his gun at Martin.

Christopher and Martin were outnumbered two guns to none. The others sat there silently watching the event from their tables.

"Listen, faggot, send that mother fucker to get my money. I want fifty thousand or they won't see you alive again." By this time Christopher had raised his hands in the air trying to prevent from being shot.

Mr. Gaston jumped up and walked over when one of the bodyguards pointed the gun at him.

"Mind your fucking business." The old man brushed his clothes off and kicked Christopher in the stomach while he was still on his knees. Christopher buckled over just like the guy he had kicked in the testicles during the grocery store robbery.

Mr. Carfagno bent over and grabbed Christopher by his hair. "Send this mother fucker to go get my money and I'll release you. You're a friend of the family," he said. "Paul, pull the car around the alley. You, monkey face, go get the money." Carfagno was pointing at Martin.

Martin looked at Christopher. "Go to my house and get the money."

Martin ran out of the front door of the bar at full speed. He looked like a little bitch running out of the bar. The Italians laughed.

Mr. Carfagno and the bodyguard lifted Christopher to his feet. They placed the gun against Christopher's back and walked him to the bar's side door.

Mr. Carfagno opened the door first and he saw the Cadillac parked, but it looked empty.

Corey walked beside him and placed his sawed off shotgun to the back of Carfagno's head.

"Raise your fucking hands."

Carfagno refused to lift his hands. "You must be fucking crazy. I'm a made man in La Costra Nostra. You're a fucking gang-banger. Fuck you!"

Just then the bodyguard pushed Christopher through the door. When he noticed the guy behind Mr. Carfagno he froze.

He saw the shotgun to the back of the old man's head.

Christopher brushed his clothes off. "Mr. Carfagno you're gonna get twenty thousand and we're gonna call this thing even. You don't fuck with me and I'll never fuck with you. Let me go. The money will be here in thirty minutes. I know the rules. I may be young, but I can protect myself and there's just as many of us as there are of you."

Christopher walked onto the other side of the alley. The Italian bodyguard didn't do anything.

Corey kept the shotgun raised but he stepped away from the old man's head. When he got next to Christopher they walked backwards towards their car, then they jumped in it and sped away.

"Where's Paulie?" Carfagno asked. That's when they noticed the other car blocking the other end of the alleyway. Carfagno walked towards his Cadillac. His bodyguard, Paulie, was laying on the ground with his hands tied behind his back unconscious.

Mr. Carfagno couldn't believe it.

"Anthony, you stay here, collect the money and don't mention this shit to anybody. Do you understand me?" If the word got out that a group of young black guys did this to him not only would it start a war, but it would be a major embarrassment for his family. "Help me lift Paulie into the car."

The other bodyguard helped his comrade into the car. He was embarrassed but he stayed behind at the bar. He entered back into the bar through the front entrance. Five minutes later the telephone rang at the bar; the person wanted to speak to the Italian guy there.

When the bodyguard got on the phone the voice on the other end said, "Your money's outside in the trashcan. Hurry up and get it."

The bodyguard went outside, got the money and then waited for Mr. Carfagno to return. Mr. Carfagno returned fifteen minutes later by himself. As soon as the bodyguard came outside and jumped in the car they pulled off.

"I'm putting a contract out on that boy's life and I want you to handle it?"

"No problem," The bodyguard replied. "But it's the responsibility of Mr. Johnson."

"You know what? You're right." They sped off.

Christopher's respect level on the street soared as word of the incident with the Italians hit the street. Things were starting to get a little crazy. The family suffered another damaging blow when the state did a drug sweep. Everyone got arrested including Christopher and Little Aaron.

Christopher, Mr. Gaston, Little Aaron, Mr. Johnson, Big Cliff and Black attended a meeting in Philadelphia.

Black was one of the bodyguards who was present when Christopher met with the Italians and he was awed. He was so impressed that he started spreading the word through the streets of Philadelphia.

"Christopher, you handled yourself well in Atlantic City," Mr. Johnson said. "The fucking Italians are heated. I told them I would handle it, but I'm gonna let you slide. Just lay low and the next time you're gonna highjack a truck let me know so I can investigate."

Christopher smiled because he was a little relieved that the situation was handled. It was going to be hard to fight a court case and a war against a bunch of Italians.

"They want fifty thousand dollars to settle it though." Mr. Johnson looked directly at Christopher to see his reaction.

"I don't have it and I'm not giving them another dime," Christopher responded without even flinching. Christopher didn't know whom he could trust. As far as he was concerned they were all out to rob him.

"Chris, I don't like to hear you talk like that. Pay them the money. It's nothing to you just to keep the peace," Mr. Johnson said and he had a valid point it wasn't worth it.

"Don't worry. I can handle myself and I won't drag you into this," Christopher said.

When Carfagno had approached Mr. Johnson about killing Christopher he refused because Christopher generated entirely too much money selling heroin, speed and now cocaine. In the early eighties cocaine started popping up everywhere slowing pushing speed into the quiet residential areas. By the time 1983 rolled around and the crack explosion in New York, speed would completely disappear in black neighborhoods and become a white person's drug.

Chapter Ten *Atlantic City, New Jersey*

Taxation Without Reaction

Several months after the bar incident Little Aaron and his fiancee had one of the biggest weddings that the entire Atlantic City region had ever seen.

Everyone in the family attended the wedding. It was held at the Second Baptist Church. The reception was held in a casino ballroom. After the wedding everyone met at Little Aaron's house in Brigantine, New Jersey. Brigantine was a small island connected to Atlantic City by a bridge. Before the casinos arrived it was a dump and most of the residents were poor, white trash. After the casinos arrived several wealthy residents built property there and the entire island's status changed. It went from a dump to a hide out for the rich and famous in the South Jersey vicinity.

Christopher, Mr. Gaston, Little Aaron and the rest of the family had a meeting at Little Aaron's house in Brigantine right after the wedding. The wedding was small and private. Everybody in the family attended.

While everyone else was celebrating at the reception, Mr.

Gaston and the rest of the family held an urgent meeting at Little Aaron's brand new house. The Gastons bought numerous properties in Brigantine because they knew that by the time the nineties rolled around Brigantine's property value would be unbelievably expensive, just like the property in the Inlet. Because the Inlet was run down people assumed the casinos would shy away from it, but they did the exact opposite and now lots that were previously going for several thousand were going for four times their value or more.

Mr. Gaston had called the meeting so that he could divide his family into mini-crews. All of this was Christopher's idea. This way they could better control distribution and remove some of the heat at the bar. There were too many of them together. They needed to separate and spread out. The others just sat there listening. They really didn't have a choice in the matter. Mr. Gaston was creating a family within a family.

Christopher and Aaron ran the Liquor House on the Westside. Lynn and Corey ran Waltz Dance Club and Bar in the Inlet. Mark ran a bar near the boardwalk called Fourteen South. Frank ran a bar called the Central Inn near Chelsea and the boardwalk. Everyone was given their own bar to operate so that their businesses wouldn't collide with each other's and it worked, because it allowed them freedom and reduced the heat.

Whatever Christopher was doing was working because they weren't getting arrested as frequently as they used to, plus the bars weren't getting hot. Each bar had a look out team and a distribution team. The only thing that messed things up was that Mr. Johnson had sent a crew down from Philadelphia and they were extorting dealers from other bars. They were attempting to practice the get down or lay down theory. If you didn't buy from them, then you couldn't buy from anybody else.

The only problem with that was, if one group controlled all of the distribution, then one group suffered the consequences. At least if there was more than one group, you wouldn't have to worry about the police easily surveilling you.

"Michael, your gonna have to tell Andre to lay back a little. He's messing everything up," Christopher said. Michael resembled his father in-law. Everyone knew that Michael wasn't Mr. Johnson blood relation; he had married one of Mr. Johnson's daughters. Mr. Johnson wanted Michael to take over the business when he retired but the older lieutenants weren't going for it. That's one of the reasons Mr. Gaston was forming a second family, in case of a war. He was going to support Mr. Johnson whether he agreed with him or not.

"I can't tell that man anything. My father in-law said to clean the city out, get rid of all the competition and that's what we're doing." Michael had been in the business for a little over five years now and he was already a lieutenant in the family, a position that usually took at least ten years to acquire.

"Atlantic City is too small for that. You're gonna make it hot for everybody. The police don't make moves on nobody unless bodies start flying and I don't want to be associated with that," Christopher said.

"Well you could never live in a big city like Philly because that's how we do it." He was trying his best to be sarcastic. He didn't see what all the fuss was about Christopher. He seemed like everybody else to him. In fact, he seemed a little softer. Half of the guys that lived in Atlantic City wouldn't survive a week in Philadelphia.

"Well, maybe I'll have a meeting with Mr. Johnson," Christopher said, and the response sounded weak. Nearly all of the Atlantic City crew thought that Christopher was a little too nice. Several of the guys might mistake that as being weak, but he had already proven he had balls when he made that move against the Italians, so important people knew he definitely wasn't a coward.

"See that's the problem with you guys," Andre said. He was a big stupid-looking guy who didn't do anything right. "You've got to start enforcing a street tax, there's crazy money in it."

"Dre, I wouldn't mind a street tax, but Atlantic City is too small for that," Christopher said.

"Well, they're paying," He said and smiled that goofy smile that he had. All the guys from Philly laughed.

Christopher decided to skip it, as long as none of the lieutenants under him disobeyed him. "Christopher, what's up with the weed?" Corty asked. His business had been suffering because Mr. Johnson hadn't had marijuana for a couple of weeks. They were so busy trying to flood the streets with heroin and cocaine that they were starting to neglect the marijuana business.

"I don't know," Mr. Gaston responded. "I talked to William and his connections don't know anything yet. They're still trying to get it," Mr. Gaston said. Marijuana was money but not serious money.

"Well, Frank's got some connections, Maybe he can do something with him. I'll call him tomorrow," Christopher said.

Franklin had been doing excellent. He was taking the heroin Christopher fronted him, and selling it in a couple of different bars in New York City. He had a couple of guy's come down from New York to buy wholesale from Christopher. He was trying to get Christopher to set up operations and start distribution in New York, but Christopher was busy, formulating things in the South Jersey area. Setting up serious distribution in New York was gonna cause a lot of bloodshed.

They all sat around discussing other little things amongst each other. Mr. Gaston took this as a sign that the meeting was over.

"Okay, gentlemen, if nobody has anything else to say the meeting is over and we'll hold another one next week. Christopher, I need to speak with you in private."

The others got up and left except Little Aaron and Michael, they sat around. This surprised Christopher because most times Mr. Gaston would discuss business with him privately.

When the last person left the room Michael closed the door.

"You guys are the backbone of this thing. I just wanted to talk with you and let you know that you have to stick together. In a few years I'll be retiring and you guys will be running everything. Christopher and Aaron will be running South Jersey and Michael you'll be running Philly. You guys are gonna be multi-multi- millionaires. The whole world is gonna want to kiss your ass. Big Aaron gulped a shot of liquor. "So stick together and don't fuck this thing up. Next week we're gonna see Mr. Johnson. You guys might be going on your own. He wants you guys to start having meetings without me." The saddest look in the world came over Mr. Gaston's face. "I'm trying to teach you guys the business so that I can successfully retire."

Christopher didn't know if he should say it but he said it

anyway. "Mr. Gee, I thought you were next in line to run everything."

The words sent something through Big Aaron and he stood quiet for a moment and smiled. "I wish, anyway we can't worry about that, that's the future and nobody knows what lies ahead of us. It's time to get back to this reception," He said and the meeting was over.

Mr. Gaston walked over to them and embraced them. It was odd how everything was working out. Sometimes Mr. Gaston treated Christopher like he was one of his sons. Christopher appreciated the father figure gesture but it was a little too late for that. His father was dead and gone.

Christopher had left Tahwan and her mother at the dinner table. He knew that they would be looking for him.

"Congratulations Aaron," Christopher said as they were walking back to the reception. Tahwan and Christopher had bought him a China dish set from Lennox China and they had presented Little Aaron and his bride with a check for twenty-five thousand dollars. Most of the other lieutenants had matched Chris's gift.

Christopher was a millionaire and he knew that Little Aaron had to be one because he got a cut of whatever his father made.

Christopher had found out that a couple of the dealers in the city were paying thousands of dollars a week in street taxes. Right after that he found out that Little Aaron was one of the collection men. All the extortion money was going to Mr. Gaston, who was taking it directly to Mr. Johnson.

Christopher, Little Aaron and Michael Donaldson, the lawyer that Christopher had hired to represent him for his drug charges, were sitting in Mr. Donaldson's office. Michael Donaldson had represented him in several real estate ventures. Christopher took most of his money and invested it into properties. His real estate company Off Shore Realty, had quietly acquired several pieces of commercial properties in various cities and was continuously growing. He was able to do this because the police didn't know much about him. All of his investments were done legally through banks with either Mr. Gaston or Mr. Donaldson co-signing for him. After acquiring his first two commercial properties he no longer needed them. Christopher had made so many wise investments legally that his children would probably never have to work a day in their lives. He just had to make sure that he hid everything properly. On paper, Off Shore Realty was a small realty company that owned a couple of properties in New Jersey. If the authorities investigated, they would realize that it was actually a growing realty monopoly. By the time they caught on to his investments, the web would be too intricate and tangled for the authorities to actually confiscate anything substantial.

"Christopher, you and the others don't have anything to worry about. I'm best friends with the prosecutor and for about thirty, forty grand we'll get all of you guy's probation, except the guys with records. I know you won't do any real time; I'm guaranteeing that."

"Can you trust this guy?" Christopher asked, dressed in another suit as he usually did when discussing serious business.

"Of course I can trust him or I wouldn't be offering him money."

"Well, maybe we should give him a bonus, sort of like a money guarantee for his assistance in the future."

The lawyer smiled. "How much are you talking?"

"At least another fifty grand," Christopher said. The lawyer was overwhelmed.

"You young guys impress me." He should have known better. Christopher owned the building on Atlantic Avenue that he was moving his law offices to.

Chapter Eleven New York City

Me Don't Run Like Dat

Christopher, Corty and Franklin rode in Franklin's brand new Mercedes Benz. Franklin was doing excellent because he had established major outlets in New York City with the help of Christopher. Christopher started distributing more heroin, in New York City than he distributed in New Jersey through Franklin. Once a week Christopher would come to New York and meet more people. There was major competition in New York City but there was always room for expansion and the market growth potential was ten times greater than the entire New Jersey. Franklin had cousins that lived in Manhattanville Apartments on 131st and Amsterdam Avenue. Franklin recruited a few new young guys that hung out in the park there and business had exploded. Christopher was thinking about starting his own family and making Franklin his number one lieutenant.

"How's business going?" Christopher asked.

"I've got 2.5 million in the trunk for you as we speak." Franklin smiled. "How's Tahwan and the baby doing?"

"They're doing wonderful. I think she's pregnant again." Christopher smiled, happy with his life and family relationship.

"What's up with Mom?" Franklin asked. "mother's doing fine." Christopher said. "You have to see the house I bought her."

"I'm coming down there but right now I'm busy. That boy in the Bronx is giving me a major headache." "Don't worry about it I'll handle it." Christopher said. Franklin was averaging about five hundred thousand dollars a week on heroin sales. A slow week for him brought in a quarter million dollars. He generated about two million dollars a month with a nice percentage of it being profit. Christopher got to see about a million a month from Franklin, but only a percentage of that was profit. Christopher wasn't complaining though because the percentage that was profit had made him a multi-millionaire before he had turned twenty-five.

"What's up with your house?" Franklin said. Corty was sitting in the back of the car silent. He didn't get to visit New York much but he was amazed when he did because it was enormous and full of life.

"I don't know I'm thinking about buying this one I saw on the Westside." Christopher said. Presently he was renting a small house in Bungalow Park.

"Which one? That mansion on the Westside?" Franklin asked.

"Why would I buy a fucking mansion and bring heat on myself. My wife's a dealer at Resorts and I'm a small grocery store owner."

"You need to move off shore or something, anywhere but that little shit hole. I thought you would see that by now."

"You want me to come up here?" Christopher asked. He knew Franklin loved his independence in New York City and didn't want Christopher within a mile of the area living wise. In New York City, Franklin lived like a celebrity. He owned a small taxi and Limousine Company. He lived in a beautiful Brownstone around the corner from City College on Striver's Row. He owned an apartment in the village and another Brownstone in Brooklyn's Park slope section where all the white people lived. One of his girlfriends stayed in each of these places. Plus, he had property in New Jersey. He had bought his mother a house.

Franklin pulled up in front of a small storefront on 128th and Lenox Avenue in the heart of Harlem, mid way between

Harlem hospital and the Apollo theater a famous theater where all the legendary acts have played and performed for decades.

Franklin, Christopher and Corty exited the car and walked into the storefront. As soon as they walked inside the store they were hit in the face, by a cloud of marijuana smoke.

A group of West Indians were sitting around listening to music. One of the guys rushed out from behind the counter.

"Bumbacylde." The Rastafarian said. "What the bumbacylde you doing boy? You ready for business?" He asked.

"Yeah, where's Dan?" Franklin asked.

"Him at de apartment. I'm taking you to it." The dark Rastafarian replied.

"Christopher, this is Simeon. Simeon this is Corty." They shook hands.

"Move it boy." The Rasta turned around and said, then another Rasta who was sitting behind the counter jumped up and they left. They were headed to the apartment.

The Rasta had a brand new BMW parked outside and he jumped in it. "Follow me." It was hard to understand his English. He couldn't have been in the country for more then a couple of years.

They drove across town to the West Riverside and made a right, drove down to Seventieth Street and pulled over in front of one of the gigantic apartment buildings.

A white doorman came out and opened both of the doors. Franklin tipped him but Simeon didn't give him anything. Some Rastafarians couldn't stand white people and Simeon was one of them. "Dem de Babylon system." He would say.

They walked into the hallway and caught the elevator all the way up to the fourteenth floor. The apartment building was lavish and Franklin admired it. He wanted to get rid of his apartment in the village. There were to many hippies running around all day and he wanted more privacy if he was going to have to pay outrageous rent.

When they walked through the hallway Simeon knocked on the door. The Rasta that was with them had greeted them but hadn't said a word since.

Two seconds later the door slid open and a pretty petite young Rastafarian answered the door. She was brown skin with flawless skin, pouty lips, round oval eyes and lemon scented dreads that fragranced the air. When she walked she switched her little hips from side to side. She was wearing a brown Ethiopian printed dress shirt and some brown tights. Her feet were bare but polished and she was gorgeous. Her name was Khalida and she was Dan's fiancee.

"Hello." She had a sweet voice of an innocent teenager but she was a grown woman. "Peace brother." She kissed the other Rasta's on the cheeks and embraced them.

"Where Dan?" Simeon said.

"In the living-room playing chess."

Christopher and the others walked into the living room. The apartment was completely furnished. There were all kinds of Afrocentric paintings hanging on the wall and you could tell that who ever lived in the apartment had money. Most of the furniture was white but some of the couches were animal prints. When they entered the living room Dan stood to his feet and extended his hand, he greeted them.

Dan was a little over five feet five inches tall. He was reddish complexion with long beautiful reddish colored dreads that hung all the way to his waist. He was handsome in a natural looking way. He looked perfect for his fiance.

"Greeting brothers." He said as he shook their hands. A couple seconds later, a white maid appeared out the back of the room.

"Will these gentlemen be staying for lunch?" The maid asked.

"Of course." Dan motioned for them to sit. "Would you like anything to drink? Juice, spring water? Anything?" He asked.

They placed their orders and then sat in the living room. Dan's fiance disappeared to another room so they could have their privacy and discuss business. Christopher admired the enormous fish tank with all the tropical fish swimming around in it. The only reason that he was here was because there was a marijuana drought and not even the brothers in Philly could get it.

"Franklin, talk to me." Franklin had been coming to Dan's shops for a couple of years now and had gotten close to him. When Christopher complained that he couldn't find any weed. Franklin contacted Dan and arranged the business meeting.

"My partners want to buy two hundred and fifty pounds.

Can you handle it?" Franklin asked.

And the Rastafarian just smiled. Two hundred and fifty pounds was a sizable deal but he was bringing tons of marijuana over on boats, ships and airplanes.

"What are they trying to pay?" He asked Franklin but Christopher was the one that responded.

"Well, what's the going price on weight like this?" Christopher asked.

"We're selling pounds from the store for five hundred but that's because it's election time and the prices are up. You know how the politicians get during elections. Your country controls everything."

"So what are we looking at?" Christopher asked getting straight to the point.

"Two hundred and fifty dollars a pound for high grade quality. You'll get no complaints. I sell it and smoke it everyday." Dan walked to a candy dish. It was filled with marijuana. He put a handful in Christopher's hands.

Christopher placed it to his nostrils, smelled it and then passed it to Corty. He had to give his approval. He was going to be the one selling it.

Dan got up, walked to the dresser drawer, pulled out rolling paper and a bong. "Let's smoke it. Which one?" Dan held the bong and the papers in the air.

Franklin pointed to the bong and Christopher pointed to the papers.

Dan placed the bong down. The paper's win. He could tell that Christopher was the boss without being told. Dan rolled a bunch of joints and each of them smoked one. The weed was excellent.

"We get to see every pound don't we?" Christopher asked. His eyes were bloodshot.

"They're packaged in five pound wraps. I was going to leave them sealed but if you want to check every one you can. If you have any problems bring them back immediately." He said it because he was having problems with customer's unwrapping the packages and switching the weed. "As long as you guarantee the quality that's what's important with me."

"You think I'm gonna blow a sixty-two thousand dollar deal. No Rasta me don't run like dat. Sin?"

Christopher shook his head yes. He liked him already.

Dan's people brought the weed over packaged in five pound packs. The pounds were wrapped in cellophane.

Christopher had a couple of bags and Corty had a couple of bags. They loaded the weed in the bags and took them to Franklin's car. Franklin drove them to a private parking lot on 149th and St. Nicholas Avenue. Christopher and Corty drove into the parking lot and then transferred the marijuana to Corty's car. From there two drivers, who had been waiting in a hotel the entire time drove the shipments home to Atlantic City.

When they left the parking lot Christopher, Franklin and Corey jumped in Franklin's car because they had to drive to the Bronx where they had another meeting with Pedro. The heroin distribution was going excellent especially in New York City. Franklin was distributing the same amount of heroin that all of the lieutenants together were distributing in Jersey.

Fortunately some of the lieutenants were establishing distribution in other major cities like Boston, Baltimore and Washington, D.C.

Christopher wanted to visit Pedro because he had passed out a couple of weeks earlier and was admitted to the hospital. The doctors were saying it was pneumonia or something they couldn't quite put their fingers on. It was the early eighties and the Aids epidemic was just starting to demand attention.

Chapter Twelve Atlantic City, New Jersey

They Couldn't Protect Me

Christopher and his crew met at Jahna's baby shower. Corty's and Jahna had been married for two years and this was their second child. They had decided to throw the party at Club Harlem. The same club that Christopher had gained his original gun charges and the same place, six years earlier where the Black Mafia had performed a famous hit.

Christopher and Franklin were driving back on the Garden State Parkway South.

"So what you gonna do?" Franklin asked.

"About what?" Christopher asked. He was puzzled, tired and not in the mood for any of Franklin's speaking in code games.

"About the cocaine connect."

"Ohhh." Christopher said. "Have you talked to him?"

"I did a little business with him."

Christopher was surprised, he didn't know that Franklin was doing side business but there was nothing that he could say as long as Franklin came through with Christopher and Mr. Gaston's money.

"How much did you spend?" Christopher said while rolling a joint. He knew they shouldn't be smoking on the parkway, especially with millions of dollars in the trunk of the car.

"I bought ten bricks for forty thousand a piece."

Christopher was astonished and the surprise that crossed his face showed it. "Impressive." Was his only response.

"So what do you think?" Franklin said pulling on the joint after Christopher lit it and passed it to him.

"That's the same thing that Mr. Gaston's charging us." Christopher said. He rolled his window down and made sure that he obeyed the speed limit. The Italians were importing cocaine from Colombia and supplying Mr. Johnson.

"I thought you said Mr. Gaston can't keep it."

"He can't." Christopher responded. "So the next time there's a drought, I'll get with you."

"You're making that motherfucker a ton of money and he don't deserve it." Franklin said. "I'm glad I'm in New York because I can't stand that motherfucker."

Christopher finished the joint and threw the roach out of the window.

"I don't know where to get any guns but we've got connections for everything else, we can break off." Franklin was high and angry. He had a group of girls meeting him in the city so that he could hang out and have a little fun as usual.

"Franklin, you've got to learn loyalty. Everything's going excellent why would I mess that up and break away?"

Franklin was pissed. "You really think those motherfuckers give a fuck about you?" Franklin was getting more upset the more they spoke about it.

"I know this is just business. I ain't crazy." They drove the rest of the way in silence, both of them reflecting along the way. By the time that they got to Atlantic City, two and an half-hours later, Christopher had his thinking cap on straight.

"In a couple of weeks I want you to connect me with this Puerto Rican." Christopher said turning off of the expressway onto Atlantic Avenue. He pulled up in one of the garages at the casino and pulled up next to his car.

"You can drive my car and I'll meet you tonight at the party." Christopher pulled the key to his car off his key chain and passed it to Franklin, then he sped off.

Franklin figured it out. Christopher was going somewhere to count that money and give Mr. Gaston his share.

Christopher drove straight to his mother's house on Green

Street. It was split level with a garage and a security fence surrounding it.

Christopher removed the duffel bags and took the bags to the office he had built in his house. He closed the door and removed the money machine. It took him an hour to divide and count the two point five million. Once he did he hid it in a gigantic safe that he had built in the floor. He would give Mr. Gaston his money later.

Christopher and Corty's marijuana business had grown prosperously. The quality was better and the price was more consistent. The only thing that he had to do was give Corty half of the money he needed for the package and Corty would split his profits with Christopher.

Two weeks later, Christopher arranged the meeting with the Puerto Rican in New York. He offered Mr. Gaston and Mr. Johnson the opportunity to become partners and they jumped on it. Their only requirement was that they would be able to meet the Puerto Rican. A first Christopher was hesitant but he agreed.

All the lieutenants had their own bars and everything was going as planned. The business had expanded way past the bar the lieutenants were in control of different cities now. Some of them had heroin customers that came and bought wholesale from out of state. They were on their way to becoming international.

Some weeks after Christopher made the cocaine deal he started spending more and more time at the bars making sure that everything was organized.

First thing every morning Christopher would jump in his Plymouth Horizon and tour the city. Then, he would go from bar to bar collecting money. Christopher wanted to make sure that everything was running smoothly.

Christopher pulled his Plymouth Horizon to the curb of Kentucky and Illinois. He didn't see the undercover parked at the end of the block until they had his car surrounded. John Martin was riding with him posing as a bodyguard and errand boy.

The police surrounded the car with their weapons drawn. Christopher and John raised their hands, they were surprised when a group of under-covers ran into the bar and started pulling guys out.

Everybody in the family got locked up except Mr. Gaston. Even Little Aaron got picked up and was charged with conspiracy. Christopher got picked up and charged with conspiracy.

Christopher's lawyer arrived at the station an hour after his arrest and his bail was posted before he could be shipped to the county jail.

Little Aaron was bailed and represented before he could reach the Atlantic County jail. The only person who wasn't picked up besides Mr. Johnson was Corty. Fortunately he had been given his own bar by Christopher and Mr. Gaston and was out of harms way.

Christopher and the others stopped for a week to meet with their lawyers and analyze things. A week after that, they were back in business.

Christopher, Franklin, two bodyguards and Pedro were sitting in Pedro's apartment in Manhattan. Pedro had a beautiful apartment in Spanish Harlem in one of those giant buildings that had just been constructed and the rent was ridiculous.

Pedro sat on the living room sofa and he looked terrible. His family wanted to rush him to the hospital but he refused. When Christopher had met him a couple of years earlier he was about one hundred and ninety pounds a nice size for his six three frame. Now, he had shriveled down to one hundred and fifty pounds and he looked terrible. His skin had darkened from the medication he was taking.

Pedro reached his hand out to Christopher. Christopher knelt down next to him and grabbed it. "Christopher, I knew you were coming." Christopher didn't know anything about this new disease but it was killing his friend. "They told me you were sick again I had to come."

Pedro smiled. The medication had him out of it. "The doctors says I'm not going to make it. This time I believe them." "No, that's nonsense they have a cure for everything. Were just gonna have to go to the government and find out what they're using."

Pedro laughed for the first time in a long time then he began coughing. "My brother Ramon is going to take over the business if something happens to me. I think I'm going to fly to Puerto Rico. I have family and children over there. I want to be near my parents."

Pedro closed his eyes for a couple of seconds and then he opened them. He released his grip on Christopher's hands and removed his thin gold chain with the small gold medallions with the Saints on them. "Here I want you to have this." He passed the chain to Christopher.

Christopher pushed his hands away. "Pedro, I can't take this."

"Yes, you can."

"One of your sons should have this." Christopher said.

"No my sons are okay. I wanted a close friend to have it. Maybe the saints will protect you because they couldn't protect me." Just then he started coughing uncontrollably and some of the other women ran into the living room. Eventually he stopped Christopher, bent over and allowed him to place the chain on his neck.

Pedro wasn't going to live too much longer and you didn't have to be a rocket scientist to figure it out.

The family was going to have to concentrate on the cocaine business. Pedro's brother wasn't smart enough to continue operating successfully so they were about to lose their heroin connection.

Cocaine wasn't as profitable as heroin but it was quieter and the family was going to need that if they wanted to stay in business.

Chapter Thirteen *Atlantic City, New Jersey*

Greed is Not Good

Christopher and Michael Donaldson were sitting at the defense table. They weren't at trial yet and the prosecution was already offering a deal. The conspiracy to possess and distribute narcotic charges would never stick unless one of the defendants decided to flip and that was not going to happen.

The only thing Mr. Donaldson was worried about was the probation violation. Even though Christopher hadn't been in trouble for years, he still had a year of probation left.

Michael came out to a conference room where Christopher was sitting. The prosecution wanted to hold a motion in one of the conference rooms in private with the judge and defense available, but the judge denied it, so they were back in the courthouse hearing the motion.

The prosecutor Hope Nicole Bailey was a nice looking white lady, who had never prosecuted any serious cases against respectable lawyers and she was already ready to make a plea- bargain.

"Your honor the prosecution is asking that you revoke the bail because the defendant is on probation." Mrs. Bailey wanted to pretend that she was putting up the fight so the next week when she offered a plea-agreement, the judge wouldn't chew her ass out.

Before Mr. Donaldson could jump up and say anything the judge corrected her. "Has parole been informed of the defendants arrest?"

"Yes, your honor." Mr. Donaldson answered.

"Then, I think we'll leave that one up to probation." Later that day, they went over a couple of little details. It wasn't the drug charges that were going to hurt Christopher. It was the gun possession.

When the police arrested him with Martin they were both carrying guns. Martin had been arrested before on gun charges so he was going to do some time, even if it was only a couple of months.

Andre and Michael pulled up to one of the bars. Several independent dealers started making money with the families arrest and Mr. Gaston not knowing how much knowledge the police had, told most of the guys to lay back. If Christopher was sent to jail, it might turn out to be a major set back.

Michael had set up a respectable distribution network in one of the bars in the Inlet that was very profitable. He was making good money selling powder cocaine and the market was growing. His only problem was that Mr. Johnson got the cocaine from his Italian connections and when they didn't have anything they were out for days or sometimes weeks and Mr. Johnson didn't trust going anywhere else.

Michael and Andre pulled up to the bar. Michael had several cars but he didn't drive them in the city. He spent a lot of time running back and forth to Philadelphia. His wife moved to Atlantic City but they still had family and friends in Philadelphia, so every weekend they went to Philadelphia even if it was just to visit.

"I don't give a fuck who you buy your bundles from. If your gonna be selling in this bar it's a thousand a week. I know you got the money." Andre was saying.

Gary looked up at him. Andre was the size of a nice size football player and Gary was small and puny.

"You trying to tell me, I buy my shit from Christopher and I still got to pay you mother fuckers to sell my shit in a bar I've been selling drugs in all my life?" Gary was pissed the fuck off. "I want to talk to Christopher."

Andre was so fast when he swung Gary saw the motion but by the time he realized what was going on Andre had already hit him. The room had exploded into a gigantic light.

Gary laid on the floor unconscious and Andre continued talking.

"Y'all think this shit is a joke, hun?" Andre was standing over Gary still talking. "Christopher's going to jail and a lot of you motherfuckers are gonna have to straighten up." Andre reached down and dug in Gary's pants. He removed his jewelry, the heroin and his money. He got to keep all the petty money that he got from extortion. Any money that a dealer voluntarily paid went to Michael and the family.

"I'm telling you mother fuckers a lot of shit is going to change." Andre looked at Michael and they left the bar.

A couple of weeks after Christopher's first court appearance Mr. Gaston called a meeting.

Christopher, Little Aaron, Michael and Andre attended. They were all sitting in Mr. Gaston's living room having drinks. Mr. Gaston's wife stayed with Little Aaron for a while because she was sick and tired of hearing the rumors about Mr. Gaston's girlfriend. For the first time in years she had threaten Mr. Gaston with divorce. Mr. Gaston waited until they got seated and then he told them. "Big Will's coming in a little while."

Mr. Johnson walked in the door, he was six three two hundred pounds. Even with the weight because of his height he appeared to be thin. He did have a little beer belly but even that enhanced his appearance.

Mr. Johnson was dark skin with blemish free skin. He had a couple of black moles that stuck out on his face, if you looked at him closely but it didn't affect his appearance. He was still handsome.

When he entered he shook everyone's hands. Clark, Mr. Johnson's underboss followed him around. He was five eleven, skinny with greasy skin and processed hair. His eyes were blood-shot red from years of not getting proper sleep. He spent most of his life chasing women and drinking heavily.

The other guy accompanying Mr. Johnson was Big Cliff Mr. Johnson's bodyguard for over twenty-five years. He didn't hold any power in the organization but he was one of Mr. Johnson's closest friends who between body-guarding and his side business made a good living.

"Christopher, what's the problem?" Mr. Johnson asked. This was Christopher's first official meeting about the extortion situation, by this time Christopher was a legend and highly respected in organized crime circles. He could make things move and shake on the streets of New Jersey.

"I don't know. I just want you to talk to Andre and them." Christopher was referring to Michael and Andre's extortion ring.

"What's the problem?" Mr. Johnson asked again.

"They're extorting every fucking body."

The others laughed like Christopher had told a joke.

"Are they extorting any of your people?" Mr. Johnson asked. Even Christopher was awed by him and the way that Mr. Johnson carried his power.

"Not really. I mean, he's extorting people that buy from me." Christopher said. Christopher was keeping his cool because he knew that he didn't have anything to worry about. He knew how to handle himself and he proved that with the Italian incident.

"Michael I don't want you extorting people that buy from Christopher. His money is my money. Do you understand?" Mr. Johnson asked.

"Yes." Michael replied and Christopher just looked at them. They were so different when they weren't around Mr. Johnson.

"But what about the guys that sell for him and come into our bar?" Michael asked because he wanted the information relayed to him clearly.

"If they sell in your bar then they have to pay that's the way it goes in Philly, right Clark?" Mr. Johnson was asking his underboss to verify some information.

"You damn right. If you sell out of a bar I don't give a fuck who you buy from unless it's Will's shit you pay a street tax for that area." Clark said. He had a drink in his hand. He was sipping from it while he spoke.

"How much are you charging everybody?" Mr. Johnson asked.

"A thousand a week."

"That's it?" Mr. Johnson said, "They can handle that. Christopher this is how we're going to handle it. If you present a name to me they won't have to pay a street tax but if this person's generating money then they'll have to pay. Do you agree?" Mr. Johnson asked.

"Kind of." Everyone looked at Christopher like he was crazy. Nobody talked to Mr. Johnson like that.

"What do you mean kind of?" Mr. Johnson asked.

"To me it's not worth it because it only creates enemies and generates snitches. If we control the entire market then we become the polices only target and I'm not comfortable with that."

"So, what do we do? Leave these guys to make money while we take all of the risk? The streets are only clean because of us." Mr. Johnson said.

"We're a family, nobody can hold a candle to us. I mean if a bar is making twenty thousand dollars a day and seventeen thousand of it is ours. Who cares about the other three thousand? We can't make all the money because it will make it easier for the police to concentrate on us. But say if that other three thousand is broken up, by other groups then they share some of the heat. If we control a bar and we're the only one's there, who are the police going to arrest?" Christopher made an excellent point and Mr. Johnson was impressed. The others were too greedy to think like that.

"Well you're one of the guys running shit, if I were you I wouldn't worry about it. If you're not the one that's getting locked up why in the fuck should you give a fuck anyway?"

Christopher just gave that calm look that he always gave when he lost in a conversation. Mr. Johnson was the boss and whatever he said was the final decision.

"Okay, enough of that. So what's up with your case." Mr. Johnson asked skipping the subject and thus leaving it finalized.

"I'm gonna beat the case but the problem is my parole violation."

"How much time are you looking at?" Mr. Johnson said. He was drinking also.

"Probably six months or less with good time."

Mr. Johnson looked at Mr. Gaston. "Is that gonna mess us up?"

"I don't know. I talked to Christopher and told him what you said. We figured it out the best way we could." Mr. Gaston didn't seem to have the confidence around Mr. Johnson that he had when they were alone.

"So, Christopher what's your idea?" Mr. Johnson asked.

"Little Aaron's my partner and he can take over. He knows everybody."

"And Michael?" Mr. Johnson asked.

"I don't think the other guys are gonna want to deal with Michael because they don't really know him."

Mr. Johnson finished his drink and settled the meeting. He was rubbing his chin trying to think for a minute.

"This is how we're gonna do it. Little Aaron's gonna be in charge and Michael's gonna be his right hand man. Andre you do whatever Michael says and when Christopher comes home we'll take it from there"

Christopher was surprised at how efficiently Mr. Johnson put everything together. Maybe that was why he was the boss.

"We're gonna have a meeting the day that you get home. Hurry home soon because my youngest daughters getting married next year and I want you there." Mr. Johnson motioned for Big Cliff to pour him another drink.

Big Cliff poured Mr. Johnson a drink and then Mr. Johnson continued speaking.

"Is their anything else?" Mr. Johnson asked.

Everyone just looked at him silently.

"Good I have some other business to attend too. Christopher I need to speak with you in private."

Everyone got up and left except Christopher, Mr. Gaston, Big Cliff and Mr. Johnson.

"Christopher, when you come home I want you and Little Aaron to run Atlantic City with Michael. I'm going to make all three of you lieutenants. Do you think you can handle it?" Mr. Johnson asked.

"I could but I would like time to think about it." Christopher said.

"Well, you'll be doing a couple of months and you can think about it then." The others laughed and Mr. Johnson was surprised. The average soldier would have jumped at the opportunity to become a lieutenant. It was every family member's dream. It assured your security within the family.

That night Mr. Johnson and his crew took their wives to the

casino gambling. Mr. Johnson lost one hundred thousand dollars that night. He left very angry.

Christopher learned an extremely important lesson there was no way, they were going to survive without a chain of command.

Later that night Christopher's crew had a private meeting at Christopher's house.

The Atlantic City police knew that Christopher and Little Aaron were taking over Mr. Gaston's operations but they couldn't prove anything. This created an invisible hate with the police for Christopher. They wanted him bad but they couldn't convince anyone to buy from him. They would have alerted the F.B.I, but they thought they could handle him. If they didn't then the new guys running around from Philly causing havoc on the streets would. They didn't know that everyone was united.

"Listen, I might have to do six months with this probation violation." Christopher said and the others looked at him pissed. It wasn't going to be the same without him. "I want the rest of you guys to leave the heroin business alone. It's too many of us doing it and the police are getting sick of it. I want Corey to control the heroin. He was the first one fucking with it since we got in this business and I know he knows what he's doing. The rest of you are going to fuck with Franklin and our Dominican connect."

The others were pissed but they trusted Christopher and they would at least listen to what he had to say.

"What about me? I've got a couple of heroin spots." Mark said. "What you want me to just leave it alone?"

"Nah, you can do both. In fact everyone can do both until I come home from this skid bid and then were going to cut our heroin operations down. You'll understand in the future when I come home I'll explain everything."

That was it. A couple of months later Christopher was going to jail and all hell was about to break lose.

Chapter Fourteen Atlantic City, New Jersey

Tax Penalty

Christopher's arrest was a powerful blow against the family. Four weeks after he left, the families unity was falling apart. Michael and Andre were on an extortion rampage approaching anybody not directly linked with the family and imposing a street tax on them. This created a lot of problems for the family. Some of the problems could be settled. Some of them got out of hand and had to be settled with soldiers from Philadelphia.

Michael and Andre took over the Liquory House on Absecon Boulevard. It was the bar that Christopher controlled when he was home. One week after he left, most of the patrons that had been drinking there for years were leaving. Within a week one of the patrons that was complaining was beat damn near to death by Andre and one of his associates.

Two months after Christopher's incarceration Michael, Andre, Junior and Gary were in the bar operating. Business was going great but there were too many distributors and Michael had just passed a rule that if you weren't buying from the family you couldn't sell anything on the premises.

The police had just stopped coming around after the last beating and things were just starting to fall into place.

Gary and Michael were sitting in a corner discussing business. "Look man. I don't have anything against what your families trying to do but if I buy it from you why are you taxing me. I pay a thousand a week and you're not doing anything for me." Gary was a little drunk and talking a little loudly.

Michael looked at him like he was crazy. "Calm down my man. Calm down."

"Nah-nah it's not that it's just that I'm tired of paying all this fucking money. It's not like I'm making thousands of dollars a week. I buy my shit from y'all. Y'all need to start extorting those other mother fuckers that's running around acting crazy."

"Who's running around acting crazy?" Michael asked.

"Mark and them over there at the Timbuktu, Anthony from Pitney village and his crew."

"Mark and them are family to us. Stick around tonight you'll learn a lesson."

Anthony Carter, the only major distributor in Atlantic City, outside of the family came home a couple of months earlier and had immediately started distribution in all of the bars that he used to sell in. His business would have grown but the family had the heroin and cocaine market cornered in the city. When he first came home Little Aaron stepped to him and tried to explain everything, and he joined forces with the family. Then a couple of weeks later Michael and Little Aaron tried to explain the street tax thing to him and he flipped out. Why should he buy heroin and cocaine from them and still have to pay a street tax. That was crazy. Instead of keeping his cool he went to Mr. Gaston flipped out on him and started trying to enforce his own street tax at a bar on Indiana Avenue a couple of blocks away from the bus station. His tactics worked within a couple of weeks he stopped buying from Little Aaron started going to New York and doing his own thing. Nobody knew that he was buying his heroin and cocaine from Franklin another family member.

Anthony and an entourage of guys walked into the bar with a couple of girls to have drinks. Anthony started drinking at the Liqoury House wanted to see if Michael and Aaron would say anything to his face. A lot of people were stepping to Anthony asking if he could help them lift the street tax off of them and he promised he would help if they purchased from him. There was a rumor going around that the family had a contract out on his life. Anthony wanted to talk to big mouth Andre and see if it was true.

Anthony took a seat and Michael sent him a couple of drinks. Anthony lifted his drink in a salute to Michael. "Thanks buddy."

Anthony waited for the bartender to return. "Tell Michael that the next rounds on me, tell him I need to talk to him it's important."

The bartender went to the end of the bar and left the message.

Michael walked over. "What's going on?"

"Nothing." Anthony responded. "The word on the street is that your people got beef with me."

Michael looked at him shocked. "Nah my people don't have beef with you. I thought you were working with us."

"Nah I'm doing my own thing."

"Oh my people never said anything bad about you. We only fucking with these cornballs that's willing to pay." They both laughed after Michael made his statement.

Anthony and his entourage sat for a couple of hours talking shit and getting drunk. Anthony, his girl, his partner and his partner's girlfriend stayed at the bar until closing which was four o'clock in the morning.

Once the bar was closed they stumbled out into the parking lot. Anthony was driving a brand new '83 Volvo. Anthony left the bar stumbling with his hands around his girlfriend's waist. She was a nice looking dark skin girl with a shapely ass.

They were laughing and joking as they walked to the car. His partner who was supposed to be his bodyguard was barely able to walk. His girlfriend had to support him in order for him to make it to the car.

Anthony opened the passenger door of his ride.

"Do you want me to drive?" His girlfriend asked.

"No. I'm all right baby." Anthony stumbled to the other side of the car after opening the back door by popping the lock button on the front doors passenger's side.

The two girls slid in the back, nobody noticed Andre step towards Anthony while he was near the trunk of the car.

"Ah man." Anthony said after he noticed the guys raising

their guns to shoot him. At first he thought it was a robbery, and he was going to say something but the gunmen opened fire. A small crowd of people watched as Andre jumped in the car with the other shooter and drove away.

Once the car left, Michael and a group of people who were in the bar came running out. Most of them walked over to Anthony and watched him until the police came. Once the police got there Anthony's girlfriend told the entire story.

"That's one of them. That's one of them right fucking there." She pointed towards Michael who was half drunk. First the police questioned him and then they arrested him. They took him downtown to further question him, and see if his statements matched anything with Anthony's girlfriends.

From Patricia's statement, they knew Michael wasn't the shooter but they were hoping they could bluff him and find out more information. It didn't work and after his lawyer got there in the morning he was released and threatening to sue without one single charge.

Chapter Fifteen *Atlantic City, New Jersey*

And Now it Begins

The six months of Christopher's incarceration were hell on the family and things didn't get better until his release. Because Christopher's charges were non-violent he was sent to a youth facility.

Corey and a group of bodyguards drove all the way to Anandale's Youth Correctional Facility in upstate New Jersey to get him. When he left the prison farm a bunch of inmates were waving goodbye to him. Christopher had obviously left one hell of an impression.

Christopher and Corey sat in the car and discussed some serious business on the three-hour ride back. When Christopher was finished explaining his plans, Corey was awestruck.

"I've got to be in." Corey was excited. He filled Christopher in on the details and Christopher was shocked. In a lot of ways it was good because it proved Christopher's genius and that he was needed in the organization. A week after Christopher's release, he called a meeting.

Christopher and his crew were sitting in Christopher's

mother's living room. They were headed down to the basement where Christopher had built an office, but they were waiting because his mother was down there removing some of the things she had left in the office after Christopher left. Christopher was home now and she had to move her stuff to another room because he would be using the business office again.

"I suggest you gentlemen get comfortable because we have a lot of business to attend too." Christopher was sitting in the large leather chair that sat behind the desk in his business room. He looked intelligent and powerful sitting behind the desk. He had been sporting a light beard and mustache.

"Corey filled me in on what's been happening since I left and basically shit has been crazy." Christopher was interrupted by a knock on the door. It was Mr. Gaston and Crazy Morris. Christopher had invited him over because he thought the meeting was important and that Mr. Gaston should attend.

"Hey, what's going on son?" Mr. Gaston walked over to Christopher and embraced him. This was his first time seeing Christopher since Christopher's release.

"Nothing I'm hanging in there. Mark run upstairs and get Mr. Gaston a chair."

Mark disappeared and several minutes later he returned carrying one of the chairs that Mrs. Larkin kept at her kitchen table.

"As I was saying. Things fell apart while I was up there and while I was there I did a lot of thinking. It's time that we become a family. I know a lot of you are use to your independence. I've explained my intentions to everyone privately and told you what I was trying to do. If anybody objects to the things I say they can leave this meeting at any time with no hard feelings." Christopher paused just in case somebody had something to say and then he continued.

Nobody spoke at the meeting until John Martin spoke up. He had been gone for a couple of months on a gun charge and was just coming home. "So how are we going to do it?" He wanted to get directly to the point. "Well, Little Aaron introduced me to the business so I want him to be my counselor and John Martin has been with me since day one so he would be my underboss."

The others didn't say anything, but they were a little

jealous. A few of them caught on that Little Aaron was being named second in command to keep the peace with Mr. Johnson and Mr. Gaston. John Martin was probably elevated because he couldn't operate independently. The only time that he did anything right was when Christopher commanded him to and sometimes he fucked that up.

Christopher continued. "Mark, Corey, Corty, Lynn and Franklin you'll be lieutenants. You'll be able to form crews and small mini-families to help operate the business. Every crew will be partners with me." Christopher said.

"What about Mr. Johnson?" Mr. Gaston asked. Making a move like this could cause serious problems.

"We're gonna form a partnership with Mr. Johnson he won't have anything to worry about. In fact he'll benefit from this tremendously." Christopher answered.

"You don't think it might cause a war?" Franklin asked. He wasn't trying to be funny. He lived in New York and his intelligence about the streets was a little stronger then the others.

"Why would it cause a war? There's nobody in this world fairer then me. Everybody's gonna benefit off of this and make a ton of fucking money. So, what's it gonna be?" Christopher had went to the cabinet and pulled out a bottle of Hennessy.

"I'm in." Mark said. He stood up walked over to Christopher and embraced him. "You have my undying loyalty baby."

The others lined up to hug him and pledge the same thing. It was official now they were a family.

After getting the last hug Christopher continued. "I don't mean to discomfort anybody but you have a week and if you change your mind you're free but if not then that's how it's gonna be. Little Aaron's second in command and John Martin's third. If anything happens to me then they take over until the lieutenants elect another boss. If you're not a lieutenant you can no longer talk to me. The guy under the lieutenant is a soldier. Every lieutenant can pick a captain that he wants to take over if something happens to him, but the soldiers under him should vote the next lieutenant in. That's how where gonna do everything. Everything is by vote. In a couple of days, Junior will get with you individually to arrange meetings so that we can go over the details. If nobody has anymore questions then the meeting is over."

One week after the meeting, Christopher made his first power move. He bought a nice size house on Ohio Avenue on the Westside. The reason that he liked the house was because two empty lots sat on each side of it. Christopher bought those lots and built a fence around the entire property. Before a construction team even started renovations they set up a sophisticated security system. The house was nice and the area was quiet. The house was worth a hundred and fifty thousand dollars. A modest fee compared to its owner's power and wealth.

Christopher suffered his first major blow against his family when he came home. Pedro died the following week of his release and his brother was indicted for selling a Federal agent a kilogram of heroin. He was facing serious time.

Pedro's brother made bail but the word on the street was that he was an informer. He told the police about his brother's Chinese connection, Franklin and what little information he knew about Christopher which wasn't much. By this time Christopher was home and had turned everything over to Corey and Franklin.

Without the connection to Pedro, Corey had to deal with Mr. Gaston and Mr. Johnson. The FBI could follow Christopher all they wanted because he wasn't dealing with heroin anymore directly and he never talked over the phone. Telephones terrified him.

Christopher and several lieutenants flew to Pedro's funeral in Puerto Rico. The federal agents in Puerto Rico were there snapping pictures and video tapping the entire incident but some how information in the United States didn't reach them in enough time, so they didn't know who to survey. The only person they knew anything about was Ramon, Pedro's brother, the informant.

When Christopher and his people popped up at the funeral they stayed as far away from Ramon as possible and nobody discussed business with him. The F.B.I had blown a beautiful opportunity. It was fate Christopher was on his way to greater things.

In '84 the heroin business was dying anyway. Crack cocaine had been introduced to New York City a year earlier and it was changing the way of the streets. Christopher was ready.

Chapter Sixteen *Atlantic City, New Jersey*

A Lesson Learned

Christopher's organizing of the family turned out to be an immediate benefit. For the next couple of months, the family had meetings to cover the details of how they were going to organize and decide who was going to control what part of what operations.

Corey, who was the second strongest was awarded his own bar and crew. The only person that had bigger heroin distribution then Corey was Franklin and he was starting to lose his grip on heroin distribution because his cocaine operations were growing. Most of the other lieutenants were investing in cocaine because it was cheaper and had a wider appeal. It seemed just as profitable.

Christopher and Mr. Johnson were walking in Mr. Johnson's yard. Mr. Johnson owned an enormous estate on the outskirts of Philadelphia. The house was a mansion. He had several cars parked in the driveway and his grandchildren were running around the estate. The day that Christopher arrived one of Mr. Johnson's grandson's was having a birthday party. The back yard looked like a mini-carnival. There were clowns, ponies and dozens of other activities. Several of Mr. Johnson's children and friends were helping his grandson celebrate his birthday. The entire event had to cost Mr. Johnson twenty to thirty thousand dollars.

"Christopher, what's this I hear about y'all organizing in Jersey?" Mr. Johnson was dressed in dress slacks and an expensive dress shirt.

Christopher was silent, he had been home for a couple of months now and this was actually his first time alone with Mr. Johnson. It had also been a couple of months since he had to have meetings with Mr. Gaston present. Basically, Mr. Gaston had been cut out of the picture.

"What's wrong, you're not happy?" Mr. Johnson was smoking on a cigar and blowing the smoke into the air.

"I'm happy were just trying to keep everything organized." Christopher responded trying his best to be careful with his words and not disrespect Mr. Johnson.

"How you going to do that? Aaron's gonna be retiring soon and your gonna be taking over." Mr. Johnson said.

For a few seconds Christopher had remained silent. He had heard all of this before and had tired of it. "I tried to wait but this is the only way that were gonna be safe and this thing is gonna last."

"You didn't forget that I'm the one that lifted that hit Carfagno put on you?" Mr. Johnson was angry but he had learned a long time ago how to hide his anger.

"I'll never forget that and I owe you for life."

Mr. Johnson smiled like he appreciated the gesture but Christopher had seen the face before and he knew that Mr. Johnson was very upset. "We're gonna have a meeting after the wedding and I'm gonna make Aaron retire. Michael's gonna be named a lieutenant and you're gonna be named a lieutenant." He looked at Christopher for his reaction.

"I've got to talk to my family first."

Mr. Johnson was shocked he felt totally disrespected he was gonna have to teach Christopher a lesson.

"You've got to talk to your family. Do you know how many people would die for that opportunity? I tried to make you my underboss but the family voted against it. They said you were to young and didn't earn your stripes yet. They want you to wait in line like everybody else." Christopher listened but he knew it was bullshit. He understood the business. The

Johnson family might hold votes but who ever Mr. Johnson initiated for a position got that position.

"So, what's up with the cocaine connections?" Mr. Johnson asked. The Italians had excellent quality but they brought it over in shipments and couldn't keep it with a consistency.

"I have to talk with Franklin but we can definitely set up a meeting." Christopher said. The cocaine business was booming and replacing heroin as the drug of choice. In eighty-four the world was introduced to crack cocaine and not only was the price dropping but the demand was increasing. Obviously, the cocaine barons were getting stronger because cocaine was arriving, factory sealed. The price for a kilogram in New York had dropped from forty thousand dollars to twenty-five thousand a sign that larger quantities were arriving.

"Arrange a meeting." Mr. Johnson commanded.

"Before the wedding or after the wedding?" Christopher asked.

"Let's make it right after the wedding. Big Aaron's retiring." Christopher was surprised and embarrassed. "Mr. Johnson I don't think Mr. Gaston wants to retire." "Do you know who's running this business? I am, William Johnson that's who runs this business and when I tell somebody to retire it's not an option it's a command. It's time for him to take a rest. I'm gonna be doing special shit with you and Michael. By the time Mr. Johnson finished they had walked all the way to the end of his property. "Christopher you're gonna be running this shit one day. I want to make you the boss right now but the older guys they'd kill us. One day your gonna be the boss and you're gonna need the support of the entire family. Are you bringing your wife and children to the wedding?"

"Of course I am. If I didn't my wife would kill me."

"How are the twins doing?" Mr. Johnson asked.

"They're wonderful." Christopher answered. "Tahwan's pregnant again."

"Are you trying to start an army?" Mr. Johnson asked.

"I don't want to die and not leave anybody these millions." Christopher fixed his tie as he walked. He had to admit he was proud of himself.

"How's the real estate going?" Mr. Johnson asked.

"I just bought a building with Mr. Gaston and Michael

Donaldson."

"What?" Mr. Johnson replied surprised. "Aaron didn't tell me that. I'm gonna put my foot in his ass."

Christopher was amused to hear Mr. Johnson speak of Mr. Gaston that way. "What's wrong Mr. Jay." A nickname that Christopher and the other family members used for Mr. Johnson.

"Nothing I just like to have my hand in everything. That's the only way you stay powerful in this business. I want a piece of all the business that goes through this family. Legal or not." Christopher had learned a valuable lesson. Mr. Johnson was dangerous and greedy.

"Oh, one more thing why did you slow down on selling the heroin?"

"To me it makes more sense. Heroin brings on intense heat and we can't have all the lieutenants doing it. It's gonna make the family hot plus this crack cocaine bullshit is escalating and I want to ride the wave."

"So you guys have crack houses and powder houses and they're not hot?"

"Cocaine gets hot especially crack but you can control it. Nobody's dropping dead over it when it's good like heroin. That heroin shit can get crazy. I mean, I'm not leaving the business I'm just restricting it to certain lieutenants in order to somewhat control the heat. I don't want the Feds coming."

Mr. Johnson laughed and placed his arms around Christopher's shoulder. Christopher was going to be initiated. Just as they started walking back a gorgeous dark skin woman dressed in a form fitting business outfit followed by two children started walking towards them.

When she got several yards closer to them, she spread her arms open for an embrace and jogged towards Mr. Johnson.

"Daddy." They embraced. Christopher stood to the side silently admiring them. Mr. Johnson was definitely a man to be envied. The children that were with her latched onto Mr. Johnson's legs preventing him from walking.

Chapter Seventeen Sugar Hill, New York City

Everybody is The Same

Christopher, Franklin, Mr. Johnson and several of Mr. Johnson's bodyguards had a meeting with Franklin's cocaine connection in order to arrange a couple of deals and establish a relationship.

The Puerto Ricans which had the cocaine market cornered, were losing control to the Dominicans. The Dominicans were new and hungry emigrants in a brand new country with unbelievable opportunity.

After establishing a relationship with Franklin's Puerto Rican connection Franklin privately introduce Christopher to Angelo Tuggerrio. Tuggerrio was a high-ranking member in one of New York's five organized crime families and he had a heroin connectionthat was out of this world.

While other people were selling kilograms of raw heroin for a quarter million dollars he was selling kilograms for one hundred and fifty thousand. Another thing was he wasn't afraid to come to Harlem and deliver which was rare with the Italians.

"How'd you like them things?" Tuggerio asked. He was one

of those obese pizza eating Italians with the expensive sweat suit and the thick gold chain, who liked to brag about his material possessions like a poverty stricken Black man.

"I thought they were beautiful." Franklin responded. They were conducting business in Franklin's living room.

"So why are you only ordering five cakes?" Tuggerio asked. He had just sold them thirty kilograms a month earlier. He figured that they'd be finished and he would see another four and a half million.

"Don't worry I'll be coming back with my partners in a minute." Franklin pulled out the money machine and started counting the money.

Tuggerio looked at him like he was crazy. "What and the fuck are you doing?"

"I'm counting the money." Franklin was sitting in the living room sporting a silk robe, silk shorts and no tee shirt.

"I'm not waiting for you to count no seven hundred and fifty grand. We've been doing business for years now. I hope your smart enough not to cheat me." Tuggerio added.

"It's not that. I just want to make sure everything's correct. You might go home and say that a couple of gee's was missing."

Tuggerio smiled. "No that's the difference between a guinea, and a nig." He caught himself before he made the fatal error. "We don't cheat people I'm about business."

Franklin smiled because he was flattered that the Italian appreciated his business.

Just as they were talking the girl that had spent the night with Franklin walked from the back of the bedroom. She walked past the living room and walked into the kitchen. She was a nice looking Spanish chick with long flowing hair and light creamy skin. She was wearing see through lingerie that clung to her body.

"Hello." She waved at them.

"Hey baby." Tuggerio had never been with a Black woman before but he was dying too. To him everybody was the same they just looked a little different. "Who's that?" He asked.

"Some Spanish chick." Frank replied.

"I've never been with a Spanish chick. She's thick like the young Italian girls I know." He said.

"You want her?" Franklin asked interested.

"Yeah." Tuggerio responded.

"Take her in the bedroom you can have her. Dalki"

"Yes." The Spanish woman answered from the kitchen.

"Come here for a second my man wants to fuck you."

When Dalki came from the kitchen she was carrying a carton of Hagen Daz ice cream and eating from it. "Excuse me." She said it with a Puerto Rican accent and Angelo almost came in his pants.

One of the main reasons that Christopher didn't want to try to hard to establish another heroin connection was because Ramon, Pedro's brother had given the FBI information about Franklin and Christopher. Franklin had to be watched because he loved doing side business with the family's money instead of paying off his debts as soon as he finished like everyone else.

Christopher had his own family now and there was nothing that Mr. Johnson could really say. Christopher wanted to keep Franklin under control because nobody knew if they were under federal investigation or not but it was always best to assume the worst.

Chapter Eighteen Sugar Hill, New York City

Meet The King

With the explosion of crack cocaine the families' business expanded into the housing developments, all the bars and several parks that were located in the area. Especially the park near Kentucky Avenue because it was located near several bars. With the crack explosion, Christopher saw the organization expand and the heroin trade get even more organized. Many of the lieutenants jumped on the crack explosion and rode the wave. A few of them stuck with the heroin. By the time that eighty-four rolled around Corey was the only lieutenant dealing with the heroin and Christopher liked it this way. Even Franklin who still ran heroin outlets in New York City started setting up cocaine outlets. In early eighty-three Christopher met with several major cocaine and heroin distributors in New York City to form a new commission. The last time a commission was formed was in the mid-sixties when Frank Matthews formed five families in New York and helped the leaders of the gangs in Chicago form families. Mr. Donaldson was Frank Matthews mentor. Franklin's cocaine business had expanded so much that Christopher sold half of the cocaine he bought through

Franklin who was flooding the streets of New York. This generated millions of dollars a month. Franklin was quickly becoming a socialite and celebrity in the process. He knew every Black rapper, athlete and R&B singer in the world.

"Are you going to the wedding?" Christopher asked Little Aaron while they were sitting in Little Aaron's basement rubber banning money. There were boxes of money everywhere.

"Of course I'm going to the wedding, if I didn't my father would kill me. He keeps asking me what you're going to do about this Mr. Johnson situation." Little Aaron loved his position in the family. Mostly, he collected Christopher's money and ran bullshit errands for the family and he got paid for it.

"How am I going to join Mr. Johnson's family and we've already got a family? They're already making money hand over fist and they still want to control me." Christopher said visibly upset. "What are you going to do with Michael?" Aaron asked. "What exactly does he want me to do?" Christopher asked.

"He wants forty bricks." Little Aaron was talking about kilograms. "He did the twenty that we gave him in two weeks."

Christopher shook his head. "That's not fast." Christopher wasn't impressed. "I don't want him mixing my money up with Mr. Johnson's." Little Aaron didn't have an idea about half of the money that Christopher was making because Christopher did some business privately. He divided his errands between Little Aaron and John Martin. "What's up with Michael's case?" Christopher asked.

"The police didn't say anything. They're still looking for Andre. They don't really fuck with Michael that much." The police had gotten on Michael so bad about the killing in the bar that he had to leave the bar and set up shop in Pleasantville, New Jersey.

"Who are you driving with tomorrow?" Little Aaron asked.

When Mr. Johnson allowed Christopher to completely break off from his father, Mr. Gaston stopped making money. Big Aaron was pissed with Mr. Johnson. He knew that one day Mr. Johnson would get greedy and cut
him out.

"I'm driving with my family." Christopher said placing the

last couple of stacks in his box.

"I hope Tahwan doesn't have that baby on the way." They both burst out laughing.

"I need a bodyguard to escort me to the crib." Christopher said.

"Nobody's here." Little Aaron said.

"Then call somebody." Christopher commanded. Christopher's cocaine business was expanding to other areas. He was trying to establish distribution in Newark, New Jersey and other northern areas. It was working.

The guy that controlled most of the cocaine distribution in Newark was an older guy name Akbar that was still connected to Mr. Johnson.

Christopher knew that with his smarts and connections he could establish something stronger with the younger guys if the Akbar didn't want to bend. Even though Christopher's prices could only be beat by the Dominicans, a lot of old timers refused to do business with him. They let their pride get in the way and it usually cost them in the end.

Christopher had made so much money that he stopped buying property and started stashing his money in Swiss Bank accounts.

Mr. Donaldson had connected Christopher with an accounting firm that was showing him how to hide his money in Swiss accounts.

He had also been introduced to Rudolph Harris the first black mayor in Atlantic City who was running for mayor. Mr. Gaston and the others couldn't stand him because he was a former cop who used to harass them when they were running gambling houses but Christopher liked him and nobody could tell him what to do. He was the leader of his own family now.

A couple of guys that he got close with in Annadale and Yardville Youth Correctional Facility were supposed to introduce him to Akbar, ran the drug gangs in Newark, New Jersey so they could discuss business. When Christopher found out how flamboyant the guy was he declined. He didn't need another Franklin in his life. The rumor was that Franklin had held a surprise party in New York. The bosses in New York had purchased a solid gold crown and crowned him. The news made Christopher sick to his stomach. "A lot of people think that selling drugs is a game and ultimately that sort of thinking becomes their down fall." Christopher warned Franklin as soon as he saw him but of course Franklin ignored him. Christopher and the others just didn't understand. New York City was a different kind of place. You could do anything you wanted in New York and the police wouldn't fuck with you as long as you paid the right people. The one thing that Christopher would hand Mr. Johnson was that he knew how to keep a low profile.

Chapter Nineteen *Cheltenham's Golf Resort*

It is Different Now

Cheltenham's Town & Country Resort Golf Club was one of the most exclusive golf courses in America. The President of the United States of America, Kings, European Royalty and dignitaries from all over the world vacationed there.

The main estate's largest building was the cathedral and it was surrounded by smaller house's that were mansions. The waiting list for membership stretched two years long and no amount of money or prestige could break it. So when Nia Johnson announced that her wedding would be held there not only were people amazed they were impressed.

Nia's wedding was going to cost two hundred thousand dollars. That was the initial estimates without the finalized cost. The guest list was at least three hundred and fifty people.

Nia came down the aisle wearing an imported antique white silk European gown that her parents had flown to Paris to pick out. Her beautiful shinny black hair was penned behind a Platinum Tiara set in Diamonds and precious stones courtesy of Winston's Jewelry of New York. Several media outlets were there including Jet Magazine with a promise that the Honorable Nia Johnson and her future husband would be in the next issue of the magazine's newlywed section.

Nia walked down the aisles of the Cathedral and her silk wedding gown clung to her body like a ballerina outfit while a diamond tiara, with a veil covering her beautiful face.

Nia was a mixture of both of her parents and probably the best looking kid they had. She was five ten, thin and shapely like an Ebony fashion fair model. She took the height from her father, and the hips and breast from her mother who at one time had a shape just as beautiful or better than Nia's.

Nia and Mr. Johnson walked down the aisle's that sat in one of the Cathedrals that rested on the estates. Mr. Johnson had to use his connections with the mayor of Philadelphia, who in turn contacted the governor, who in turn contacted a close friend to the President of the United States of America. This with an under the table payment of ten thousand dollars in cash got Mr. Johnson and his family a day at the Golf course.

Nia and Mr. Johnson marched to the front of the church ignoring the flashes that were constantly being released from cameras of well wishers and professional photographers.

Mr. Johnson marched his daughter all the way up the aisle into the arms of Marshall Lester Doughty III and released her. Mr. Johnson wasn't exactly to fond of his daughter's new husband to be but he would do. Marshall completed four years of college and had received a degree from Temple University. His father was a wealthy attorney, his mother was a former political activist and homemaker. Mr. Johnson thought that his daughter could have done better but his new son-in-law was growing on him.

Mr. Doughty, his wife and children were in the front row. Mrs. Johnson and her children were on the left side of the church the side reserved for the bride's family.

Nia had six gorgeous bride's maids. Marshall had six handsome groomsmen, all of them educated with promising careers.

The Pastor, a famous black reverend that Pastored at Mrs. Johnson's church, presided over the wedding. He was short, fat and black with a screaming voice and a devoted congregation that followed him everywhere he went.

The Pastor walked up to the bride and groom then read them their vows. He loved presiding over beautiful weddings it added to his history and the church's reputation.

"Do you Marshall Doughty the third take the honor Nia Johnson to be your lawfully wedded wife?" "I do." replied Marshall.

"Do you Nia Kristina Johnson take Marshall Doughty to be your lawfully wedded husband?"

"I do." sobbed Nia. Tears were streaming down her face.

"Then I pronounce you man and wife. You may kiss the bride." The audience started clapping. The Reverend had only been speaking for a couple of minutes and he was already sweating profusely. He wiped his brow as he continued.

Mr. Johnson was standing next to the groomsmen. He looked tall and handsome in his black tuxedo. The only thing that exposed his age and differentiated him from the other men was his salt and pepper hair.

Mr. Johnson stood there with pride beaming on his face watching his youngest daughter cry her fears away. Now that his last was married and educated he was happy. When Nia turned around and the audience saw her ring they gasped.

Mrs. Johnson was sitting with her daughters in-laws wiping tears from her face the entire time. The last time that she was this happy was at her own wedding almost thirty-five years earlier.

"Pop-Pop." Mr. Johnson's youngest granddaughter ran up to him and jumped in his arms. The entire cathedral burst into laughter.

The brides groom and the bride walked down the aisle. The flower girls were Nia's little nieces and they were carrying Nia's twenty foot train. Without looking back or making a word the new Mrs. Nia Doughty threw her bouquet in the air and one of the prettiest girls in the wedding party grabbed the bouquet. Screaming to the top of her lungs, she immediately ran over to her boyfriend.

At the reception hall, the dinner tables were set beautifully. The wedding had cost her father a small fortune, not counting what it was going to take to establish an accounting firm for his new son in-law if he decided to practice accounting in Pennsylvania or New Jersey on his own. If he searched for his own job and didn't go into private practice it would save

Mr. Johnson a lot of money.

At the reception Nia and Marshall had disappeared and returned wearing casual clothing. Mr. Johnson had rented the reception hall for twenty-four hours, plus a honeymoon suite for his daughter and son-in-law for the next day. After that the newlyweds were flying to Las Vegas because Marshall had never been there. Then they were flying to Hawaii before they did a small tour of the Virgin Islands.

Two weeks before the wedding several IRS agents, FBI agents and ATF agents surrounded Franklin's brownstone in Park slope Brooklyn. Several IRS agents with weapons drawn raided his house. The agents found a little over a million dollars in cash at the Park slope residence.

At the other three houses they found more money and drug records. They were raiding Frank's house because he had deposited over six hundred thousand dollars in several banks but only reported an income of fifty thousand dollars the previous year stating his sole income as ownership of a limousine service. When initially arrested, he told the agents the money in the bank was tips he made by driving his limousine but had forgotten to report, they laughed. All together they confiscated four million dollars in cash.

The four million-dollar lost was a powerful blow against the family not counting what it was going to cost in legal fees. Mr. Johnson immediately called an emergency meeting.

Mr. Johnson, Mr. Gaston, Crazy Morris, Little Aaron and Big Cliff were sitting in Mr. Johnson's garden drinking lemonade.

"What the information on this kid?" Mr. Johnson asked. Little Aaron responded. For the first time he was going to get the opportunity to start talking at the meetings.

Christopher had refused the position of lieutenant in the family and Mr. Johnson was counting on Little Aaron to convince him to change his mind.

"Franklin's a piece of shit we should have killed him a long time ago. The first time Christopher went to jail he left Frank and John Martin twenty thousand a piece and both of them fucked it up. Now he owes you a million dollars and I think he owes Christopher a million dollars." Little Aaron didn't mention that Franklin also owed Mr. Gaston a million dollars because that would prove that they were doing side business behind Mr. Johnson's back and in the family that was a no-no.

"So he was doing side business?" Mr. Johnson asked.

"He sure was." Little Aaron added in. "He's a selfish mother fucker and I don't trust him. I think he would snitch in a heart beat."

The others were drinking from the lemonade pitcher and silently listening.

"That's all I've got to hear then. In a couple of weeks I'll arrange a meeting with him and we'll handle it." Mr. Johnson said. He was referring to his crews in Philadelphia.

"I think Christopher warned him." Little Aaron said angrily. Rightfully Little Aaron was supposed to be the head of the family in New Jersey and his father never let him forget it.

"Christopher's fucking up I've got to teach him a lesson so that he knows to never go against the family. Were the only mother fuckers that he can trust."

"I think if we kill Franklin he'll get the message." Little Aaron said.

"What do you think Aaron?" Mr. Johnson was referring to Mr. Gaston.

"I think we should kill them both. I don't trust either one of those motherfuckers."

Mr. Johnson didn't even entertain the thought of killing Christopher. They needed him too much. He generated entirely too much money. "Nobody ever touches Christopher. After he sees his friends dying one by one he'll come around. I don't care if we have to remove his entire power structure. Now who's gonna replace Franklin in New York once we get rid of him." Mr. Johnson asked because whether they realized it or not Franklin's outlets in New York were generating millions of dollars.

"Christopher will get somebody from New York to replace him."

"Well make sure you get close to this somebody." Mr. Johnson said and he ended the meeting with that. "If you gentlemen are finished I want to call my girlfriend up. We're flying out to Mexico for the weekend. If Mooney calls one of you looking for me, I just left on business." Mooney was Mrs. Johnson's nickname but only the older lieutenants knew that.

Two weeks after the wedding Nia and her husband Marshall threw an appreciation party. Everyone in the Christopher Larkin Crime family and the William Johnson

Crime family attended with their wives. No children allowed. Mr. Johnson, his son in-law Michael, Big Cliff, Black and Christopher were outside of the garden watching Nia thank everyone personally. She looked so happy and Michael remembered his own wedding only a couple of years earlier at a much smaller church.

Mr. Johnson looked handsome in his tuxedo at the wedding and now he looked just as good in his business suit. He was a handsome man with a handsome family. He had everything the others admired and envied him. "Christopher I want to have a little meeting with you Friday if it's possible?"

"Can we make it two weeks from now because I got word that Dan got arrested in New York. His parents want me to fly to Trinidad."

"Damn, what happened?"

"Somebody set him up with an undercover and he sold them two hundred pounds."

Mr. Johnson shook his head. "What in the fuck is this world coming to? You can't even sell marijuana without somebody snitching on you. This shit is getting crazy. They're too many hustlers. It didn't use to be like this in the seventies. As soon as that shit left the bars and spilled out in the projects I knew this was the beginning of the end. They've got crack house on every corner in Philly." Never did Mr. Johnson take notice that he was largely part of the blame.

"You've just got to be careful." Mr. Johnson continued and then he gulped his drink.

Chapter Twenty Port of Spain, Trinidad

Trini Vacation

As soon as Christopher got word of Franklin and Dan's arrest he called an emergency meeting and then he disappeared. He wasn't even in town when Corty the family's main weed distributor got word of the arrest. Christopher decided to fly to Trinidad to meet with Dan's family right away.

In Trinidad Dan's family owned a majority stock in a Government and Private Petroleum refinery. They also owned a small but profitable Petrochemical plant, a steel mill and a company that produced fertilizer. They owned a company that produced processed foods, beverages, textiles, electronic equipment and plastic goods.

All of this didn't include their real estate portfolio, which included thousands of undeveloped acres of land, hotels, condominiums and apartment complexes. Legally Dan's mother was worth more then two hundred and fifty million dollars.

Dan's family was the richest and most powerful family in Trinidad. They lived and were treated like royalty.

Ever since the island was discovered by Spanish explorers marijuana had been widely used. The Arakawa and Carib

Indians that lived on the island used it for medicinal purposes. Once the explorers discovered it and it's intoxicating power the plant started being used for pleasure.

By the early twenties, Dan's grandfather was exporting it to America with a group of businessmen he had met during the Prohibition era. The drug became especially popular in the sixties, widely used and widely accepted.

By the time that the early sixties rolled around Dan's grandfather was a multi-millionaire who had invested heavily in Trinidad. He also had real estate in America, houses in Miami, Florida, Dallas, Texas, and New York City. He ended up teaching all of his children the business and they excelled.

Dan's grandfather had a severe stroke in the early seventies and died a couple of months later. By the time that Elijah died he had amassed a legal fortune worth almost sixty million dollars through restaurants, real estate, shares in oil refineries and real estate in America. A few years before he died he pushed his family into Trinidadian politics. Like most powerful men he wanted his family deeply involved in politics something that would allow his family to continue to operate and flourish.

When Elijah died his empire was divided amongst his children and they became rich beyond their wildest dreams. Several of them had already entered the marijuana business and were trying to establish their own wealth.

Christopher caught a small plane from Atlantic City airport in Pomona, New Jersey to Philadelphia. In Philadelphia he boarded a flight to Miami, Florida. From there he was flown by private plane to Trinidad. Dan's grandfather and several of his partners owned a majority share in Trinidad Airways the biggest airline in Trinidad and Tobago.

Several bodyguards carrying assault weapons met Christopher at the airport and escorted him to Dan's family's estate. Trinidad is tropical and mountainous, Christopher had never seen a country so beautiful.

The escorts drove the vehicles through the jungle Christopher got to see the small huts that the country and city people lived in. It was obvious that there mass poverty in the Country but the people didn't seem affected by it they worked and moved around with a smile on their faces.

It took several hours but they arrived at the compound and

Christopher was shocked. He thought it would be designed like the Plantation houses that he saw built in the South.

The compound was beautiful and modern constructed out of large white stone. Its architecture resembled an Egyptian Villa. It really surprised Christopher when he found out that Mrs. Ebby was raised in the house as a little kid. Christopher was given the option of staying at the compound or one of the condominiums in the city of Port of Spain.

The truck drove up to a security gate and several Rastafarians carrying assault weapons walked up to the jeep and peered inside. They waved the truck through after a thorough inspection.

The truck rode over the stone pavement and parked beside a group of houses and Dan walked outside. He was wearing a white linen suit and his hair was tied behind his head. He had been arrested in an undercover sting and had decided to visit Trinidad before he had to serve his federal time. Dan wasn't suppose to leave the country but after the lawyers worked the plea agreement he decided to go on vacation. It was only a marijuana case. The FBI had awarded him a reasonable bail. He was only going to stay for a month and then turn himself in to the authorities in America. A couple days after his release government soldiers came to the house and informed him that America had issued an international warrant for his arrest, then they left. The government was on his family's payroll.

Christopher and Benjamin, Dan's youngest brother, walked into the front door of the estate. The doorman who opened the door wore a tuxedo and white gloves. The doorman smiled and Christopher couldn't help but to think of the butlers he had seen in the movies of the thirties.

"Master Benjamin, may I take your bags?" It was more of a demand then a request.

"There are no bags, Alan." Alan was one of the butlers that lived on the outskirts of the estate. He had been a butler at the estate every since Dan was old enough to remember and even though they told him to stop calling them master and madam he refused. He felt as though he owed it to Master Elijah Dan's grandfather.

Christopher wasn't carrying any bags, the morning before he'd put ten thousand dollar's cash in his pants pockets and disappeared.

Before they could hit the steps a maid appeared. She was Arakawa Indian with a distinct mixture of African. She was tall and stocky compared to the other woman in the house.

The maid Adiyah, was about five ten, had a square shaped face and beautiful tresses of silky hair. She had long beautiful brown limbs and a wide behind. She was so beautiful Christopher almost lost his breath admiring her. Adiyah escorted Christopher to his room. Dan noticed the way that Christopher looked at Adiyah.

Adiyah threw the doors to the bedroom open and Christopher was pleased. The bedroom looked like a luxurious apartment. In one section there was a bedroom and in another section, a living room and television. In another section there was a balcony. Christopher walked over to it pushed the silk curtains aside revealing a breath taking view of Trinidad and one of its famous mountains.

Christopher was blown away. He glanced out of the window on the balcony, he heard laughter and walked to the edge of the balcony when he glanced over he saw several women wearing bathing suits lounging around the pool side with drinks in their hands. It looked like they were having a party.

"Swimming." Adiyah's voice was the most beautiful voice that he had ever heard. Even when she talked it sounded like she was enticing him.

"I have no bathing suit." Christopher responded mad now that he had rushed out of the house.

"Can you take me to the city to shop?" Christopher asked.

"No." She shook her head and her beautiful hair temporarily covered
her face.

"Why?" Christopher was hurt. "Please. You'll be safe with me I promise."

Either she really wanted to go or Christopher's sad eyes had convinced her because she said. "Okay ask Master Benjamin." She turned to walk away and a whiff of her perfume fragranced the air. Her smell and beauty were intoxicating. When she whirled away she left Christopher dizzy.

When Christopher's senses came to a second later he ran to the steps and yelled out. "Dan!" Several servants from different rooms ran outside of the rooms they were working in and Dan came racing from the kitchen up the steps with a smile on his face.

"You want to fuck her don't you?" Dan was speaking with a heavier accent then usual but Christopher understood every single word he said.

"No." Christopher lied. He immediately began thinking of his family. Tahwan was pregnant with another baby and he loved his family more then anything in the world. "I want her to escort me to the city." Christopher said.

"Okay be careful she will break your heart." Christopher caught the message. Christopher walked into his bedroom placed his money in his dresser draw. "Will my money be safe here?" He asked.

"Of course. The servants will not enter your room unless you're present. I'll see you tonight." Dan disappeared and Christopher jumped in the shower.

This two-week vacation might turn out to be really special Christopher thought as he showered.

After Christopher jumped out of the shower and dressed he had a meeting with Dan's mother at the poolside. Another nice looking maid took him to his table. This maid was dark skin with thick course dreads that fell down her back.

When Christopher exited his room and took a seat at the table there were women everywhere. One of the ladies an older one with a beautiful youthful body and long reddish dreads stepped out of the pool and snatched a robe from one of the tables. She walked towards Christopher he was mesmerized. The bathing suit that she was wearing clung to her body and her nipples were hard. She smiled as she walked towards him and extended her hands when she reached the table.

"Christopher." She said with a slight accent. "I'm Dan's mother Mrs. Ebby."

Christopher jumped to his feet in order to show respect. "Mrs. Ebby how are you doing?" She was beautiful and Dan resembled her greatly. Christopher couldn't help it. He glanced between her legs because she had left the robe opened and he admired her gap. She had the body of a twenty year old.

Mrs. Ebby smiled it flattered her that he was secretly

admiring her. "My husband is on the way. Are you going to swim?" She asked. The only jewelry that she was wearing was a gigantic wedding ring. The first time that Christopher flew to Trinidad was for the wedding but he didn't meet her then.

Naptali and Benjamin walked out of the back doors of the house with another group of dreads following them. Everyone was wearing linen outfits.

Naptali greeted Christopher he was Dan's father and he looked exactly like Benjamin. He was thin only a little older with a belly, dark skin with thick black dreads that looked like cords.

"Christopher greetings Mon yes Jah-Rastafari." He said extending his hand and Christopher returned the greetings.

"You and you're people are gonna have to fly down to Florida to conduct business with Benjamin and Dan's uncles. Once we find out what's up with this New York mess, we'll resume business as usual." Dan's father was wanted on old federal drug charges in the early seventies but he had skipped town and opted never to return to New York to live. He always came to visit most of the time on false identification. "Another thing that we wanted to talk to you about was flying the money over here on private planes so that we could give you better prices and you could some what cover the New York market until we stabilize. We just want to know what the authorities know. If it's nothing like we think we'll be up and operating in New York again in six months."

Christopher listened and then he spoke. "It doesn't matter to me. I'll do whatever I can to help but first I have to talk to my man Corty and see what he says, he handles the weed."

"Ganja." Benjamin corrected him and the others laughed. Throughout the entire meeting the others sat silently listening.

"Tomorrow we might be flying out to Colombia to have a meeting with Senor Cachas his family controls a lot of the ganja in Colombia. A lot of time when our harvest runs out we deal with dem." Naptali said.

"Okay let me know what we're going to do." Christopher said and the meeting was over.

Chapter Twenty One *Trinidad & Tobago*

A Mind Miles Away

Christopher and Adiyah were afforded the opportunity to visit the town. Adiyah was the tour guide and they viewed the area on horseback first. Christopher was surprised at how small the island was and how easily it was to get around on horseback.

The morning after Christopher arrived, Adiyah and Christopher rode all the way to Port of Spain to the shopping district. The market place was ancient looking but very romantic. The first thing they did was stop for morning breakfast.

Adiyah wore a shear see-through linen dress that clung to her body with some tight panties and no bra. Christopher got to see Adiyah's firm round breasts through the material Her beauty was intoxicating. After eating breakfast Christopher and Adiyah went to the market place and bought everything. There was no way they were going to get everything back.

Christopher was riding on his horse, his black hair was sticking up like a porcupine, two days in the country had turned his brownish complexion dark. His teeth were white and he had nice bone structure. Together they looked handsome.

Adiyah with her domestic exotic beauty and Christopher with his plain good looks, they would've made a beautiful couple. Christopher and Adiyah drank coffee at a small antique coffee shop while a Muslim scholar sat outside serving drinks and reciting the Qu'ran. A lot of the villages in Trinidad looked like Morocco because of the Islamic influence. Christopher couldn't count the number of women he saw running around wearing Hijab the female clothes covering worn by the Muslim women.

"How am I going to take all of this stuff back?" Christopher asked. They had rented another horse from the village just to carry their presents. Christopher saw a lot of presents that he would have loved to buy for Tahwan but he didn't want to hurt Adiyah's feelings. He would return to the shopping district later on his own.

Adiyah and Christopher had gotten very close. They talked about their past. Christopher didn't tell her the details of his business but he told her some might consider him an important man she understood.

She told Christopher about her parents. About how they had disclaimed her when she decided to work. How she wasn't Arakawa and her father was an Indian from India. Her mother was Indian and African, two races that sometimes mixed in Trinidad. Later that afternoon they had lunch and then Adiyah took Christopher to one of the condominiums that Daniel's family owned in the city.

When Christopher and Adiyah arrived at the condominium they made love it was a quick and distant lovemaking session, a tension reliever. Christopher and Adiyah were lying in the bed Christopher had his back turned to her.

"What's wrong Christopher?" Adiyah asked. As beautiful and intoxicating as she was Christopher could not stop thinking about his family or the fact that he had broken his marriage vows again. "Nothings wrong. I'm okay." Christopher said lying next to a window where the breeze was blowing a curtain in.

"You lie." Adiyah said. "You're thinking about your wife and your family."

The words made Christopher spin around. His mind was a million miles away.

Adiyah was just as heart broken not because she had someone else's husband but because she looked at her beauty as a curse. Most men could not see past it and it prejudiced them towards her.

Later that evening they spent more time together and they had a serious talk. Christopher told her about his wife and children but she didn't care. Adiyah ignored all of that. As far as she was concerned she had found her husband and she was going to marry him and have his children.

Adiyah took Christopher to the resort section and showed him where he could purchase property and build houses. She showed him other little hidden areas but they had to drive there in cars. She also told him that Franklin came to visit often and that he was famous with all of the local women because of his generosity.

Benjamin and the rest of Dan's family were like celebrities in Trinidad because of their wealth and good looks. Later that night before they separated Christopher told her about the advances that Mrs. Ebby had made and Adiyah explained that she was not surprised. Dan's father Naptali was a famous womanizer that had women and children all over the island. Maybe Mrs. Ebby wasn't very happy.

Chapter Twenty Two *Trinidad & Tobago*

Ten Million Friends

The day after Christopher and Adiyah's rendezvous Daniel's family threw a party on Daniel's estate.

When Christopher and Adiyah arrived at the mansion he was surprised at how many people had come to the party, it was incredibly crowded. Christopher was wearing a black tuxedo and Adiyah wore a beautiful evening gown that they had bought in the city. She also wore a diamond bracelet that Christopher had purchased for her. Her evening gown clung to her body and her beautiful silky hair was penned up she looked marvelous.

There were several bodyguards standing against the walls carrying assault riffles. Christopher smiled amazed at the fact that these men carried their firearms openly in public and on the estate. In some ways it gave Christopher an uneasy feeling. Lately he had gotten a little home sick. Trinidad was a beautiful country but Christopher missed the security of America. When he called home his wife informed him to contact Mr. Donaldson. When Christopher contacted Michael, Michael informed him that he would have to return to America as soon as possible because the IRS wanted him to answer some questions pertaining to his relationship with Franklin and their limousine service.

There had to be about five hundred people attending the party and half of them were beautiful island women. Everywhere Christopher walked a woman grabbed him and demanded he danced or passed him a drink. Christopher stood next to the punch bowl observing the party. Daniel's little brother Benjamin had told everyone that Christopher was their cousin from New Jersey and every single women there wanted to meet him.

Benjamin and Salvio Henrique Omar Luis Cachas walked directly over to where Christopher was standing. "Christopher let me introduce you to Senor Henrique Luis Cachas."

The Colombian man extended his hand. Christopher extended his hand and they shook hands for a second admiring each other. "It's a pleasure to met you Senor Cachas."

One of the bodyguards translated for Cachas in English. Cachas shook his head and then said something in Spanish. The bodyguard translated.

"It's a pleasure to met you Mr. Larkin." Christopher was shocked when Senor Cachas responded in broken English. "I understand English but sometimes if you speak fast." Senor Cachas threw his hands in the air in frustration. "Then I lost."

Christopher smiled.

"My father is waiting for us in a private room let's disappear."

Adiyah was standing there. She glanced at Christopher.

"Mommy I'm going to see you later." He kissed her on the cheek and she disappeared. She knew her place.

Benjamin walked them to a private room and they all took seats. Naptali was already waiting there.

"Senor Cachas my partner from America wanted to purchase two thousand pounds of marijuana." Naptali said.

Christopher was going to fly home the next day and have the money shipped through Naptali's people to Trinidad.

"You make me mad I don't fuck wit marijuana." Senor Cachas said. He was 5'10 with a large face, salt and pepper hair. He had arms like a construction worker and a large round belly. He had been selling cocaine since the early seventies, it wasn't until the early eighties that his associates revolutionized the business. They grew from making pounds of cocaine in Colombian kitchens to building factories that could produce thousands of kilograms a week.

"You let me fly my cocaina here and I'll give you the weed as a present." Senor Cachas said. He had been flying tons of cocaine to Trinidad for the last couple of years but he was always getting robbed of his material. He needed a partner that had connections with the government so that his shipments would not pop up missing.

"I told you Henrique this is my wife business and I cannot do it without her permission."

"You let your wife run you." Senor Cachas said. His assistant sat there quietly as Senor Cachas tore Naptali apart. Senor Cachas was wearing a dress shirt and slacks with a diamond bezel Rolex.

Christopher had to interrupt. "Senor Cachas if I were to buy a kilo from you in Trinidad how much would you charge me?"

Senor Cachas turned to his assistant and started speaking in Spanish. "I believe a key here goes for three or four thousand but we're not looking for customers in Trinidad."

"But you are looking for customers in America."

"No not really we have enough customers we don't deal with small customers. If you can't spend five or ten million there's no need for you to talk to us."

"I can get five or ten million with no problem and I might be able to help you with your storage problem here if you give me the chance."

The bodyguard began speaking to Senor Cachas in Spanish. Then he turned back to Christopher. "Do you have planes and means to transport to America?"

"No I do not."

"So we would have to fly the product to you."

"Yes, but this is the deal. How much would I have to pay in Florida if you delivered it?"

"Eight or nine thousand a key. If you pick it up in California it's cheaper. Five or six thousand a key but you have to get the money to Trinidad to get these prices."

Christopher smiled. "No problem and you have to spend at

least five million in cash up front."

"How about this I'll start out by spending ten million in cash. After we establish trust, I'll spend twenty to forty million every time I come."

Senor Cachas smiled. At least his visit wasn't a wasted trip. "Well tomorrow you fly to Colombia with Benjamin, and we'll talk about it." The bodyguard turned to Senor Cachas and said something in Spanish.

Senor Cachas responded.

"El Padrino says he's gonna give you a thousand pounds of marijuana as a gift and charge you only a hundred dollars a pound for the other one thousand."

That put a smile on Naptali's face.

Later that evening when they returned to the party Christopher couldn't find Adiyah. So he stayed for a little while and then he retreated to his room.

Christopher jumped in the shower when he came out the lights in his room were off and that alarmed him.

Christopher walked out of the bathroom into his room and started drying himself off. Then he looked in the corner and something moved.

Mrs. Ebby walked from the corner of the room where a chair was sitting. She was completely naked. Christopher's heart dropped into his chest he was about to run for the door but she was in front of him.

"Mrs. Ebby, no please, not in your house. Your sons are my friends."

She silenced him with a kiss and pushed him against the bed. Christopher didn't want to do it but something told him if he fought her she was going to make a scene.

Mrs. Ebby laid him on the bed grabbed his penis and slid it inside of her without any hesitation.

Christopher couldn't deny it, being inside of her felt good. Mrs. Ebby began pumping quietly like she was sneaking around. She stayed on top of him for what seemed like all night until she quietly came. By the time she reached her climax and slid Christopher in her mouth, he was so frightened he tried to act like he was asleep. He didn't want to be conscious when any of this happened.

It might have been the fear or the shock but Christopher fell asleep immediately after she finished. He didn't even know if she left or not.

The next morning while he was sleep Adiyah came in the room and slipped out of her maid's uniform. She went under the sheets, kissed his stomach and then slid him in her mouth.

Christopher jumped up and yelled out. "Help." He was shocked.

He lifted the cover and saw Adiyah sucking on him. She stopped and smiled at him.

He pushed her off. "Were you here last night?" He asked her.

"No." she cooed, referring to the blow job.

"Let me take a shower." He jumped up and went to the shower and she followed him.

Chapter Twenty Three West Philadelphia

New Found Respect

The week that Christopher returned all hell broke loose. The family was intact and strong but Michael and a group of guys from Pleasantville were having a drug war over turf.

The real problem was that Pleasantville was smaller than Atlantic City and the police knew everything. Michael couldn't leave his house without the police pulling him over.

Christopher and Mr. Johnson's family held a meeting at one of Ernest Clark's house in West Philadelphia.

Christopher and Little Aaron arrived last because Mr. Johnson started the meeting two hours earlier. There were things he had to tell his family that Christopher and Little Aaron couldn't hear.

Christopher and Little Aaron walked into the office room that Clark had set up in the house. When Christopher walked in everyone in the room embraced him. Mr. Johnson let him take a seat and then they started the meeting.

"What's up Chris?"

"I'm hanging in there." Christopher said.

"What are you drinking?" Mr. Johnson asked.

"I just want a rum and coke." Christopher loosened his tie and slouched in his seat.

"So what's going on? Have you heard anything about Franklin yet?" Mr. Johnson asked.

"I talked to his lawyer and they arranged a meeting for me with the IRS."

Mr. Johnson just shook his head. "Is he going to be all right?" Everybody was worried because initially they thought it was a federal investigation. "I lost a lot of money fucking with that kid, Christopher. He messed up real bad."

"How much does he owe you?" Christopher asked.

"Why you gonna pay him?" Clark asked. He was pissed off at the fact that Christopher would even have the heart to ask Mr. Johnson a question like that. Like maybe he could interfere with what was about to happen. The young had no respect. In the olden days a remark like that to the boss might have gotten you killed. "Maybe." Christopher said.

"Maybe what?" Clark replied sarcastically. He didn't know why they didn't teach Christopher a lesson when he broke off and formed his own family.

"Clark, please. We're grown men." Mr. Johnson gave him the eye. How
was Clark going to be the boss someday when he couldn't even disguise his hatred?

"Franklin owes me a million dollars."

"The man's arrested. It's not his fault." Christopher added in trying to protect his friends honor. "He owes me a million dollars too."

Mr. Clark sucked his teeth he couldn't believe for one minute that Christopher would defend somebody that owed him a million dollars.

"Well that's between you two. What's pissing me off is I've been calling for my money for a couple of days now and he said he didn't have it." Mr. Johnson was drinking liquor from a shot glass. Then he continued. "He just proved he couldn't be trusted, he was flipping our money. He lied to me and asked me to front him work on consignment. When he comes home he's gotta die."

Christopher was shocked. He could barely swallow his rum and coke. "I'll cover his debt." Christopher said.

Clark shook his head. "Christopher, you just don't get it do you?"

"Clark, be quiet. Franklin made bail right?" Mr. Johnson asked.

"Not yet but he's gonna make it according to his lawyer."

"And you believe that?" Mr. Johnson responded. "If he makes bail on this case he's a snitch, he has to die and that's final. He stole from the family and he brought heat on us. He's too risky and I'm ordering his death. If you don't have the balls I'll have Michael do it." Mr. Johnson finished his drink poured another one and then looked towards Michael. "Michael can you handle it?"

"Of course I can. It will be my pleasure." Michael was sitting in a chair picking his teeth with a tooth pick. "Is that how you want to handle it Christopher?" Mr. Johnson asked.

"Nah. I'll handle it myself don't worry about it."

"Don't play with me, Chris this is serious business."

Christopher didn't like how Mr. Johnson said it but he swallowed his pride.

"I'll handle it." Christopher repeated. Christopher saw a smile come over Mr. Johnson's face like maybe Mr. Johnson was trying to teach him a lesson. "What's up with your Florida connection?" Mr. Johnson asked.

"I've got a connection in Florida where we can get the keys for ten thousand dollars a piece delivered."

"Holy shit." Mr. Johnson said. He was impressed. He wanted to speak with Christopher privately so the others wouldn't know the details of his business then they wouldn't expect favors.

"I'm going to need you to collect a couple million so that we can take the money down south then, we can fly it to Colombia." Christopher said with a slight smile on his face proud of his business achievements.

"So you're connected directly with the Colombians?" Mr. Johnson asked.

"Directly." And the words sounded like they echoed. That's how powerful having the connection with the Colombian's was especially with Christopher's genius.

"Ten thousand dollars a kilogram. Do you know what we could do with that?" Mr. Johnson repeated aloud.

"Sometimes the price is gonna fluctuate but basically that's what we'll be paying and I'll handle delivery. They're bringing it to Florida and we're bringing it out." Christopher said.

"So how much money do you want to start out with?" Mr. Johnson asked.

"At least ten million and you put up three."

"And your gonna put up seven?" Mr. Johnson asked shocked that Christopher's family could generate that kind of money.

"Well all the lieutenants in my family are going in as partners we're putting up a half a million a piece so that's our seven million." Christopher didn't tell him that he was putting up his own seven million dollars in cash. It might make the others jealous. "How are you going to get paid if the lieutenants are spending their own money?" Mr. Johnson asked.

"After they finish they're gonna buy all of mine for about fifteen thousand a key." Christopher said. Mr. Johnson was impressed, as were the others in the room. "So your gonna make five thousand dollars a key?" Mr. Johnson asked.

"Yup." Christopher responded. "Five thousand dollars times fifty keys is a quarter million dollars. It's gonna take a while before I finish mine but cocaine is a lot less quieter then heroin so I'll make money." Christopher was purchasing a ton of cocaine on his own and Senor Cachas was going to front him another ton on consignment. Christopher was going to use the money that Mr. Johnson spent to cover his debt. If Christopher sold the kilograms for ten thousand a piece, he was going to make eleven million dollars in profits for himself. His goal was to make at least six shipments a year. Within two years he would indirectly control fifty percent of the cocaine distributed in the Tri-State area.

Christopher was using Mr. Johnson's money as a safety net.

"I want to meet the Colombians?" Mr. Johnson said.

"No problem." Christopher said. They were about to make millions of dollars because of him and everyone whether they liked him or not had a new found respect for him. Even Mr. Johnson was impressed.

Clark couldn't believe his ears, he had completely underestimated Christopher and the Larkin crime family.

Within two years Christopher's distribution outlets would indirectly control the entire Tri-state area. Christopher would establish distribution in New Jersey, New York City, Philadelphia, Baltimore, Washington D.C, Chicago and some other cities on the East-coast.

Chapter Twenty Four Atlantic City, New Jersey

For The Good of The Family

Christopher took seven million dollars in cash and collected another eight million from the lieutenants. Mr. Johnson only sent a million because he refused to lose anymore money. All of this became the advantage for Christopher, who had the keys delivered to the lieutenants for ten thousand a piece. Once they were finished they had to buy from him. He was going to charge them fifteen thousand a kilogram with a restriction that they couldn't sell the kilos for more then twenty-five thousand or less then twenty thousand without his permission. This would control the prices on the market. Kilograms had already dropped to the twenty to twenty-five thousand dollar range in 1985 and that was a drastic drop from the old price of forty thousand a kilogram it had been several years earlier.

Christopher flew to Colombia for vacation and he was afforded the opportunity to see Senor Cachas cocaine empire. Impressive for a man, who was still in his late thirties, Christopher brought Maria, Pedro's sister as his translator.

Christopher and Franklin were sitting in a car in North Jersey. One of Franklin's soldiers was attending college in the area and flooding the market with cocaine.

"Franklin, I'm retiring you?" Christopher said. It was a rare occasion but Christopher was driving. Franklin was sitting in the front seat and Corey was sitting in the back seat. They were all multi-millionaires except Franklin who had just fallen into the upper six-figure bracket. Nobody sold as much cocaine as he was in New York City.

"You're retiring me? What and the fuck does that mean?" Franklin asked. He was pissed off. Off of this one shipment he had made a couple of million dollars in profits but a lot of it was going to legal fees and other responsibilities.

"First of all you owe two million dollars." Christopher said and Franklin turned away embarrassed. He didn't want Corey to hear his business.

"Plus the IRS is watching you and if they alert the Feds this could turn into a federal investigation. Don't worry about money. I'll pay your lawyers and put you on an allowance."

"An allowance." Franklin was shocked and hurt. "Christopher that's fucking me up. I need money. What's up? You don't trust me?"

Christopher looked at him. He could see the hurt on Franklin's face. "I trust you but I don't want Mr. Johnson to put a contract out on you."

"What?" Franklin yelled. "I can handle myself."

"I know you can handle yourself but you're a lieutenant in a family now and you have to do what's best for the family. You have to think about the big picture now. Say for instance the feds are on you and you don't know it. Then your subjecting us to a federal investigation that we know nothing about."

Franklin was pissed but he understood and before he could say anything Christopher continued. "When you come home you'll still be a lieutenant and you'll still control whatever areas you control. Right now they don't have anything on you but tax evasion and I would like to keep it that way. It's not fair to endanger the others. You understand me right. You know those bastards in Philadelphia want an excuse to murder you. They're pissed off about their money."

Franklin just held his head down. He was still embarrassed because he was doing side business with all of them. They didn't know it, until his arrest, then they all found out. He even owed Mr. Gaston a million dollars. If he wouldn't had spent his money on all of that foolish materialistic stuff then he would have had millions saved. Hopefully if he beat the case he could sell some of his property and make some hard cash when he came home.

"So, what do I do with the money I was gonna give those mother fuckers?" Franklin asked. "I made two million dollars off of this shit."

"How much were you going to give them?" Christopher asked. Corey was still sitting in the back silent and for the first time in his life Franklin realized how dangerous his comrades were. They could easily kill him and leave his body but Christopher would never do it. Tahwan was Franklin's first cousin.

"I wanted to give them the whole two million." Franklin stated and Christopher was impressed. He smiled.

"Give me the two million and I'll divide it up. They'll be happy." "Frank, I'm giving you a pass because you're like a brother to me and I love you. Please don't put my life on the line. It's taken a lot for me to get this. I'm going to let you rock until we finish this shipment and then your retired. You'll make all of your money through your soldiers." Christopher said and then he continued. "Who's gonna take over for you?"

"My brother in-law Beanie from Manhattanville apartments." "Wise choice." Christopher said. "All of this has to be presented to the family and when you're gone we're gonna name him acting lieutenant until your release."

Franklin shook his head. "I hope I don't have to kill that mother fucker after he starts making all that money. You know how these mother fuckers get."

Christopher took another pull from his joint. "He's a soldier you're a lieutenant. He knows his position."

Christopher started the engine and they sped away leaving behind the small hotel they were talking in front of, Christopher had to return to South Jersey, he was driving around with millions of dollars in the trunk of his car.

Franklin should have been happy that Christopher didn't kill him because he had already burned his bridges with the other lieutenants by alienating himself from the others and thinking that he was better.

Everyone knew that he wanted to start his own family but he was too flamboyant and bringing a lot of unnecessary heat from the police. The one thing that the family had going in its favor was that the authorities didn't know they were organized or how massive their business actually was.

Chapter Twenty Five South Jersey Area

Second to None

Christopher, Mr. Johnson and his crew were sitting in Christopher's living room having a meeting. The bodyguards were left to sit in the kitchen while the leaders conducted business. Little Aaron arrived a couple of minutes after the meeting had started. Little Aaron had told Mr. Johnson that Christopher took seven million dollars on their first trip to Florida and Mr. Johnson was impressed. It couldn't be prevented anymore Christopher had to be initiated into the family or the Johnson family would lose a powerful asset and moneymaker.

"Christopher I'm making you a lieutenant." Mr. Johnson said with his fedora sitting on his lap.

John Martin just smiled. These people still underestimated Christopher. John Martin didn't say anything because Christopher told him not to speak during the meetings, just to listen.

Christopher shook his head.

Mr. Johnson continued. "I wanted to make you second in command but it might start a war so this is how we're gonna do it. I'll retire in ninety. Clark becomes boss, Tommy Cans." Mr. Johnson's real right hand man. "He'll become Counselor then they're gonna name an old timer Underboss. You, you'll be made lieutenant over the entire New Jersey area and Michael will be your right hand man."

The others just stared silently amazed.

"By two thousand you'll be running everything.' Mr. Johnson added in. "But you have to give me your answer now because I have to make some arrangements and connect you with some people. Big Aaron and Crazy Moe retire the day you're initiated. They'll have no power or connection with the business."

Christopher glanced at Little Aaron and he didn't flinch he was finally learning to hide his emotions a powerful trait for business.

"Mr. Johnson." Christopher got up from the seat he was sitting in and grasped his mentor's hands. "I would never disrespect you but once your gone I can't work under any of these men. I would rather keep it the way it is now."

Mr. Johnson was pissed but he kept his composure. "Christopher, when I retire they're gonna come after you if you don't turn over your connections. I like you that's why I'm trying to help you and prevent a war." He said it like he carried the concern of a worried father.

"I can handle myself." Christopher said.

Mr. Johnson placed his hand against Christopher's face like he was going to caress it. "Christopher, you're like a son to me." He paused after he said it. "In fact, better because were in the same business. I just want what's best for the family. We've got to stick together or everything's gonna fall apart and I don't want that to happen even after I'm gone. I don't want anything to happen to you." Mr. Johnson said.

"I'll be okay. I know when ninety rolls around to be ready." Christopher said it like he was taking the meeting as a warning. Christopher had only been dealing with the Colombians for two years and had only made six shipments, with those six shipments he was dominating the cocaine business in the South Jersey and North Jersey area.

"When's Franklin coming home?" Mr. Johnson asked.

"In another year." Christopher said.

"That contract on him stands." Mr. Johnson added in. He was going to kill Franklin in hopes of waking Christopher up.

"He paid the money." Christopher said. "He doesn't owe

anything."

"Yeah but he's a snake in the grass and I can't stand him." Mr. Johnson said.

Andre had turned himself in a couple of months earlier and he was home on a quarter million dollar bail placed up by one of Christopher's properties. The only thing that was pissing Christopher off was that Andre was still running around extorting people when he came home.

Michael and his crew had settled down a little bit because they were making so much money selling cocaine. Michael was doing business with Christopher and Mr. Johnson.

Mr. Johnson was taking his kilograms and cutting them. Christopher sold his the same way they came from Colombia. Factory sealed and high-grade fish scale white or beige Christopher was becoming a force to be reckoned with in the business. He still lived in the modest home with the security fence around it.

Chapter Twenty Six Atlantic City, New Jersey

We're About to Visit Hell

Two years after dealing with the Colombian's and a couple of months after Franklin's release, Tahwan gave birth to Christopher's fourth child Aaron Larkin named after Mr. Gaston. Now they had Christopher junior, Najwa and Inayah the twins and Little Aaron. Tahwan hated the name but she loved her husband so much that she didn't want to displease him.

Christopher and Corty drove out to Ocean City, New Jersey, a small town located a couple of miles from Atlantic City. Corty usually traveled with Christopher and helped him collect his proceeds. Sometimes, he even did bodyguard work for Christopher even when he didn't have too. Corty had ten to twenty soldiers under him and they would have gladly protected the boss but sometimes Christopher didn't want it that way. He liked to keep himself surrounded by the originals. For Corty it was an honor, whenever they were together he learned something.

Christopher's business had excelled and covered the entire New Jersey area. He had major distribution in Newark, Patterson, Passaic County and Atlantic County to name a few areas.

Through Franklin's crew he had distribution outlets in all the five boroughs of New York City. Christopher was making multi-ton cocaine deals and buying commercial real estate in several major cities across the United States.

Christopher and Corty pulled up to Michael's apartment. Christopher had given Michael one hundred kilograms of cocaine for ten thousand a piece on consignment he was here to collect his money.

After Christopher established the cocaine connection with the Colombians Michael started getting consignment from him, and proceeded to sell the cocaine in Philadelphia where he still had outlets.

A couple of months earlier Mr. Johnson had officially made Michael a lieutenant over New Jersey. Mr. Gaston was forced into semi-retirement with Crazy Moe where they quietly tended to their legal businesses.

Michael was sitting in his living room counting money on his money machine. Michael was unwrapping the thousand dollar stacks and placing them in the money machine to be recounted and then rubber banding them again.

"How did everything go?" Christopher asked.

"Beautiful." Michael had a ten-man crew from Philadelphia that had distribution outlets in Atlantic City, Pleasantville, Ocean City, and Millville. Christopher's prices were better than the Dominicans that were running New York City at the time.

"Chris I need more consignment." Michael said. "That shit is flying off of the hook in Philadelphia." In Philadelphia Michael sold the kilograms for twenty thousand a kilogram to lieutenants or soldiers in his family. Sometimes he would have to go cheaper because the lieutenants would buy his entire package in cash and want some kind of deal.

"How much do you need?" Christopher asked. He had heard the story before. The Cocaine business was just like heroin. You'd make millions if you know what you were doing.

"At least two hundred keys." Michael replied. He was a nice looking young man with a raggedy smile until recently having expensive dental work done.

"That's a lot." Christopher added in he knew that Michael was still selling for Mr. Johnson. "You sure you can handle it?"

"Of course I can." Michael was making side deals with the

young lieutenants in the family and he needed much more than two hundred. He wanted to get the new lieutenants under his wing before Christopher did it.

"So what's up with Mr. Johnson?" Christopher asked.

"He's still bugging. Charging twenty a brick and cutting the shit out of it. Now, he's on that re-rock shit." Michael said.

"I don't know why. It's only gonna hurt himself." A lot of people were cutting the coke and baking it in the oven to bring it back to rock form but the quality was garbage. Christopher had made it a rule as soon as they started heavy distribution anybody caught cutting his material would be killed immediately.

"Why don't you talk to him?" Michael asked like maybe Christopher could help.

"There's nothing I can say to him." "You know he's mad at you for refusing that lieutenant position and charging him what you charge everybody else." Michael added in. Christopher was surprised to hear Michael repeat that, not because he didn't believe it but more shocked that Mr. Johnson would express his dislike for Christopher verbally to another lieutenant. "I know he's pissed but I've got a family." Christopher said. Corty was sitting silently in the corner minding his business.

"A lot of mother fucker's want him to retire?" Michael added in trying to feel Christopher out. "But who's gonna challenge him? The only person strong enough to take over the family is you." "I don't know." Christopher kind of ignored it and skipped the question.

"What's up with Franklin?" Michael continued.

"He's alright."

"Mr. Johnson wants him dead." Michael said and Christopher was about to stop him. Christopher trusted Corty completely but he knew that something's weren't meant for everybody to hear. The other lieutenants in the Larkin family wanted to strike first and kill Mr. Johnson just on general principle alone. Nobody liked him and they trusted him even less. To them he was a jealous, greedy snake in the grass but Christopher didn't see it and if he did he wasn't showing it to the others.

Michael counted the last of the money and placed it in the duffel bag. "So, what's up with the two hundred keys?"

Michael asked.

"You got it tomorrow." Christopher said picking up the bag and throwing it to Corty. Corty caught the bag and stood up. This was lightweight. He had driven around with Christopher and picked up ten million in one day from about four different states. When they drove to New York, they would fill up the flat bed of a truck with duffel bags.

"What time you want me to call you tomorrow?" Michael asked walking Christopher to the door. It was dark outside and getting late. Michael planned on calling his girl to the house. He was slowly falling out of grace with Mr. Johnson because his relationship with his wife was falling apart, she had caught him cheating and they were thinking about separating until he got himself together. Mr. Johnson was infuriated, to him Michael's behavior was a slap in the face. Michael didn't understand why it was such a big deal. Mr. Johnson had been cheating on his wife since Michael met them.

Christopher and Corty left Michael's condominium and walked down the steps. Ocean City was an extremely quiet area which played to Michael's advantage. The police weren't sophisticated enough to capture somebody of Michael stature.

Andre was on his way home from jail because the state had awarded him an appeal on his murder conviction with bail. Corty passed Christopher the bag as they walked down the steps. When they got down the steps they walked around the corner to the parking lot to Christopher's Mercury Topaz. Christopher bought cars like this just for business. His wife was driving a brand new Mercedes Benz.

Christopher placed the bag in the trunk of the car and walked around to the passenger side. Corty followed him and opened the door. Corty closed the door. Christopher didn't see the men come from around the trashcan until Animal raised his weapon.

Animal started firing and the first shot went through the passenger's window and entered the side Christopher was sitting on. Christopher's body slammed against the steering wheel splattering blood against the windshield. Animal fired several more shots into the car and most of them landed in Christopher's body.

Black and two other guys came from the opposite side and

they started shooting at Corty. Corty saw them pop up from the side of a car parked next to his but it was too late. They riddled his body with bullets and he crashed to the ground.

When Michael had heard the gunshots he turned up his stereo. He had already told the landlord that he was moving the month before when Mr. Johnson reaffirmed the order. This way the police wouldn't be so suspicious if he left after the shooting.

After listening to the gun shots Michael fought against going outside to view the bodies. He was gonna have to wait until the police came. He wanted to see the bodies just to make sure they were dead. After dealing with Christopher for several years now he knew how powerful the Larkin family was, even if Mr. Johnson didn't understand all hell was about to break lose bodies were going to start flying. When Mr. Johnson gave Michael the order to kill Christopher at Nia's wedding Michael contemplated warning Christopher but where would he live. He was married to Mr. Johnson's daughter? Something in his heart told him to warn Christopher and side with the Larkin crime family but what if Christopher didn't believe him? Or what if Christopher wasn't smart enough and didn't kill Mr. Johnson? In the long run he would be the one blamed and he would eventually pop up dead so Michael went with what he thought would be the best odds. He would just have to wait until the war was over to find out if he made the right decision or not. One thing he was sure of, the Larkin's were nothing without Christopher and his cocaine connection. Compared to Mr. Johnson and the others they, were babies.

Animal walked to the back of the Mercury Topaz he aimed his gun and shot the lock off the trunk. He lifted the trunk and removed the duffel bag. Then jumped in the get away car and they sped away.

They removed their ski masks and immediately jumped on the Garden State Parkway North.

Chapter Twenty Seven *Ocean City, New Jersey*

No Body Touch Him

It took a couple of minutes before the first cops arrived on the scene and a couple minutes more before the ambulance arrived. Corty was lying near the back of the car and Christopher was sitting in the front seat. The windshield was smeared with blood.

A few minutes after the cops arrived on the scene a crowd of elderly white people that lived in the condominiums surrounded the crime scene. The next law enforcement to arrive was the forensic truck. They taped the area off, zipped Corty's body up and rushed Christopher to the hospital, from the looks of his wounds he wasn't going to make it.

Christopher and Corty were carrying identification. The Ocean City Police department notified Atlantic City's homicide department and the Prosecutors office as soon as they discovered out who the victims were.

Corey was the first one to receive the call. He was sitting with his soldiers in a building they sold drugs out of in Atlantic City. After the crack explosion drugs had left bars and had spilled into parks and some of the low-income housing developments.

Corey's crew was working out of a house that made every bit of fifty to twenty five thousand dollars a day depending on the time of the month. The closer to the first of the month the better. Sometimes the lieutenants would take kilograms that Christopher gave them and quadruple their money. About 8:35 that night Corey got a page on his beeper. The message was call Red at 344-6111 extension 47. Corey's heart started racing that was his connection at the police department.

Corey ran outside to use a pay phone. When a operator picked up the phone he asked for the extension. Five minutes later his police connection was on the line.

"Hello."

"What's up I got your call?"

"I called because two of your people got killed. One made it to the hospital but he ain't gonna pull through. Go past the hospital as soon as you can.." His police connection said. The family was paying him a thousand dollars a week just for information.

"Did you get their names?"

"I think the one that died was named Christopher Larkin and the other one's name was Corty Taylor he's not related to you is he?" "Shit." Corey said smacking the phone against his hand.

"Listen honey I have to go it's busy down here I'll call you later." Corey knew that was the signal that another officer had walked in and his police connection couldn't talk. Right after the officer said that the line went dead.

Corey was shocked. He stared at the phone for a couple of seconds trying to grasp his composure.

"Corey you alright?" His bodyguard asked him. They had been friends since childhood and they were very close.

"Yeah, everything's alright." Corey was in a daze. "This is what I want you to do. Go to your house and beep Lynn. Tell him to meet me at Christopher's house, and it's extremely important." Corey repeated Lynn's number to the soldier and the soldier ran off without another word. Corey and another bodyguard drove his other car to Christopher's house. When they got there all of Christopher's cars were parked in his parking lot. Maybe the cop had relayed misinformation or his sources weren't correct.

Corey jumped out of the car and buzzed the security alarm.

"Who is it?" Asked a pleasant voice over the intercom.

"It's Corey Mrs. Larkin can you open up?"

The alarm on the gate buzzed and Corey pushed the gate open while his bodyguard drove the car on the property.

Corey walked to the front door and the door swung open. Mrs. Larkin was standing behind the door crying.

"What's going on?" Corey asked.

"The police called, Christopher and your brother are dead." Mrs. Larkin started crying uncontrollably. Corey wrapped his arms around her to comfort her.

The words made Corey's legs weak he was completely shocked like it was his first time hearing the news. He thought that he would be able to handle the situation better but he was trembling. Corey paused for a second to get his composure. He had lost his twin brother and his best friend in one night. What was he gonna tell his mother? She was going to be destroyed. Then the thought hit him. What was he gonna tell his brother's wife and kids?

"Mrs. Larkin did anybody go and identify the bodies?" Corey didn't want to but he had to ask.

"I couldn't go Tahwan's not going to be able to take it she been upstairs crying every since the police called."

"Call down there let them know I'm coming and I'll handle everything. I want you and Tahwan to get the kid's dressed. You're staying at my house with my wife until we get to the bottom of this. My bodyguard is going to take you there, he's safe." Mrs. Larkin nodded her head and retreated upstairs. Corey had never noticed how much Christopher resembled her until today. He couldn't believe that his partner was dead.

Just as Corey was returning to his car Lynn pulled up and jumped out of his car. The security gate was left wide open.

"What the fucks going on?" Lynn asked.

"Christopher and Corty are dead and we have to identify the bodies."

Lynn was shocked. "Are you sure?"

"Not until I see the bodies for myself."

"I'm telling you right now if they killed my brothers I'm killing every fucking body." He didn't say any names but Corey knew whom he was talking about. They jumped in the car and sped away.

Lynn and Corey went to the administrative desk in the

hospital told the nurse their purpose and she directed them upstairs to the hospital morgue.

Lynn and Corey walked to the elevator, caught the elevator to the 8th floor. When they got to the 8th floor they went to the nurse's station and told her they were there to identify a body. The nurse called the doctor and a young doctor appeared.

"Are you gentlemen here to identify the body that came in from Ocean City today?"

"Yes we are."

"Follow me please." The doctor was short and a little older then Corey and Lynn. He was neatly dressed and carrying a clipboard and wearing a white lab coat.

The doctor opened the door and led them into the room where they stored the bodies. He removed the slab that Corty was lying on. The back of his head was torn to pieces from bullets. Corey almost fainted seeing his little brother lying on a slab like that. He bit into his own fist to stop from screaming. His mother wasn't going to make it. She worshiped the ground they walked on. Her life centered around them.

"Is that him?" The doctor asked and both of them looked at each other shocked before nodding their heads in the affirmative.

"Where's the other one?"

"The other one's in surgery but we're not sure if he's going to make it."

Lynn flew out of the door he had to make some calls immediately.

By the time that Lynn and Corey got downstairs to the main phones the hospital was packed with all of the lieutenants. Corey's mother and father were there. Seeing his father surprised him. When his mother saw him shaking his head she immediately started crying and yelling. Just as she started crying Corty's wife Jahna walked in. When she saw her mother in-law crying she fainted dropping her baby in the process. The family rushed over to her.

Then Mark walked over to them. "What's going on?" Everyone was still in shock over the news.

"Christopher's in surgery and Corty's dead we need to have an emergency meeting."

"No." Mark said shocked. The other lieutenants surrounded Corey and Lynn. They started embracing each other. The family would provide Corty's family with a steady income and make sure that his children had the financial assistance to receive an education whether Christopher made it or not. None of this was needed because Corty was a millionaire.

Five Atlantic City Hospital surgeons were standing over Christopher performing emergency surgery.

The head doctor, a young female named Heather Williams was overseeing the operation. "Come on gentlemen were losing him." The doctor looked over at the monitor that monitored Christopher's condition and started yelling commands to the other doctors attempting to assist her.

"Keep on breathing for me baby." The lady kept saying.

Just as she said it the monitor went flat line. "Oh shit were losing him."

Another one of the doctors ran out of the back with the shockers and shocked Christopher's chest. He jumped but his heart wasn't beating.

"Do it again." The main surgeon commanded.

The other doctor did it again, and nothing happened. "Don't give up on me baby. Somebody needs you."

The doctor hit his chest again and nothing happened.

"Shit." The doctor punched Christopher's chest. "Goldstein, hit him one more time."

Doctor Goldstein looked at her. "Heather he's gone."

"Please, shock him again for me." One of the hardest things for a new doctor to do was give up on a patient or declare a patient dead.

Doctor Goldstein walked over to Christopher again and hit him. Nothing.

Another one of the female doctors that was in the room placed her hands on Doctor William's shoulders and walked her to the corner. The doctor started crying.

Another doctor placed a white sheet over Christopher's face. As they started walking out of the room the monitor beeped again. Everyone froze in their tracks.

They ran back over to Christopher removing the sheet that covered his face. "Nobody touch him." Doctor Williams said. "Let him breathe on his own." The doctors sat there silently while Christopher's breathing slowly improved showing his increasing vital signs on the monitor.

Chapter Twenty Eight *Atlantic City, New Jersey*

Cross Your Fingers

By the time the lieutenants and their bodyguards had assembled at Christopher's house, the house was littered with cars that belonged to soldiers and lieutenants. Lynn had turned the alarm system off and set up a bodyguard team to guard the gate of the house. Somebody had tipped off News Center Forty. There was a small group of news reporters with cameras outside of the residence attempting to interview lieutenants as they entered the property. The only reason that the shooting got media coverage was because Christopher was a small time construction tycoon in the city. Franklin was the last lieutenant to arrive because he had gotten the word in New York about an hour after Corey had left from identifying the body. He had driven down in a car with a bodyguard. They were staying in the casino.

A group of undercover cops were parked up the street across from the house copying license plates and gathering information.

The family decided to hold the business meeting in Christopher's office. The one he had built a year after he purchased the house.

Little Aaron would have started the meeting but they were

waiting for Franklin to arrive and as soon he did they started.

"Christopher and Corty got shot up real bad tonight." Little Aaron said. He hated to take the position as head of the family but it was something that he had to do. Christopher would want it this way.

"Are you sure?" Franklin said, because he operated out of New York he was like an outsider to most of them. A couple of them didn't like him because they knew that Christopher let him get away with owing millions of dollars, which he wasn't attempting to repay.

"Corey and Lynn identified Corty's body. Christopher's having emergency surgery as we speak. The doctor said he might not make it." Little Aaron said. His father was sitting quietly in the corner with Crazy Morris. They were silent because they didn't actually belong to the Larkin family.

"So, did anybody hear anything?" John Martin asked. He was not qualified to run the family. The only reason that he held the position of Underboss was because he was very close to Christopher. Now that position might be challenged.

"The only thing I know was that he got shot in Ocean City in one of those condominiums." Corey answered. Still in shock after hearing the news and identifying his twin brothers body.

"Who was he with?" Franklin asked highly upset.

"Corty." Was Lynn's response.

"And he's dead?" Franklin asked shocked. He still couldn't believe the news even though, it was being reported to him by reliable people.

Mark spoke he was the quietest one in the family. "Doesn't Michael live in Ocean City?"

"He sure does." John Martin responded. "You think he set Christopher up?"

"Most likely." Corey responded. Corey was the most powerful lieutenant after Franklin who lived in New York. Distribution wise Franklin was the strongest he sold more cocaine and heroin then all the other lieutenants combined or at least that was what he claimed. "But why?" Corey asked. "Mr. Johnson." Franklin responded and everybody looked towards Mr. Gaston. "That's not correct. If Mr. Johnson was gonna kill Christopher he would have informed me. Maybe it was a robbery?" Mr. Gaston said. It sounded like a cop out. "I called Big Will and didn't get an answer yet but I know he wouldn't have done it without informing me. He loved Christopher like a son." The words seemed promising but something wasn't correct and the others could sense it. "I'm gonna call him until I reach him tomorrow." Mr. Gaston sat back and gulped his drink. He was going to need it because it was going to be an incredibly long night.

"First thing we have to do is calm down and make sure that everything's all right. There are a bunch of cops parked down the block. I don't know if they're cops or Feds but we have to be careful because they're expecting a war and they want to pick us up in the process. The first thing we have to do is think, just like Christopher would think. We have to keep the family stable, especially if were gonna find out who did this to our man." Aaron said attempting to assert his authority and control over the situation.

Corey smiled but he was pissed off. "I don't give a fuck what anybody says if he got killed in Ocean City he was probably collecting money from Michael or doing business with him. If Michael had something to do with it, then we have to handle it." "Corey you're right but what if it wasn't Michael and it was just a robbery? That's why I don't want anybody making a move without consulting with me first." Little Aaron continued.

The others were pissed because Little Aaron seemed to be taking the situation lightly. Little Aaron was given his position he didn't earn it like the rest of them had too. The family was already dividing and Christopher had only been hospitalized for a couple of hours.

"I say we don't vote on the new positions until after we find out whether Christopher is going to make it or not. Little Aaron's the family boss until we vote on a new boss." Corey said. He was drinking straight out of a whiskey bottle. He hadn't rested since receiving the telephone call from his police contact. "The next meeting should be after the funeral but we should immediately start an investigation. Mr. Gaston can call Big Will, get information on that end relay it to Little Aaron and he can relay it to us."

The other's looked at him.

"Dad you have to contact Mr. Johnson and find out what's going on because we need some answers. Then somebody has to get with Michael and arrange a meeting so that he can explain what the fuck is going on."

"Explain what and the fucks going on? I say we put a bullet in Michael's head and make Mr. Johnson explain later." Mark was pissed off and teary eyed.

"Mark you have to calm down. Let's get the facts first. The next meetings after the funeral and then we'll vote on the boss and the next lieutenant." Little Aaron said. Rightfully, he was the boss. He wanted to control the family. Even Christopher wanted it that way that was why he had made him second in command. "Is there anything else we need to cover?" Little Aaron asked anxious to end the meeting and get some rest. It was damn near two o'clock in the morning.

"Yeah, do you think we should set up a bodyguard team at the hospital?" Franklin had made a valid point.

"Not right now because the police are guarding Christopher but if they remove the guards will appoint a bodyguard team." Corey said.

The others were silent. The meeting was over. The family would not find out Christopher's situation until the next morning. The police were already stationed outside of his room waiting on his recovery. Because it was a shooting they placed him under guarded protection.

That night Tahwan and Mrs. Larkin were sitting in the hospital waiting room waiting to here the news on Christopher's condition when a nice looking African American female doctor walked into the waiting room. She looked at her clipboard. "Is there a Mrs. Larkin here?" She asked and both Mrs. Larkin's stood up smiling at the action.

"Yes I'm Mrs. Larkin." Tahwan said. "And this is Mr. Larkin's mother the other Mrs. Larkin." The doctor smiled while extending her hands. "Well it's nice to meet of you." "So how's he doing?" Christopher's mother asked.

"He just came out of surgery and we're running tests. We lost him for a couple of minutes so now we have to run tests and make sure he's not brain dead."

Even though it didn't sound good it was good enough news. At least he wasn't dead.

Then she hit them with the bombshell. "You guys are gonna have to pray and cross your fingers because there's no guarantee's on whether he's gonna make it or not."

Chapter Twenty nine *Atlantic City, New Jersey*

Message Number One

Corty's funeral was held on a beautiful day in January. For the seven years that Christopher dominated the cocaine and heroin trade in South Jersey, Corty was a trusted lieutenant. The family made sure he was buried properly.

At the time of the shooting Christopher owned commercial property in Trinidad, Florida, California, New York and real estate in Atlantic City, New Jersey so providing for Corty's family would be no problem.

Christopher also owned a small but profitable Construction company, Off Shore Construction Corp and several commercial properties that he was renting out. If Christopher would have died, his children would have received his property; his wife and mother would have been named guardians over his estate.

While Christopher lay in the hospital he gave his lawyer instructions to give his mother and his wife his will. A vault had been constructed under his mother's house, where three million in cash was stashed. It was for his mother. In Tahwan's letter she was instructed to go to Idaho where

Christopher owned a small farm that she knew nothing about. When she got there she went to a closet that had a secret compartment slash elevator, after pressing the codes and the switches, a steel door slid open. There were blocks of money wrapped in plastic with some of the plastic blocks being the size of beds. He had another twenty million in overseas bank accounts.

It was a little over one hundred and fifty million dollars. The week after the funeral Christopher's wife and mother flew to Switzerland and opened up Swiss bank accounts. When Christopher came home from the hospital, nobody but his immediate family and his most trusted lieutenants knew.

Corty's funeral was held exactly one week after he died at the Second Baptist church in Atlantic City, New Jersey.

All of the lieutenants, their wives, children, guys from out of state that did business with him and all of Corty's friends came. Luckily the bullets had only tore the back of Corty's head apart and left his face intact. His family gave him an open casket ceremony.

Corty's family wanted to bury him quietly the day before without a crowd but John Martin told them Christopher was coming home and wanted to be there. The Reverend that over saw the ceremony said a few words. They spent time at the church viewing the body and then it was off to the cemetery.

Corty looked terrible. His wife went to the funeral parlor and took his favorite suit but his body looked dark and shriveled up. A couple of hours after making sure everyone viewed the body. Jahna stood up and ordered the casket closed after she let the children go up and kiss their father cheeks. Corty's children were young and really didn't understand what was going on. Christopher had surprised everybody when he arrived at the funeral. Nobody had noticed him at the viewing a couple of hours earlier because he was surrounded by a group of bodyguards and he was wearing a hat. From the shooting he had lost a considerable amount of weight but beside that he was fine.

Mark walked over to Christopher. "What's up now?"

"Take Tahwan and the kids home." Mark nodded his head yes. "Mark, have two bodyguards follow her everywhere she goes you understand me." Christopher asked. Mark had only to be told once. He took his orders from Christopher extremely serious.

"You ready Tee?" Mark asked. "Yes." The words were a whisper.

Mark looked over at one of his men raised his hand and Christopher's family was shielded by a group of bodyguards, taken to the limousine where a car would take them home and bring Tahwan back to the cemetery. Tahwan didn't have to come but she had gotten close to Corty's wife Jahna and wanted to show her support. Her husband had lost his life saving Christopher's. One hundred and fifty people had attended the funeral when it was over they piled up in cars. There was so many cars that they blocked the highway. When they got to the gravesite the Reverend said a few more words and then slid the casket into the vault. Christopher had purchased an enormous vault, big enough for Corty's immediate family to be buried in when they died. Christopher was sitting in the seats reserved for Corty's family, surrounded by a bodyguard team when Lynn walked over to him and whispered something into his ear.

"Christopher, I just got the call he's sitting outside of the projects."

"You know what to do then." Little Aaron watched Lynn as he walked away.

The day of Corty's funeral, Michael and one of his most trusted soldiers, were sitting in a car parked outside of a housing development that they controlled in Millville, New Jersey. The development was extremely small, but the business there was massive they sold large amounts of crack there.

Michael was sitting behind the wheel of a brand new Mercedes Benz. It was a gift from Mr. Johnson for his good work. There was a good-looking woman wearing acid jeans with a very nice shape blocking his view from the window. Her name was Citrus and she danced in the strip clubs on the weekend. The driver pulled next to Michael and asked for directions. He was driving a stolen commercial van.

Lynn slid out of the van when it stopped from the passenger's side. He was carrying a double barrel sawed off shotgun. He kept the gun to his chest in case he had to fire immediately or if Michael spotted him while he was running towards him.

Michael had placed his hands on the girl's ass and was squeezing it. They were tongue kissing and saying goodbye.

Lynn walked over to the girl and pushed her out of the way. For one second their faces locked and Michael's eyes displayed his horror of knowing that he was about to die.

Lynn pulled the trigger and Michael's face exploded. A couple of seconds after the first shot Lynn pumped the gun and shot Michael in his chest then ran back over to the get away van.

Then entire time Michael's bodyguard stood frozen in the passenger's seat.

The Larkin family sent it's first message.

After Corty's family slid his black mahogany coffin in the stone encasement they began to walk to their cars.

The bodyguards had already alerted Christopher that a group of undercover cops were parked behind the last car snapping pictures.

Nobody noticed the van parked outside of the gravesite with the tinted windows video tapeing the entire incident. Two federal agents were sitting in one of the cars parked behind the other cars snapping pictures. One of the agents lifted his walkie-talkie.

"Alan, did you get somebody to follow the guy that sped out of here?"

"No we couldn't because he left too fast and we didn't want to make a move and alert anybody to our presence."

"Damn." The supervising agent slammed his fist against the dashboard of the car he thought that something important might be happening.

Tahwan and Jahna drove to Corty's house in one car while Christopher and a bodyguard team drove in a separate car. Christopher wouldn't drive to Corty's until security checked the area out first. The entire family was on war alert, especially a day later when they found out Christopher made his first move against the Johnson crime family by killing Michael.

Chapter Thirty Atlantic City, New Jersey

Who Are Your Friends

Michael's death was a powerful enough blow against the Johnson family to warrant a semi-peace agreement. It wouldn't be Michael's death that would hurt the Johnson crime family the most but the lost of Christopher's cocaine connection. Losing Christopher's cocaine connection forced Mr. Johnson to reconnect with the Dominicans he used to deal with in New York and there was an enormous price difference. Business in Philadelphia suffered and a lot of the younger lieutenants were pissed because they were losing money. Nobody knew that it was actually Christopher himself who was the connection to the Colombians.

Two weeks after Corty's funeral, the Larkin Crime family gathered at Christopher's house in Atlantic City. Christopher was still sick but the meeting couldn't be prevented. Police surveillance had stepped up and the family was put under federal investigation. The FBI assumed that Mr. Gaston and Little Aaron controlled everything, so they placed the bar and their residence under twenty-four hour surveillance.

The Larking family was sitting in Christopher's den.

Nobody could believe how quickly Christopher recovered.

He had lost a good amount of weight but besides weight lost he had completely recovered and he was ready to take his position as head of the family. This was the Larkin family's first war and hopefully it's last. Before being shot, the police didn't really know anything about Christopher. Now they kept coming past his real estate office trying to harass him about the shooting incident. Christopher just referred them to his attorney he was too smart to let them question him. "Mr. Gaston, have you talked to Mr. Johnson yet?"

"Oh course I have and he's ready to talk. He said Michael sanctioned that shooting on his own. William wants to hold a peace meeting because he had nothing to do with it."

Mr. Gaston was no longer allowed to attend meetings that the family held but right now he was the only link that Christopher had to Mr. Johnson and they had to get to the bottom of the situation in order to secure peace.

"So what did he say about Michael?"

"He doesn't give a fuck about Michael. Michael was an unworthy piece of shit. Why would William risk destroying the money machine we put together. He would have never put a contract out on you. He would gain nothing."

"Maybe he thought with Christopher gone that he could take over the cocaine connection." John Martin said. John Martin was light skin with an enormous nose and curly hair. He was still Christopher's right hand man but he held no true power in the family.

"Big Will's not greedy like that plus what about the rest of you? You think he's dumb enough to think you're gonna sit around. He's been doing this shit since the late fifties he's smarter then that."

"Why didn't Mr. Johnson come to the funeral?" Lynn asked.

"I told him not to come to the funeral because I knew that one of you might fly off the handle and do something stupid. You guys are underestimating Big Will. He's been doing this for years. What if one of you clowns did something like tried to hit him? Then you would have started a war and I don't think you could handle that. Killing Michael, that's small time but killing Mr. Johnson now you're fucking with a legend who's backed by an Army." Mr. Gaston said.

"Fuck Mr. Johnson." Mark said upset about the attempt they made on Christopher's life. "If you ask me we should go after his ass, too."

"No." Christopher interrupted. "Mr. Johnson's smarter then that. We make too much money together. Michael was an airhead he was probably setting me up to get robbed."

The other's looked at Christopher shocked, he could be so naive sometimes. Mr. Johnson was an unworthy piece of shit and everybody knew it. "Mr. Gaston, arrange the peace meeting as soon as possible because next month I'm flying to Colombia on business."

"Christopher I'm glad you made it. If anybody knows Mr. Johnson, it's you. He would never do anything to harm you ever. Is there anything else you need me to do? If not I'm going home now I'm tired." He was ready for the meeting to end. All those years of drinking and chasing women were finally catching up with him.

"No, that's it just arrange the meeting for me please." Christopher stood up to embrace his mentor.

Mr. Gaston stood up to hug him.

"Thank you." Christopher responded.

Two hours after the meeting with the family was over, Mr. Gaston and Crazy Moe met at Little Aaron's house in Brigantine. They were all sitting in Little Aaron's business office drinking.

"I can't believe Black and his crew fuck that hit up. I hope Mr. Johnson kills them." Big Aaron was still shocked that Christopher survived the shooting. Mr. Gaston wanted to set the meeting up for a month later but with the change of business came a lot of unexpected things. It would be nearly three months before Christopher would even agree to have a peace meeting and after that the meeting wasn't arranged until July or August, seven months after Corty's untimely demise.

Chapter Thirty One Atlantic City, New Jersey

No More War

Mr. Gaston arranged for Christopher to have the meeting to establish the peace with Mr. Johnson. Christopher knew that most likely the reason that Big Will didn't make anymore moves was because without Christopher's cocaine connection he lost a strong hold. Most of the Italians were in jail facing racketeering charges so he couldn't turn to them and he didn't have the spunk to take trips to New York. A lot of his families drug business was left to the soldiers and lieutenants that still wanted to indulge in it. Losing Christopher had turned out to be a tragic mistake. The family members that were selling cocaine and heroin were not going to give Mr. Johnson a fair share of the proceeds unless he supplied them with the product. By placing the hit on Christopher, Mr. Johnson had lost his strong hold over the cocaine business. The Johnson Crime family was losing its powerful grip on crack distribution in the Pennsylvania area.Big Aaron arranged for the meeting to be held in the casino mostly under Mr. Johnson's urging. To his knowledge nobody had the heart to commit a murder in the casino with all that security and top notch surveillance.

Mr. Johnson divided Philadelphia into three sections. In each of these sections there were four lieutenants who operated for the family. The Johnson family consisted of a boss, an underboss, a counselor and twelve lieutenants. Fifteen people held administrative positions not counting the one hundred and twenty soldiers that worked for the family.

The Larkin crime family was a tad bit smaller. There was a boss, an underboss, a counselor and seven lieutenants, and seventy soldiers. Christopher had closed the books and the only way that somebody could be initiated was if they committed a murder for the family. This way the family wouldn't grow to enormous proportions and be out of control. It was better to be small and efficient, than colossal and sloppy. Christopher had constituted the theory and it worked.

Big Will had control over the Philadelphia underworld since the early seventies, when Mr. Donaldson elevated him to counselor. He completely took over during the extortion wars of the early and mid seventies. That's when a militant group, that was supposed to be following the teachings of the Honorable Elijah Muhammad broke off and started extorting drug dealers. They challenged the Donaldson family and they lost. Mr. Johnson became a hero. It was him and a crew of men who had did the shooting in the club Harlem back in Seventy five. Mr. Donaldson had named him acting boss the following year and then retired after suffering from a string of slight heart attacks. That was almost fifteen years earlier and Mr. Johnson was still running strong.

In the early forties Mr. Donaldson had collected all the African-American number runners, loan sharks, petty criminals built an allegiance and formed one of the first African-American crime families. There were other brothers in New York who were doing the same thing so by the time that the early fifties rolled around an African-American crime family was permanently established in the Pennsylvania and New Jersey area. With connections to the one's established in New York City. It was a beautiful thing when it spread to Chicago and other areas.

In the beginning the family controlled gambling houses, loan sharking and number running. It wasn't until maybe the Mid sixties that they really started indulging in the drug business and back then it was mostly heroin. Cocaine was present but expensive and hard to acquire so there were people that dealt in it but not many. The main drugs were heroin, speed, marijuana and hallucinogens.

Mr. Gaston didn't pop up in the picture until about nineteen sixty when his father died and he took over his father's gambling operations and other illegal activities. In the sixties the Gaston's ran the biggest Casino, prostitution ring and numbers racket in the South Jersey area. The only other Casino and whore house that could rival theirs in the South Jersey area was the one's in Camden, Trenton and Asbury Park but those area's had a high crime rate and most of times if a business man relaxed or vacationed there he was robbed.

When Christopher arrived he was escorted by, Little Aaron and John Martin. There were at least seven casinos in Atlantic City by the late eighties and most of the black Mafia members gambled in them.

Mr. Johnson, Clark his counselor, Charles McCant his underboss and Mr. Gaston were sitting at one of the table's playing cards. Crazy Moe was standing near the table as a bodyguard. He was attempting to help Mr. Johnson win. Crazy Moe was a professional ass kisser.

When they walked in Mr. Johnson stood up and walked over to greet them. "Black don't search them."

Christopher looked at Mr. Johnson like he was crazy he wasn't going to let Black search him if he tried. Through Michael, Christopher had established connections with some of Mr. Johnson's lieutenants. Christopher was feeling them out before he continued to do business with them. He wanted to gather as much information as possible about the contract that was on his life. A lot of the lieutenants were infuriated with Mr. Johnson because he had almost completely destroyed their cocaine business.

Mr. Johnson and Christopher embraced and patted each other on the back. "How you feeling?" Mr. Johnson asked like he was truly interested.

"I feel excellent." Christopher responded and he looked better too.

Christopher smiled and it sent a chill down Mr. Johnson's body. For the first time in their relationship Mr. Johnson felt a true sense of mistrust for Christopher. He was gonna have to be very careful.

They walked over to the table and Mr. Johnson cleared the table himself. "Black get Christopher and his partner a chair." He couldn't remember John Martin's name and didn't care too.

Black returned with several chairs and then exited the room. He walked into the living room with the big screen television. "Holla, if you need me." He said as he was walking away.

"Talk to me Christopher." Mr. Johnson said.

"What's there to talk about." Christopher said. "We want the peace and we want an assurance that when Andre comes home he doesn't start extorting people because were not going to accept it." It was definitely a warning. "Were not allowing the street tax in New Jersey anymore." It was a final warning.

"The extortion game is over." Mr. Johnson said and then he continued. "You don't have to worry. I'm killing it." He was lying through his teeth and Christopher knew it. He had already replaced Michael with his cousin Jeremiah who was still running around trying to extort people. "That's good to hear cause if I catch anybody extorting any of my people. I'm killing them. It's as simple as that."

Mr. Johnson ignored him. "I need to see you and start conducting business again. We've got connections with some Colombians in Mexico but those slimy bastards are cheating me. What would you charge me for a key if I gave you the money up front?"

"It's still ten thousand but I'm not doing anything for a couple of months. I have other business to concentrate on but as soon as I'm ready I'll contact you." It was Christopher's turn to bullshit Mr. Johnson. The family had just flown sixty million dollars to Trinidad. They were waiting to hear from Senor Cachas.

"So who am I going to talk to, to conduct business?"

"I want you to deal directly with me that way we can alleviate a lot of, misunderstandings. No middle man."

"I'm sorry about Corty. I swear to God, I didn't know that Michael was going to do it. I was a little blinded because of my daughter and grandkids. I trusted that motherfucker and he was a piece of shit." For a second it looked like Mr. Johnson was going to cry and if Christopher didn't know better he would have believed him.

"Well, that's water under the bridge. Mr. Gaston told us you had nothing to do with it and we took it from there. It's time for our families to reunite and conduct business again. I'm sure you don't want to end up like the Italians. They have nothing. I want a guarantee of peace the extortion to stop and then business can resume as usual. Michael paid for Corty, but if ever any of our people are hit again its gonna be all out war."

Mr. Johnson nodded his head in agreement but actually he was pissed that Christopher had the nerve or the audacity to threaten him like that. Times were changing the Johnson family didn't hold the power and prestige that it used to hold.

"You have my word. The war is over." Mr. Johnson got up and walked over to Christopher. They embraced.

They discussed a couple other things and then the meeting was over. Mr. Johnson and his crew were going to stay and gamble. They had brought their girlfriends and loads of money so that they could have fun and enjoy themselves.

The Johnson family kept a lieutenant in the South Jersey area but without Christopher's cocaine connection Mr. Johnson's illegal interest in Jersey died.

Later that night Little Aaron met privately with his father and Crazy Morris.

"I'm not going to do anything."

"What you mean you're not going to do anything?" Mr. Gaston had suffered a slight stroke and had lost a considerable amount of weight. He no longer looked the same. He had been in the hospital for the last two weeks. He forced himself out for this meeting. The way that he was starting to forget things, he might have been developing Alzheimer's. "I'm not making a move against Christopher the families too organized and too powerful. I think we've underestimated Chris. The only way we're ever gonna be able to kill him is if we do it ourselves."

Big Aaron looked at Moe. "You think we could do it?"

"Hell yeah."

Little Aaron shook his head. As much as he loved his father he realized that his father was washed up and no longer capable of running the business. "Don't even think about it, it's not worth it. The only person that's benefiting off of any of this bullshit is Mr. Johnson and he's not worth it. Everything is nice, and quiet. I like it this way. I'm happy with what I already have. I don't have to control everything. It's not like the old days Dad, things have changed."

Mr. Johnson was the true genius. He used Michael's death as his scapegoat to remove the blame off himself.

Now he had to find out from Little Aaron whether Christopher believed him or not.

An Eye For an Eye

A couple of months after the Christopher Larkin and the William Johnson war ended the F.B.I, disappeared and things turned back to normal. Christopher wouldn't sell Mr. Johnson any cocaine directly so Mr. Johnson had to go through Little Aaron which proved difficult because Little Aaron couldn't sell large amounts without Christopher questioning. Eventually Little Aaron lied and said that he was making side deals through his father with Philadelphia lieutenants. Christopher believed him but didn't completely trust him.

Mr. Johnson, Ernest Clark his underboss, Big Cliff Mr. Johnson's loyal bodyguard, Black and Jubbie were sitting at a dinner table in Julia's a famous restaurant that Big Cliff's family owned in West Philadelphia. The restaurant had become famous because it was a famous jazz spot and musicians from all over the world came there to eat when they played in the Philadelphia area.

Big Cliff had named it after his mother who was a black film star in the late forties and early fifties. There was not one major black star from the forties through the seventies who hadn't eaten there. Bill Cosby and his family. Harry Belafonte,

Sidney Poitier and Dorothy Danbridge the lady that played in Carmen Jones. The place stayed pack especially on the weekends.

"How's business going?" Mr. Johnson asked.

"Terrible." Black and Jubbie had walked in carrying a suitcase full of money. Black had set the suitcase next to Mr. Johnson like he did every single week when it was time to pay him.

"What's wrong?" Mr. Johnson asked. He was in his mid sixties and still very good looking. A couple of days earlier he had celebrated his sixty-fifth birthday in a big celebration bash and the entire family came. He didn't look sixty-five, maybe fifty.

"I can't make no money. There selling bricks in New York for twenty thousand and you're charging me twenty thousand which is excellent but the most I can make off of it is five thousand profit because everybody that comes to me buys weight."

"What's weight?" Big Cliff asked.

"Weight is like saying you sell wholesale."

"Oh." Big Cliff responded. He usually kept quiet during business meetings because unlike the others he wasn't a lieutenant he was only a bodyguard. The only money that he made was what Mr. Johnson paid him a week. In the early seventies he use to run numbers and whorehouses but he could never manage the money. So he loved the bodyguard position. He could make a couple thousand a week from Mr. Johnson and then run little errands and make more side money. Sometimes he would go places and collect money for Mr. Johnson, and Mr. Johnson would pay him more. When his mother died she left him the bar and Cliff changed it to her name to honor her.

"So what do you want me to do with this motherfucker, Christopher is holding that Michael shit against us."

"So let me talk to him make a side deal and act like I'm cutting you out he'll deal directly with me and we can become partners. I'll split all my profits with you."

That was a good idea but what if Black betrayed Mr. Johnson and set him up for Christopher anything was possible. Then Black would get away with everything. "How much money do I have to invest?" Mr. Johnson asked. "A million dollars." Black replied. They were sitting at the table eating dinner. The waitresses always gave them excellent service because they knew who Mr. Johnson was and if they didn't they know he was like a brother to the owner Mr. Clifford.

"I'm gonna need two months."

"That's a long time. I wanted to do something immediately."

"Well you have to wait and I don't want you making a move without my permission is that understood?" Mr. Johnson had to assert his authority sometimes and let them know who was the boss.

"No problem. Whatever you say you're the boss."

"What's your problem?" Clark asked. He was tall and dark skin with processed hair something that went out in the sixties with terrible greasy oily skin. "You got a problem or something?" He wouldn't let Black answer.

"Mr. Johnson's the boss, what and the fuck is wrong with you? You don't answer him like that. If this were the early seventies and another lieutenant even heard you respond like that you would have gotten killed."

Black was shocked because Mr. Clark was flipping out. "E.C, I didn't mean it like that."

"See what I'm talking about? I'm you're superior. I'm old enough to be you're father and look how you're talking to me? You're just like your father he was a ignorant piece of shit too."

Black looked at him pissed, he had disowned his father years ago and didn't want to have anything to do with him.

"Fuck you and my father you're both pieces of shit. Clark you know what pisses me off about you? You don't do shit and you get paid for it. You're probably the one who told Mr. Johnson to hit Christopher and look what it did. It fucked our business up. Nobody can make money and all the young guys that hustle to make a living can't make shit."

Clark laughed, his breath reeked of alcohol and it smelled horrible. "Oh you're pissed. Well I'm pissed because if it was up to me I wouldn't let you do side business I don't trust you or Christopher."

"Clark please." Mr. Johnson tried to stop him because even though Clark had been in the business for thirty years he still didn't know how to hide his animosity towards someone and that could get you killed.

"You motherfuckers don't know nothing about loyalty. Like I said you're just like you're father." He almost slipped and said 'And that's why we killed him,' but he caught himself.

"Clark enough."

"Sorry William but when we found this guy he was selling smack out of a fucking building and look at him now we made him a millionaire. Look how he shows his appreciation."

Just as they were saying it Animal, Black's hit man walked through the entrance of the restaurant towards the table Mr. Johnson and the others were sitting at. He was carrying a small liquor tray with nothing on it. His gun was resting next to his leg so that nobody would immediately notice it. The gun looked extremely long because it had a silencer on it.

Animal walked to the table and lifted the gun. He pulled the trigger and the first shot hit Mr. Johnson square in the middle of his face. The blow from the impact pushed Mr. Johnson back out of his seat and his feet flipped the table. The entire restaurant exploded in pandemonium.

Animal was about to reach over the table when Clark his second target got up and started to run. Animal looked at him aimed the gun and shot him right in the back. His legs froze. Animal walked right over to him while he was trying to crawl to the exit and shot him in the back of his head.

Clark collapsed and let out a sigh.

Animal walked back over to Mr. Johnson and raised his gun to put another bullet in his face when somebody trying to run out of the door pushed him to the floor. Animal was about to raise his gun and shoot the innocent bystander but he didn't, even though he wanted too. Mr. Johnson wasn't moving he had to be dead.

Animal stood to his feet and ran out of the back of the restaurant like the others. He glanced around for a second and noticed the get away car jumped in and sped away. The next morning the shooting was in the newspapers.

"Black Mafia Chiefs Assassinated."

The Christopher Larkin crime family had finally got their revenge and unlike the Johnson family they were going to be ready for the war and wouldn't stop warring until the Johnson family begged for peace.

Chapter Thirty Three *Atlantic City, New Jersey*

No Time to Explain

The news of Clark's murder and Mr. Johnson's attempted murder spread through the underworld in a matter of days. The first thing that Black did was arrange a meeting with Christopher. They talked privately for several hours. When Mr. Gaston received word of the attempt on Mr. Johnson's life he became terrified and disappeared for days. He didn't open the bar or go anywhere near the construction business that he shared with Christopher and his son. Black was promised financial support for arranging the hit on Mr. Johnson. Christopher was going to supply him with cocaine and a small but very effective hit team if needed.

Christopher was sitting back in his home office with John Martin and another lieutenant making Black repeat the story.

One week after Clark's homicide and the Johnson crime family was all over the papers, the Fed's worked with the media in order to blow the ordeal up.

"Philadelphia Rackets Being Taken Over By Black Mob"

The newspapers were having a field day. They did articles on Mr. Johnson and his blood family. Exposing him as a real-estate magnate whom actually controlled major distribution of drugs in the Philadelphia area.

The feds stepped up surveillance and started harassing members of the family.

The newspapers kept printing articles about different lieutenants and positions they played in the family. Several of their businesses were listed as Mafia hangouts. Even Black made the papers and the Philadelphia Enquirer stated that an unknown source identified Black as the leader of a break-off fraction that the papers decided to label the "Junior Mafia."

Mark and a group of his lieutenants were sitting in Westside Groceries having lunch when a call came in. The cocaine that Mark sold in Atlantic City was nothing compared to what he sold in other cities like Bridgeton. What business he did control he did it with Little Aaron, unofficially they were partners.

Business was good and building every single day. The Housing developments were off the hook with Casino employees, prostitutes, pimps and junkies running in them all day. Cocaine and heroin had gotten so big that children were selling on the streets but the family didn't sell to children. They sold wholesale only most of their money was generated in other cities and states. A lot of people didn't even know that an organized crime family existed in the Atlantic City, South Jersey area until the papers printed it.

Little Aaron pulled up to Westside Groceries in his brand new black Mercedes Benz. A couple of cops that they had on the payroll informed him that the F.B.I were investigating his father Big Aaron, especially with the war raging in Philadelphia.

The newspapers were trying to make it the young mob against old Black Mob and in a lot of ways they were correct.

Little Aaron pulled up to the curb and blew the horn. It took a couple of seconds before Mark had the store gates pulled down but he walked out carrying a bag. Probably a couple hundred thousand that he had collected that week from cocaine sales and a smaller package. Probably cereal or something for his wife and kids.

One of his soldiers was following him. Mark turned to him. "Anthony follow us in your car I've got some business to take care of."

"I'll follow you."

Mark jumped in Little Aaron's Mercedes.

"What's that?" Aaron asked. His Mercedes was a brand new 87' and Mark loved it. Mark owned a string of foreign cars but rarely drove them. As soon as he saw Aaron's car he bought his wife one. He usually drove his Nissan Maxima and he thought that was too flashy.

"Five hundred thou. Half of the money, I owe you." Mark responded.

"Put it in the trunk." Aaron said.

"Nah, let's wait. You're dropping me off at the Absecon train station and then I'll drive my man to his crib right up the block from there." Mark said.

Little Aaron drove and they discussed various things, especially the war that was raging in Philadelphia. "I'm glad my fathers not caught up in the middle of this bullshit." Little Aaron was trying to be nonchalant and get as much information as possible.

"What's up with Big Will?" Mark asked.

"I think he's in a coma. My father went to see him and said he's alive but fucked up real bad."

Nobody in the family knew that Little Aaron and Thomas McCant the new Acting-Boss of the Johnson-Donaldson crime family were secretly having meetings about the hit they were going to attempt on Christopher.

Aaron pulled up to the train station, which took them ten minutes to reach. The train station was so new that some of the sections were still under construction. There was a platform that sat on a hill with what looked like a thousand steps leading down to the parking lot. Empty cars were sitting in the lot and a security guard was in a booth at the end of the parking lot in the only area that was lit.

"When you gonna call me?" Little Aaron asked.

"I don't know." Mark responded exiting the car. "Pop the trunk and the locks." Mark had sat the five hundred thousand dollars in the back seat. He opened the back door and raised his gun with the silencer on it.

Little Aaron was looking directly at him and smiled. Within a second he understood everything. Somebody had told them that he had arranged the hit on Christopher. He was about to open his mouth and explain but Mark pulled the trigger. The side of Aaron's head exploded.

Mark grabbed the bag and emptied the rest of the clip into the back of Aaron's seat. After the clip was empty he walked over to the car where his driver was sitting and he jumped in. They had security cameras but it was so dark in the parking lot that it would be impossible to positively identify him.

They sped away. "Read the paper tomorrow and see if they say they have leads. If they do get rid of the car, if they don't park it in storage for a couple of weeks."

Anthony didn't say anything. He was a soldier in the family. Another position was just opened and Mark might be getting elevated.

Mr. Gaston, Crazy Moe and the others would find out about the killing that night but the rest of the family wouldn't get the information until they read the papers the next morning.

The Johnson-Larkin war had started again and wasn't going to end until Mr. Johnson got murdered. There was no turning back from this point on. The night that Little Aaron was murdered Christopher was in Las Vegas having a with a group of construction companies.

When Christopher returned from Las Vegas the family had a meeting and named two new lieutenants. The family voted Corey in as underboss to take over Little Aaron's position. Then they elevated a guy named Anthony Woods to take over Corey's crew and Alexander Smith became the lieutenant that took over Corty's crew.

Little Aaron's death made headlines: "Black Mafia Wars Spill Into New Jersey."

Chapter Thirty Four *Philadelphia, Pennsylvania*

Two Birds One Bullet

Several weeks after the assassination attempt on his life Mr. Johnson was released from the hospital and the family called an emergency meeting. The meeting was being held at Thomas McCant's house in Glenside Pennsylvania and all the lieutenants were commanded to attend except Black. His entire crew were outcast because of the war.

Mr. McCant lived in a modest English styled Tudor Mansion compared to the other houses they were building in the area Mr. McCant mansion was small. He had been living there since the early seventies.

The property was littered with foreign cars because all of the lieutenants attended. Ray Guns was there, Aaron Gaston, Jeremiah Lewis, Fat Albert Wagner, Black Andy Stewart, Charles Cores, Crazy Moe, Eddie Gordon, Cootie Cameron the lieutenant that controlled Lancaster and York. Philip "Frog" Hammond and Joseph Cecil the lieutenant that was running Pittsburgh and Scranton attended.

When they walked into the living room where the meeting was being held Mr. Johnson, Big Cliff and Andre were already sitting at the dinning room table. Mr. Johnson was sporting a beige suit with a matching Fedora concealing the white bandage that covered his head wound. He had lost a considerable amount of weight and still looked like he should be hospitalized.

When the lieutenants walked into the living room they immediately walked over to him and embraced him. It was the first time anybody had seen him since he had come home from the hospital. When the last lieutenant arrived they took their seats and started the meeting.

The meeting was held at Tommy Can's house because the family had elevated him to acting boss until Mr. Johnson's hospital release. He was in his early fifties. He had been underboss since Mr. Donaldson had retired in the early seventies and he was highly respected amongst all the lieutenants. Unlike the young ones he always kept a low profile.

Even though he lived in a mansion and drove expensive cars, legally he had the wealth to acquire these things. He owned a string of Laundromats and dry cleaning businesses that provided him with several million dollars a year. Mr. Johnson was his legal partner in all of the businesses.

Mr. Johnson had a bowl of fruit and a glass of wine in front of him but he didn't touch them. Every time he ate he got a headache. "I called this meeting so we could organize everything. I proposing Tommy as second in command and Ray Guns as my underboss. If nobody objects to this proposal then we can vote on it now." He waited for a couple of seconds and no one said anything. "I take this silence as a fact that nobody opposes." he said.

Then he continued. "Ray, your gonna have to pick the soldier that you wanna raise to lieutenant and then we'll have to pick another lieutenant to cover Blacks place. In a couple of weeks I'll be having a meeting with Christopher Larkin so that we can settle this thing then we go after Black. I would like that motherfucker dead before we even sit down with Mr. Larkin." The others were silent because as long as Mr. Johnson was alive and well he was more then capable of making decisions and heading the family. "I want everyone to concentrate on Black. After this meeting I need to speak with you Ed." Everyone knew what that was about. Crazy Ed and Black were close. Edward was gonna have to set Black up.

"Aaron's officially retired and any business handled in

Jersey goes through Jeremiah," Mr. Johnson said placing a grape in his mouth. As soon as he bit into it his head began hurting.

"Will I need to talk with you for a second it's important." Mr. Gaston said.

"After the meeting I have to speak with Ed and then I'll speak with you." Mr. Johnson said. His head was pounding but not as bad as days before maybe he was getting better. "Every lieutenant is expected to have a meeting with me at least once a weak like it was before but I don't know if I'll be holding big meetings at the house because the Feds are gonna be all over the place until they think this thing is settled down. If nobody doesn't have anything major to talk about I'm ending this meeting. Tommy will set up individual meetings with everybody." Mr. Johnson went to stand up and could barely stand up. "Oh one more thing Andre welcome home."

Andre was sitting behind him. "Thank you Mr. Johnson," the others clapped and Mr. Johnson's head immediately started pounding.

After the meeting the lieutenants walked over to Mr. Johnson and embraced him. Then Mr. Johnson, Tommy Cans, Ray Guns and Crazy Eddie went into Mr. McCant's business office and had a thirty-minute meeting, when they came out they were laughing and patting each other on the back.

"Aaron you ready?" Ray Guns asked motioning Big Aaron and Crazy Moe to follow him into the private office.

When they walked in Mr. Johnson was sitting behind the desk and the others were sitting in chairs. Big Aaron and Crazy Moe took empty chairs.

"Aaron what's going on?" Mr. Johnson asked.

"Nothing I'm chilling. I wanted to talk to you about Christopher. I didn't hear you say anything about that cock sucker. You know he supported Black's move against you. They've been doing business on the low for a while now."

"How do you know?" Mr. Johnson asked.

"I have my sources," he said. "Christopher killed my son that mother fucker has got to pay and I don't need your help. Me and Moe can do it."

"Aaron listen to me we're gonna handle Christopher but first things first we have to handle Black, he's right here in

Philadelphia. Black doesn't have Christopher's power, we share the same territory so he's more of a threat believe it or not."

"I say we hit both of those mother fuckers and leave it at that."

"Then it's gonna cause another war and right now we can't afford that because the police are all over the place." Tommy Cans added in. Tommy was second in command, and it was time for him to act like it and voice his opinion.

"So this mother fucker slides because of the police. I could handle the shit myself. I'll go visit him and kill the mother fucker myself."

"No first will handle Black a year or two from now when we're directly connected to the Colombians will handle Christopher. I'm never gonna forget what he did to me." Mr. Johnson said. The ironic thing was Mr. Johnson was acting like he forgot that he had originally started the war by trying to have Christopher killed in Ocean City. If he hadn't been so greedy the war wouldn't have even started.

Two weeks after the meeting in Philadelphia Andre returned to New Jersey and started his extortion business back up but this time he came with an even tougher crew.

Jeremiah was scared to death because he thought that Christopher might think he had something to do with it and kill him. He sent some of his most trusted people out to contact Christopher. He was gonna have to have a meeting and let Christopher know he didn't want any problems.

Wilber Duberry and his partner Mark were at the small hotel twelve o'clock in the afternoon for their meeting with Andre.

Wilber knocked on the door and Andre answered it. "Who the fuck is it?" He asked from the other side of the cheesy door.

"It's me Wok," Wilber said. They called him "Wok," because he sort of resembled a Chink.

"What's up?" Andre swung the door open and let them into the room.

They walked in and took seats. Wok reached in his pocket and pulled out an envelope and passed it to Andre. "Here it is ten thousand cash."

Andre grabbed the envelope and opened it counting the

money in the process. Just as he almost finished counting the money his girlfriend came out of the bathroom wrapped in a towel. She was a nice looking girl who's curves couldn't even be concealed by the towel.

"Oh I didn't know you guys were here." She said.

"Don't worry they leaving." Andre said.

Cassandra sat on the small bed just like they weren't there she didn't want to anger Andre he could go crazy sometimes.

The brothers left and then Cassandra got dressed. Andre counted the money to show off and then he threw her one of the stacks, a thousand dollars.

She picked it up. "What you want me to do with this?" She asked. "I want you to go to the Gucci shop and do some shopping. Make sure you buy me another pair of Gucci sneaks."

"Okay," she smiled.

"Hurry up."

Andre and Cassandra boarded the small elevator a half an hour later to go to the lobby downstairs and pay their bill. As soon as they stepped off of the elevator Anthony, the new lieutenant and two of his soldiers were standing in the lobby. They walked over to them before they could exit the elevator and opened fire. They were carrying semiautomatic assault rifles.

Cassandra was screaming to the top of her lungs before one bullet even hit her, the shooting was over in seconds and the elevator was filled with smoke. The clerk that was standing behind the lobby counter was on the ground praying he didn't even see them when they exited.

Chapter Thirty Five *South Philadelphia*

It's Only Business

When the war started Edward Gordon was just a lieutenant associated with Black, and the family had no personal beef against him.

Mr. McCant held a meeting with Crazy Eddie because they knew that he was close to Black. Mr. McCant asked Eddie to set Black up or just murder him, Edward agreed but when he took to long Mr. McCant took it as a refusal.

In the beginning Black's strength was that he had cocaine connections and the rest of the family didn't. They would have to go to New York and purchase cocaine themselves which would naturally cut the boss out of a lot of profits. The first thing Black did was arrange meetings with lieutenants, captains and soldiers in the family.

Like most of the lieutenants, Crazy Ed's illegal activities were not limited to one section. He had business in North, South, and West Philadelphia. He also ran small but very profitable crack houses in Scranton and Pittsburgh Pennsylvania. In the late eighties, he controlled the biggest heroin outlets in Lancaster and Chester Pennsylvania. He had soldiers there under his command and all this money was in partnership with Black.

Income wise, Crazy Ed was Black's strongest asset. Once a week, usually when clothes shipments would come in, Crazy Ed would go to the store that his family ran for him in South Philadelphia and help.

Cute Kid's clothing store was located a couple of blocks away from South Street in the old factory district. A majority of the area were factories and business offices.

The white people that lived in the area bought the factories and converted them into business offices so there was constant traffic in the area besides the residential row houses that Italians and newly arrived emigrants lived in.

Crazy Ed had always stated that it amazed him how an emigrant could move into this country and move to one of the most exclusive sections of Philadelphia. If a black man wanted to pay twice the property value he was always refused or turned away.

Crazy Ed and several men that worked for the Koreans that supplied his store were stacking boxes. Ed was the person that was standing outside of the truck passing the boxes onto the curb. His father and another one of his employees would run to the curb and haul the clothing away. Business was good because of the location and the quality of clothing that Edward carried. Edward's mother was behind the cash register helping customers that had already entered the store.

The entire block was filled with quaint little boutiques, flower shops, adult clothing shops, restaurants and cafés. Most of the Cute Kid's clothing store clientele were well to do whites and Blacks.

Edward was outside of the store stacking the boxes, he didn't see Ray Guns and a group of his men drive pass the delivery truck in a metallic colored van.

Ray Guns was in his late sixties but he had the chest and arms of a construction worker. A trade that he still did whenever he wanted to help his son operate their construction business.

Ray pulled the van a couple of yards away from the truck and two men jumped out wearing masks. Ray had killed dozens of people he didn't need to prove himself to the family.

It was time for the young one's who would eventually be taking over the business to earn their stripes.

Ray sped away and the sound of the tires peeling off was the only thing that got Crazy Ed's attention. When Edward turned around to look in the direction of the sound the gunmen were standing next to him with their masks on holding semi-automatic assault weapons. They opened fire and one minute later before Edward's body could even hit the ground it was riddled with bullets. Chunks of flesh were ripped off as the bullets hit him. His face was destroyed and completely unidentifiable.

After shooting him the gunmen ran to the corner and jumped in a get away car and the car sped away. The killing made the evening news.

"Black Mafia Old-timer's Strike Again."

This time the article talked about Crazy Ed and his connection with Anthony Miller a.k.a. Black. It also showed pictures of several of the men who could have ordered or actually did the shooting. There were pictures of Fat Albert, Tommy Cans, Ray Guns and Christopher. It was Christopher's first time being in the papers connected to the war. The article also named the men as possible leaders of the Philadelphia Black Mafia.

When Black got word of the shooting he was sitting in a Chinese restaurant with his lawyer Alan Blaubein, a prominent Jewish attorney.

"Anthony, I'm not going to be able to get these people to go less then that. You got the IRS investigating, which is actually a small thing but you don't want the feds to connect you with this. The advantage of taking the Ninety-day plea is that you're pleading guilty on the case. If those guys in the house don't snitch and don't say the gun was yours we can beat this thing with just the six months. With the way your names in the paper getting away may be just the thing you need."

"What do you think, Jubbie?" Jubbie was sitting there stuffing his face with his arms wrapped around his girlfriend's waist. Jubbie was a light skin guy with a chubby face who walked around wearing a Kangol. When people saw him on the streets they thought he was the young rapper L.L. Cool Jay.

"I say go, me and Animal can handle everything."

Animal was sitting in the corner with some pretty half Asian half Spanish looking girl who had just moved from New York and started attending school at Pierce Junior college. She was gorgeous, just like the other ladies there. "Black, you know I can handle it."

Ever since Animal did the hit on Mr. Johnson and Clark, he had become a legend. His only problem was that he bragged about it to too many friends. Then they bragged about it to close friends, until eventually it hit the ears of an informant. If Animal was more professional he might be considered the best hit man in Philadelphia since Ray Guns. Ray Guns was a street legend, by the time Mr. Johnson had become boss Ray had murdered more then twenty five people by himself. People in the family that knew him personally called him the Angel of Death.

The next week, Black got his court date pleaded guilty and disappeared. The first thing Animal gave Black's codefendants a visit. Black's incarceration opened up the doors for a meeting between the Christopher Larkin Crime family and the William Johnson crime family.

Arranging for the five families in New York, the Larkin crime family and the Johnson crime family to hold the meeting without F.B.I surveillance was going to be hard, so Franklin waited until after Run D.M.C, threw a concert at the Madison Square Garden. Franklin threw an after party at a club on West Riverside Drive and they used the back room to hold the meeting so that all of the Bosses cars in New York would blend in with the customer's automobiles. The party lasted all night and nobody had an idea that a mob summit was taking place in the next room that morning.

Because Christopher was the head of the family, he brought John Martin his counselor and a four-man bodyguard team. Mr. McCant and Mr. Johnson were there with a small bodyguard team. They also brought Andrew Stewart, Mr. McCant's acting counselor for the family. Franklin came to represent Manhattan even though he was still a lieutenant in the family.

The other representative for Manhattan was a man named Sean "Ruffy" Coles. The man representing Brooklyn name was Shawn "Cray-Z" Carver. The man representing the Bronx was named Peter "Pete Guns" Terrence, the man representing

Queens was named Fredrick Dupree and the Boss representing Staten Island was named Raymond 'Raekwon' Bules. All of these men in one way or the other were associated with Christopher Larkin and loyal to him. It was Christopher like Frank Matthews before him who had thought of organizing the families or drug gangs as they were previously called.

Thomas had heard about the other families that Christopher formed but when he actually saw it with his own eyes he was impressed and awed by Christopher's power and genius. Mr. Johnson was so fortunate that Christopher was humble and hadn't decided to strike first because he would have won. United the Black Mafia families had to be at least one thousand men strong.

Christopher waited until everyone was seated he was wearing a dark pinstripe suit with an expensive tie and nice shoes. He had slowly gained all his weight back. Lately he had been sporting his straight black hair low. It resembled a military cut.

Christopher started the meeting. He whispered something into John Martin's ear and then John Martin stood up and whispered something to another man. That man disappeared and closed the doors when he left.

Christopher waited for everyone to be seated before he started the meeting. "Mr. Johnson I want to thank you and Mr. McCant for coming, this war is costing everybody too much money and too much heat. I hope that we can settle everything today."

Mr. Johnson sat back in his chair for a second. He had lost a considerable amount of weight since the assassination attempt but he was healthy. He was wearing an expensive blue pinstripe suit with a dark colored shirt and a nice tie. "Christopher you're right. The more we war, the more heat we bring on each other. I made a mistake. I'm not gonna say what that mistake was but I'm gonna admit it. Things went too far. It should have never went the way that it did. This shooting incident has made me see the light." Mr. Johnson pointed to his head. He was wearing a bandage to cover the scar. "Everybody is allowed to make mistakes in their lives as long as they learn their lesson and I've learned mine."

The other men in the room sat there quietly. They didn't

really have anything to say in the matter. The commission meeting was called by Christopher so that all the different families could see how see profitable this business could be if they all stuck together.

"Christopher I need to start conducting business with you again. Without your connections my business is suffering and it's causing a lot of confusion." Mr. Johnson wasn't lying either. Without him controlling the narcotic industry in Pennsylvania a lot of nuts were popping up and fighting over territory. With the right connections and proper material he could put a stop to all of that and reorganize everything.

"Mr. Johnson I have no problem doing business with you but first you have to recognize my families independence and second you have to realize you can not control everything. Fate didn't put the connections in your hand, he put them in mine." Christopher said pouring himself a glass of wine from the bottle that was sitting in front of him.

"I know things have changed. I know its time for me to think about retiring but before I retire I have to put certain things in order. I don't want to be coming out of my house or eating dinner with my wife and somebody walk up and put a bullet in my head." Mr. Johnson chuckled and the other commission members laughed with him. It was an honest statement.

"I think you should know by now that I'm a fairly decent man and I don't hold grudges. If I know your not plotting against me then you have nothing to worry about."

"So can we make the peace?" Mr. Johnson asked. "I mean real peace where we know we're really not coming after each other?"

"Of course we can I'm not an animal. You think I like popping up in the papers or having FBI agents follow me every where? No I hate it. I want the peace and I'm always sincere it's you who has to check himself."

Mr. Johnson smiled and he looked devilish. "Your right. If we make peace can we really resume business?" Mr. Johnson asked.

"Yes we can." Christopher replied.

"Chris I have some other request. If we make the peace I want you to cut your ties with all of the lieutenants in Philadelphia that you do business with and let them deal directly with me like they use too."

Whoa that was a deep one cutting them off could mean losing millions of dollars. "Mr. Johnson I'd have to think about that one but I'll tell you one thing. The more you prove your sincerity about peace the more I'll pull back."

Mr. Johnson smiled. " And there's one more thing. You can't interfere when I handle this situation with Black."

Christopher pushed back in his chair and he had to think on that one. "Black's my friend."

"Yeah but he's also a lieutenant in my family and he crossed the line when he placed that hit on me." Mr. Johnson didn't even mention Christopher part in the event. There was no need too. "Christopher I can't have him running around doing as he pleases if I seriously want to get this thing back in order. Black crossed the line and I understand that it was just business but as long as he's alive I won't feel safe. Just like what he did to me is business what I'm about to do to him is strictly business but I wanted to let you know first. So that you wouldn't think it was an act against you."

"What if I say you can't have Black?" Christopher asked.

"Then I couldn't make the peace. Black is never gonna feel safe as long as I'm around and I won't feel safe until he's gone. I know you know how it feels to have a close friend betray you. You have to handle it no matter how much you love them. What Black did to you in Ocean City was only business and what I have to do to him is only business. I'll be retiring in a couple of years but I'm not going anywhere as long as that cat's around. I don't trust him." Mr. Johnson touched his head, "And as you can see I have good reason."

Christopher paused for a second listening quietly while John Martin whispered in his ear. "Okay I'll stay out of that affair because he's in your family but I pray you're a man of your word and you keep this peace. It's really hurting everybody and nobodies happy. Things were so much better before this war."

"Christopher, I'm not an animal. When I give you my word then you have my word. I know you're about peace and so am I. Like a said I made a mistake and I learned from it."

They covered a couple of other things and then Christopher introduced Mr. Johnson to everybody. The Christopher Larkin and William Johnson war was officially over. Now they could get back to making millions. Hopefully they wouldn't have to worry about each other, watching out for the authorities was enough of an headache.

Chapter Thirty Six *Atlantic City, New Jersey*

Get Rid of Him

Two years and six months after the United States Government almost completely decimated the Philadelphia/South Jersey Italian Mafia, the FBI made there first move against the Christopher Larkin and William Johnson Crime families.

After establishing the peace with the William Johnson Crime family things got extremely peaceful for Christopher. Franklin and Christopher were fighting a small but serious heroin war in New York City with an young Spanish guy that ran the Bronx, beside that everything was going perfectly.

"Off Shore Realty and Construction Co.," was located on Christopher's property in Atlantic City. Because a small board actually operated the business, Christopher conducted most of his legitimate business with them from his house. He didn't want to establish a pattern by travelling to his offices on Atlantic Avenue in Atlantic City because it would be to easy for his enemies to attack him or the FBI to surveillance him.

The first thing Christopher would do is wake up, shower and then come into the dinning room to eat breakfast with his growing family.

Little Christopher had just turned seven and was in the second grade. The twins would be starting school in September Little Aaron was still to young to start school. So he spent most of the day being carried around by either one of his parents.

Christopher was sitting at the dinning room table drinking coffee when the doorbell rang at seven o'clock in the morning. The ringing of the doorbell alerted everyone because no one came to the house unannounced. The Larkin family had friends but besides Christopher's business associates, they lived very quietly.

Christopher's maid answered the door and several white men were standing outside of the house wearing business suits. They were federal agents.

"Good morning Miss., Is Mr. Larkin here?" One of the men said holding papers that stated the FBI had a federal warrant for Christopher's arrest.

"Yes, what can I do for you?" "Excuse us, we have a warrant for his arrest." "Mr. Larkin." The maid screamed to the top of her lungs. More trying to warn Christopher then summon him. The federal agents pushed right passed her and Christopher met them at the steps.

"Excuse me can I help you?"

"Yes." One of the agents said. "Are you Christopher Larkin?"

"Yes. I am." Christopher replied, pissed that these men had entered his house without his permission.

"We have a federal warrant for your arrest would you come with us, please?"

"No problem." Christopher slipped out of his robe and walked into the circle of agents. Tahwan and the children were standing there silently watching. Christopher had slipped on a pair of slacks when he heard the maid scream his name. The agents walked him outside before they cuffed him.

Christopher just looked at them. How did they get on the property? Climb over his security fence. The regular police would be arriving eventually because his alarm system was about to go off. The agents walked Christopher through the entrance gate and placed him in a car.

At the same time that the agents were arresting Christopher Larkin, they were arresting Mr. Gaston at the bar where he had stayed all night in the upstairs apartment with his mistress. Mr. Johnson was quietly tending to his garden in Philadelphia when the agents arrived.

They arrested several other guys and everyone was charged with High-jacking and robbery. Until they were arraigned in federal court and awarded bails nobody actually knew what was going on.

By the end of the day everything was explained. When the FBI had arrested several high-ranking members in the Italian Mafia, one of them Salvatore Carfagno had been awarded the witness protection program and he told the government about the high jacking and grocery store robbery that Christopher orchestrated. The information wasn't really enough for an indictment but with the right rubbing of political elbows an indictment was handed down. Christopher and the others were arrested.

The newspapers went bananas and the Atlantic City press made the arrest front page news.

"Federal Agent Nab High Ranking Black Mafia Lieutenants."

The article went on to state that the FBI had arrested Christopher Larkin and Aaron Gaston two high ranking mob captains in the William Johnson Crime family that both men controlled Atlantic City and South Jersey racket's for the William Johnson Crime family.

The papers stated that the William Johnson Crime family was an organization that controlled ninety percent of the narcotics distributed in the Philadelphia and South Jersey area. It also stated that a high ranking captain in the Nicodemo Scarfino family had testified that both men had committed the robbery at Shop More Grocery store on Absecon boulevard and had committed a string of high-jackings in early 1980. The defendants pleaded innocent.

Mr. Johnson, Crazy Moe, Big Aaron and Big Cliff sat in the law offices of Donaldson, Harris and Davis speaking with Big Aaron's attorney Harold Baker a small intelligent looking white man who had represented Mr. Gaston on a lot of his civil cases.

Mr. Baker was sitting behind an enormous mahogany desk cluttered with papers and law degrees on the wall. He had practiced law in Pennsylvania in the early seventies then moved to New Jersey to be closer to family when he joined the Donaldson Davis and Harris law firm. He hated working there mainly because he couldn't stand Rudolph Harris a partner in the firm, who had just run for Governor and lost.

"Well in a couple of weeks they should be sending the discovery and we'll know exactly what you guys are facing." Baker was sitting on the end of his desk holding a file in his hands.

"You know you guys could have gotten a lower bail if you would have waited in jail for a couple of days." Baker continued.

Mr. Gaston just laughed. "Have you lost your mind? I've been working hard all my life so that I don't have to sit a day in jail."

"Yeah but a million dollars bail is kind of drastic." Baker replied.

"But it's worth it, plus we'll get the money back."

"I don't know, sometimes the Fed's play dirty when they know you can generate that kind of money they try to fine the shit out of you so they can discover a money trail for the IRS." "Well, it don't matter because were not going to jail and your gonna make sure of it." Mr. Johnson said. He had been sitting there quietly the entire meeting listening to Big Aaron talk to his attorney.

"I can't make any promises but I'm gonna try my best." The attorney said.

That was their cue Mr. Johnson stood up and extended his hand to the lawyer. The other men stood up and shook hands with the attorney before leaving.

Mr. Johnson waited until they got out to the hallway to voice his real opinion. "I don't like that mother fucker and I don't trust him. He's one of those lawyers that will sell you out before you even start the case. Aaron I advise you to get rid of him."

"Yeah he's a fucking bum." Big Cliff said holding the door for his superiors. "That's the kind of lawyer where your codefendants are found innocent and this cocksuker convinces you to take a plea." They all burst into laughter.

They walked out of the office and jumped into Mr. Johnson's brand-new '87 Lincoln Continental. They drove straight to the bar so that they could have sort of a mini meeting.

It was a nice sunny day, so instead of going inside they decided to take a nice little walk. They didn't want to talk in the bar just in case the FBI had broke into the bar and set up wiretaps.

Chapter ThirtyYSeven Barranquila Colombia

The Public Eats it Up

Three months after Christopher and the others were picked up on federal charges the federal prosecutor dropped the charges for lack of evidence. The papers ate it up and ran several articles on different members. The Philadelphia Inquirer did several articles on Mr. Johnson and the Atlantic city Press did several articles on Christopher, naming him Mr. Johnson's right hand man and successor. All of this was misinformation but the public ate it up.

Christopher, John Martin and Corey flew out to Senor Cacha's villa in Barranquilla Colombia. Senor Cacha's villa was an enormous Greek style villa overlooking Barranquilla's mountains and the Atlantic Ocean.

Christopher and Senor Cachas were walking on Senor Cacha's grounds. They were surrounded by a group of Don Cachas', bodyguards. The grounds were beautiful. There were several servants working on the grass and visitors in the back yard swimming in Don Cachas's pool.

Don Cachas was wearing a white linen shirt, white linen slacks and black sandals.

Christopher had on powdered blue linen, an outfit very

similar to Don Cachas's.

"Christopher, what's going on?" Don Cachas asked as they walked around the grounds.

"Nothing, just trying to concentrate and stay focused." They were both smoking cigars and relaxing.

When they got to the pool several women got out and walked over to them. "El Padrino, get in the pool with us. Come play with us," one of them said.

"Later. Don't interrupt me I'm discussing business," The Don said.

They walked away and continued talking. "I hope you're ready to resume business," the Don said. Christopher had become one of his strongest lieutenants. He could ship cocaine to America, give it to Christopher on consignment and have half of his money sometimes in days.

"I'm ready."

"So are you gonna bullshit or are we gonna do something heavy?"

Christopher smiled. He was a little darker then usual because he had flown to Colombia and stayed a week with Tahwan and the rest of his family. After he left Colombia he was flying back to Tobago to overlook construction on his house.

"We can do something heavy but when you say heavy what are you talking bout?" Christopher asked.

"Well, me and my partners have fifty tons stashed here in Colombia and we haven't been able to move them because of those damn guerillas fighting in the forest, and then Don Pablo's running around blowing shit up making the government mad, but things are getting better. We've calmed him down and we're ready to resume business."

Don Cachas had taught Christopher so much. He didn't know that the narcotic business was so entrenched in politics until he came to Colombia and got this deeply involved in the business.

"So what are you thinking about doing?" Christopher asked again.

"I figured I'd ship twenty tons over and give you ten of them for five thousand a key."

Christopher could do nothing but shake his head. Sometimes he couldn't believe how deeply he was involved in the business. "How many keys in ten tons?"

"About ten thousand keys."

"Ten thousand keys times five thousand is..."

"About fifty million," Don Cachas said.

"How much money do you want up front?" Christopher asked.

"At least twenty five million," Don Cachas replied, like he was speaking about twenty-five thousand.

"Then how long you want to wait for the other twenty-five."

"Give me three or four million a week," He said.

"I don't know?" Christopher said.

"Christopher, what's the problem?" Don Cachas asked.

"Flying all that money is becoming a risk," Christopher said.

"You know what? I have to fly to Mexico next week. I want you to meet me there. Maybe we can nip some of this in the bud. Get the money to California I'll have my people in Mexico do the rest."

Christopher smiled. "That's a lot better. If I drive it to California I can easily get you the five million a week."

"Excellent," Don Cachass said. "Bring the twenty-five million and I'll have the cocaina." They shook hands and the meeting was over just like that.

They walked back to the pool and the beautiful women. As they were walking back Christopher reflected on how quick their relationship had changed. When he first met him Don Cachas pretended he couldn't even speak English. Now they took long walks and talks all by themselves.

After the meeting Christopher flew back to Trinidad with Tahwan and his children. The houses that he was building in Tobago were Colonial houses on one of the beaches. Christopher was having twenty of the houses built, along with docks and small cottages. He was creating a Martha's Vineyard in Tobago. The colonial house he was having built was so big it looked like a mansion and the property that surrounded it was big enough to build several more smaller houses, which he intended on doing for his children once they reached adulthood.

They already owned the duplicate to the one in Tobago in Boothbay Harbor, Maine, but the white people got so mad that Christopher moved and built a bigger one in Tenants Harbor where the population wasn't as big and the white people were more tolerant.

The mansion that Christopher built there was surrounded by hundreds of acres. Tahwan loved it. She had started her own landscaping and interior decorating business. Christopher was letting her fly all over the world to conduct business as long as she took the children. It gave her something to do and kept her out of his hair.

Mr. Gaston and two federal agents were sitting in an office having a meeting. Mr. Gaston had agreed to become an informer so that he could get revenge for his son, the same revenge that Mr. Johnson wouldn't allow him.

Two supervising agents were sitting outside of the office listening to the meeting. "So is he telling anything?" the younger less experienced agent asked.

"Right now he isn't giving us anything because he's still trying to figure us out. He's telling us all this information about Christopher Larkin but we want Mr. Johnson and for some reason he's not trying to hear that. Right now I don't know, but he's coming around."

Chapter Thirty Eight *Tenants Harbor, Maine*

Who Needs Protection

Christopher Larkin and Tahwan Jones Larkin cordially invite you to the honorable Rudolph Harris III governor's fundraising bash. The invitations were simple with gold lettering. More then five hundred people were invited.

Mr. Harris, his campaign party and several organizations were invited to Christopher's beach house mansion in Maine for a fundraiser to raise funds and awareness for the Rudolph Harris governor's campaign race.

The mansion sat on the edge of the rocks overlooking the beach in Tenants Harbor, Maine. On the front entrance was the beach, in the back was a private road that lead to the property. The estate was gorgeous and the grounds immaculate. Tahwan had arranged everything except security. Christopher insisted that he be in charge of that. Some of the future governor's guests had complained that they heard the host was heavily involved in narcotics, but once they saw the estate and the elegance of the place they kept quiet.

Rudolph Harris walked to the middle of the living room and

began tapping his wineglass to get everyone's attention. He was dark-skinned with thick salt and pepper hair. He had won a term as Mayor then stepped up from there to a representative in congress and now he was running for governor of New Jersey.

"Excuse me. Ladies and gentlemen, may I have your attention please?" Slowly quietness fell across the room.

"Excuse me. May I have your attention?" he repeated. "I want to take a moment to thank my partner at my firm, Michael Donaldson of Davis, Harris and Donaldson, and his special friend Christopher Larkin for hosting the event." Everyone began clapping.

Christopher was standing in the corner next to Tahwan carrying a wineglass. He looked elegant in his black tuxedo with the matching cummerbund and bow tie. Tahwan was wearing a beautiful dress that showed off her figure.

Michael Donaldson walked over to Rudolph Harris and said a few words. Christopher took this as his opportunity to disappear. He waked down the hallway into a section of the house with private doors. When he came to his study hall Anthony and Alex, his new lieutenants, were guarding the doors.

"Big Christ, what's going on?" they asked simultaneously.

"Nothing. I'm just checking on you guys. How's everything going?"

"Excellent."

Christopher could see the bulge of their guns underneath their tuxedo jackets. He reached in his pockets and removed an antique key. He placed the key in the door and entered the room. It was pitch black until he turned on the light and when he did the room was filled with blocks of cellophane wrapped money, the twenty-five million dollars that he was going to drive to California.

Christopher finished his drink, sat his wineglass on one of the blocks and left the room. "What are you guys doing tonight?" Christopher asked.

"Guarding this door in four hour shifts," Alex replied. He was tall and handsome, a former high school basketball star.

"Maybe I'll see you guys in the morning." Christopher returned to the party and his guests.

Anthony and Alex were in charge of security along with

their ten man crews. Twenty-two people for security. Two people were at the front and back doors. Another eight were ordered to surveillance the grounds and make sure that nobody was able to sneak onto the property. Surprisingly, there was media coverage at the party but only the ones invited.

A group of the men were assigned to guard the boathouse and the docks. Another group was guarding his small private airstrip that was located a couple of miles from the property. The people that came to the estate were more than impressed.

The next morning, Christopher was flying the money to his estate in Trinidad; not the one he was having completed in Tobago but, the one he actually live in, in Trinidad. He wanted to be in Tobago. He was building facilities for his overseas construction company and postal service. His real estate company had opened a package delivery service just like U.P.S. and business was going excellent.

Mr. Gaston, Crazy Moe, Jeremiah and his little brother Mikal were sitting in Mr. Gaston's having a meeting.

"Jerry, I need your help," Mr. Gaston said. Jeremiah didn't know that the conversation was being recorded for the F.B.I..

"Mr. Gee talk to me," Jeremiah said. He was tired of the bullshiting. He wanted to get rid of Mr. Gaston, as soon as possible he had become a hassle.

"You've got to help me get rid of Christopher. He killed my son. And William knows but he's sitting around here making all that money with that grimy mother fucker and treating me like shit."

"Mr. Gee, I can't harm that boy without Mr. Johnson's permission. He would kill me. If I make a move against Christopher I might start a war and somebody's gonna have to pay for that shit and it's not gonna be me."

"What if I gave you money?" Mr. Gaston asked drunk. He had been drinking all day.

"What kind of money you talking about?" Jeremiah asked like he was interested but he knew better. He had to act like he was interested so that he could keep Mr. Gaston off guard.

"A hundred thousand."

Mikal and Jeremiah laughed. "A hundred thousand? What am I gonna do with that? You think starting a war with somebody like Christopher is worth that?"

"Listen, I'll pay you half a million," Mr. Gaston said.

"Now we're talking. Listen, give me a couple of weeks and I'll let you know what I can do, but you've got to be careful. You can't talk to everybody because that half a million might be my retirement money. If Mr. Johnson doesn't agree, me and my brother might be using this money to run for the rest of our lives and five hundred grand would be peanuts then. If I make a move against that man, Mr. Gaston, I'm gonna handle it myself, that way if anything goes wrong I only have myself to blame." Jeremiah gulped his drink and turned to his brother. "Come on Mikal. Let's get out of here."

Mikal grabbed his brother's jacket and placed it around his shoulders. Jeremiah walked back over to the bar and extended his hand. "Mr. Gaston, I'm gonna do it, but I want half of the money up front and the other half the second you hear about it. Cash."

Mr. Gaston smiled. It was the best news he heard all day. His wife had a nervous break down and she was in Ancora hospital seeking mental evaluation. This war had destroyed his life. He couldn't help but think about his son telling him that the only one benefiting from the war was Mr. Johnson, and he finally realized that his son was right.

As soon as the men left Mr. Gaston poured himself another drink.

"Moe, walk me to the car. Charlie, you gonna close up?"

"Of course," the old man responded. He had been closing up the bar for the last thirty-five years every single day including the holidays.

Mr. Gaston slipped his jacket on and waked outside followed by Crazy Moe. Mr. Gaston had treated himself to a brand new 190 Mercedes Benz. One of the deals he made with the feds was that Crazy Moe wouldn't have to do anytime. Mr. Gaston hadn't told him that he was an informant but he was going to. First, he wanted to make sure he got Christopher just in case he couldn't trust Morris as much as he thought.

"Moe you got any money?" Mr. Gaston asked.

"Yeah, I've got a couple of dollars on me. You need some?"

"No I mean money saved," Mr. Gaston said.

"Oh, course." They were both smoking Newport cigarettes.

"I'm leaving everything I got to you and my grandkids."

"What about your wife?" Crazy Moe asked.

Mr. Gaston just shook his head. "Viola's out of it." Mr. Gaston got in the car and turned the ignition on. The car exploded sending Crazy Moe crashing against the wall. He was in flames. When the fire department put the flames out Mr. Gaston's remains were ashes. Crazy Moe was propped against the building burnt to death.

The next week the feds and the papers were all over the place.

Three weeks after the bombing Black, Frog, Ray Guns and one of his soldiers were sitting in a quiet dinner on the outskirts of Philadelphia having a secret meeting. Ray Guns and Black's father were best friend. Ray Guns had told Black when he first entered the business, "Never let anyone know how close we are. This is a business where you can't trust everybody," and Black never forgot the warning.

The group sat down, ate and went over small matters. When they were finished eating and were about to pay the check Ray Guns spoke. "Black we have to take a ride so we can figure out what's going on and what's the next move."

"Okay," Black said.

Frog gave Black a look. He was security. "You want me to come?"

"Nah, I'm alright. I'm sure Uncle Ray wants to speak in private."

Ray smiled, Black got up and followed him. Ray was driving a brand new Mercedes Benz, he jumped into the drivers seat and Black jumped into the passengers seat.

"Black, I told William what you said about offering the peace."

And what he say?"

"He said he would guarantee you the peace if you arranged a meeting through Christopher and if you sacrificed two of your people so that he knew you weren't bullshiting."

Black was shocked and pissed but he had to listen. Fighting this war and watching his back was wearing him down. Twice, hit men had cornered him and shot his car up and both times he barely escaped with his life. Now that Mr. Johnson had cocaine connections again his influence over the streets was returning and the ring was closing in tighter and tiger on Black.

"What do you think?" black asked. He trusted Ray Guns because he knew if he wanted to Ray could have easily killed him.

Frog, Ray's bodyguard and Animal were following them in Black's rental car.

"I say take it. If you get Christopher to approve the peace Will's giving you a chance to make the peace with the promise that as long as you pay a reasonable street tax he'll leave you alone.

"So why does he want to kill my people?"

"So he can make you weak. If America goes to war with another country when they make the peace they force the other country to destroy their weapons."

Black was hurting. "Which two would I have to give up?" He asked.

"Frog and Jubbie, everybody know you won't give up your brother and we're not expecting you too."

"What if I give up my partners and Mr. Johnson double crosses me?"

"He can't"

"Why?"

"Because Christopher devised the peace agreement and if you agree with it he's gonna make Mr. Johnson guarantee that peace, plus you'll return as a lieutenant and nobody can lift a finger against you without Christopher's permission."

Black was shocked. Frog was right. "I see Christopher every couple of days. Why hasn't he said anything about this offer to me?"

"Because we just ironed it out and you know Christopher. He's extra careful. He doesn't get involved in too many things. If you ask me, he's saving your life. I think it's a good deal and I think you should take it."

Black looked over at Ray, he looked so evil when you knew his history. He was devilish. He had to be. He had killed entirely too many people not to be.

"Okay, I want to have a meeting and hear this repeated." Black said, " Just to be safe," then he looked behind him just to see if Frog and them were still following him. He could be getting set up right now for death and wouldn't have known it.

"Good," Christopher said "Everybody can meet at Mr. Gaston's funeral and we'll repeat the deal just as I said, but don't bring Jubbie to the funeral. We're gonna handle him first."

"What should I tell him?"

"Don't worry. I know you'll think of something." Ray Guns pulled the enormous Mercedes over to the side of the road and let Black out.

Frog pulled over and Ray Guns' bodyguard jumped out of the car. The way he walked toward Black it looked like he was about to shoot him but he didn't, he just extended his hands.

When Black got back in the car Frog started questioning him. "What happened? What did he say?"

"I'll tell you later. I'm tired. It's good news though. We're gonna have a meeting at Mr. Gaston's funeral in Atlantic City, but I can't take all of y'all. It might be a set up. Jubbie, I want you to stay home just in case something fishy happens."

Animal was sitting in the back of the car doped up. He didn't give a fuck. He would kill anybody. "Am I going?"

"Of course you are because I know if they start shooting your gonna shoot somebody."

"And I won't?" Jubbie asked offended.

"Jube, you're the brains. I need somebody that's gonna be able to run this shit if something happens to me. I would be a fool to take everybody with me. You and Blue are gonna stay in the city."

One week later the entire family gathered at St. Monica's Catholic Church on Pennsylvania Avenue in Atlantic City and listened to the sermon. The priest only said a few words and then they left escorted to the cemetery in Pleasantville.

Black was nervous but animal and Frog were even more nervous. They were both thinking the same thing," Is this nigga worth dying for?"

The only thing that eased Black was that he was allowed to follow Christopher everywhere.

Jubbie had stayed in Philadelphia all day laid up in the bed with the girl he had met at Pierce Junior College. She was his fiancée now.

Early in the afternoon he got a beep from his mother's house and he kept trying to call but got no answer. Something was wrong because he kept getting pages. He woke his girl grabbed his gun and drove over to his mothers house in West Philadelphia. He wanted to buy her a house but she refused to move.

When they pulled up to the house Jubbie placed a gun in his waistband. His girlfriend was sitting in the car applying makeup.

Jubbie ran up to the small steps that lead to his mother's door and knocked on it. When he got no reponses he screamed out her name and opened the door with his key. As soon as he turned the knob the door exploded, Jubbie was blown to smithereens.

Everyone was at the gravesite when one of Mr. Johnson lieutenants got the gage; he walked over to Mr. Johnson and whispered something in his ear.

Mr. Johnson smiled and whispered something to Ray Guns who walked over to Black. "Your man Jube's gone. We're ready to have the meeting after the funeral at Christopher's house."

"Okay," Black said. He had talked with Christopher earlier that day and the only thing Christopher said was that he thought it was an excellent deal.

Frog looked at Black after Ray whispered something in his ear. "What he say?" Frog asked when Ray Guns walked away.

"They're ready for the meeting."

"Okay," Frog said he was a little uneasy. Something wasn't right, but he couldn't place his fingers on it.

Chapter Thirty Nine *Trinidad & Tobago*

Turn Around and its Gone

Mr. Johnson and Black made peace at the funeral meeting and then Christopher flew to Trinidad to finish his business with Senor Cachas.

Christopher, Don Cachas and his bodyguard team were driving in a old raggedy pick up truck. The back was loaded with blocks of cellophane money. Christopher and Don Cachas rode up to Christopher's estate. In the distance, construction teams were working on the other mansions and dock, which Christopher was going to sell to a real estate company that would rent the mansions out as beach house rentals in the winter and summer.

Don Cachas was using one for a base of operations on the Island. The mansion that Christopher owned in Trinidad was finally sold to a real estate developer who was turning it in to a cottage/hotel resort for tourists.

Christopher went to the boulevard and opened Reliable Postal Services a legitimate company that was going to deliver mail and packages all over the world. Surprisingly, before they even opened, they had millions of dollars of orders. Christopher loved it. Several magazine articles had listed Off Shore Realty Co as an up and coming real estate development company.

Christopher, Don Cachas, several associates and Robert Greiner were sitting in Christopher's business office. The twenty-five million-dollars that he owed Don Cachas was sitting on the table. They ignored it like it wasn't even there.

Robert Greiner was one of the government officials from America that was working with Senor Cachas to run their business on the islands successfully. He was an administrator at the drug enforcement agency.

"Christopher, I have that information that you requested." Mr. Greiner reached in his briefcase and passed Christopher the envelope.

"Excellent," Christopher said. "How much is it going to cost me?"

"Two hundred and fifty thousand."

"What?" Christopher replied.

"What you mean? Do you know how valuable that information is? It might come in handy twenty-five years from now. I know for a fact it's not going to change."

Christopher paused for a second. "Okay. John, go and get this man the money. Mr. Greiner, I'm gonna talk to you later. Mr. Martin will take care of you."

Robert Greiner walked over to Christopher and extended his hand. They shook hands. "Thanks for everything. I'll see you Monday. We've got things to cover."

"Okay."

As soon as they left the room Christopher began talking. "Senor Cachas, here's the rest of your money."

"Christopher, how and the fuck did you get the rest of that money so fast?" Don Cachas asked impressed.

"Well, I already had about twenty-five million stashed for business, then I made some of the customers in America pull a couple of million together, and here you have it."

"I have another ten tons. You want it?"

"No, I'll wait. I don't have any loose money right now," Christopher said.

"Don't worry about it. You don't need it. I'll fly it to Mexico and have it waiting in America when you're ready for it. Just give me a time after you take it how long I'm gonna have to wait for my money. I don't want it in Colombia because who knows if I'm gonna be able to get it out next month."

"What happenned to those other forty tons?"

"I sold thirty, now I want to get rid of this last ten before the factory produces another hundred."

"Don Cachas, I'll probably wait."

"Suit yourself. I'm gonna convince you to take twenty tons next time." He smiled.

Black, Frog, Blue and Animal were sitting in the funeral palor in North Philly that Jubbie's viewing was being held in. It was their first time together since Jubby's death. When they returned to Philly, Black ordered them to disappear and meet at the funeral. Frog thought the request was odd but he followed his Boss's orders.

"I can't believe that bullshit that we ain't gonna do nothing? They made a move against us after we arranged the peace. They killed Jubbie while we were having a meeting and you're just gonna accept that?" Something was fishy but Frog couldn't put his finger on it.

"Frog we'll talk about it after the funeral, now just relax," Black said. They were sitting in the funeral palor behind Jubby's family. His baby's mama was there and several of his girlfriends.

Actually, Black didn't know what to do. He was about to have another meeting with Mr. Johnson and start reporting to him and sharing his proceeds. One of the parts of the deal agreement that Black favored was the fact that he didn't have to buy his material from Mr. Johnson. He was gonna be able to deal with Christopher and he explained himself when he was alone with Christopher.

"Christopher, I hope you're not blaming me for that shooting in Ocean City. Believe me, I didn't know you from a can of paint. All of that was on the orders of Mr. Johnson. Don't let him fool you," Black said.

"Black, listen to me and listen to me straight. I'm probably the most honest businessman you know, right?"

Black looked at him for a second then shook his head in agreement.

"Don't you think if I wanted to kill you I could have had you killed a long time ago? This is straight up business. One of the reasons I'm keeping you alive is to spite Mr. Johnson and teach him that none of this is personal. I know he's dying to have his way with you but this is my way of keeping him in check and truly showing my power."

"So I'm a chess piece?"

"No, you're proof that Christopher Larkin knows how to properly conduct business and not let his feelings prejudice him. Don't forget if I wanted you dead I can send a crew against you that would fight you everyday. I would be a fool to charge you personally with coming against me." Christopher smiled and caressed Black's face. "All of this is business and you're gonna live because you do honest business. It's like honor among thieves."

Black smiled because he believed him, but he was more at peace because he knew Christopher's character. You could live by his word and Black agreed with his philosophy.

Two weeks after the meeting the most amazing thing occurred, the feds made sweeping arrests. They arrested Mr. Johnson at his home office in Pennsylvania, Thomas McCant at his Laundromat, Raymond Jones at a construction site, Fat Albert at his house and Andrew Stewart opening the flower shop.

The most shocking arrest was Christopher. They arrested him leaving his house, on the way to the airport. His bodyguard was arrested and released for carrying a concealed weapon. This hit was as deadly as the blow the family received when Christopher was almost murdered several years earlier. Black was arrested in Baltimore in a hotel room with a young lady and Jeremiah was arrested coming out of a restaurant having breakfast with his soldiers after a late night out.

The media ate it up, "F.B.I. Make Powerful Attack Against Black Mafia- Jersey and Philadelphia Leaders Arrested."

One week after the arrest the Christopher Larkin crime family had it's first meeting at Corey's house in Absecon, New Jersey. All of the lieutenants were there.

"It's up to you guys whether we're gonna vote somebody in as acting boss until Christopher comes home," Corey said.

"Well, John Martin's the underboss. Isn't he supposed to take over?" Mark asked.

"Yes, I am, technically, but I don't want to leave this position

I'm trying to die with it," John Martin said. "I can be of more assistance as a counselor."

"Well, Core, that leaves you," Lynn said. Corey was every body's choice anyway. After that, Lynn was voted in as acting underboss and Gary Duffy, Lynn's right hand man, was voted in as an acting lieutenant.

"Hopefully, these positions will be temporary. Everyone's going back to their position once Christopher makes it home. If he doesn't, then we'll have a second vote and change everything or make it official. Everyone has to be real careful," Corey added in.

Later that week Michael Donaldson, Franklin and John Martin were sitting in a federal conference office having a meeting with Christopher. Michael had them sneak in under the guise that they were private investigators working on Christopher's case. If the federal agents found out what he was doing, he could be banned from practice.

John Martin and Christopher were sitting across from each other at a table. "What do you want us to do?"

"I want y'all to move like I don't exist. I'm not trying to worry about running no family from here. The ball's in your hands, and let everybody know from this point on nobody comes to visit me but you and my lawyers. You're my mouthpiece. If I need to see anybody else I'll call for them."

John smiled. It was business as usual. Christopher was still a leader.

A prison guard was standing a couple of feet away and even though by law this was the only office that the feds couldn't set up wire taps Christopher had a feeling that if they got a court order they could do it.

Franklin walked over to Christopher and they embraced. Christopher told him he shouldn't visit, but he insisted and came to visit anyway.

"Cousin, what's up?"

"Nothing. I'm hanging in there, still having to put these New York mother fuckers in check."

"So, what's going on? Talk to me. They said it was an emergency."

"I just wanted to let you know if something happens to you I'm breaking off and forming my own family but I want your blessing because I don't want to kill anybody. Those mother fuckers know they should have made me at least an underboss. They're jealous of me. I'm your real right hand man I should be running the family," Franklin said, pissed that the other lieutenants had voted over him.

"Don't worry about it. You can form your own family but I'm asking you two things. First, make sure that you pay debts off with me. I'm gonna need my money, and wait to see if I'm convicted. I don't want you guys fighting while I'm on trial. Do everything properly and I'll make sure nobody fucks with you when you form your own family."

That was all Franklin had to hear. When he returned to New York he started formulating his plan. He called the first commission meeting without the Larkin family present. Now that Christopher was gone there were gonna be a lot of changes.

The charges against William Johnson's family nearly destroyed it but they had to have a meeting and they had to appoint an administration. That was the term member's used for each family's ruling body.

In Philadelphia, Charles Cores was voted in as boss, Dwayne Philip Hammond was voted in as counselor and Joseph Cecil was voted in as underboss. Now they had to get together and vote eight new lieutenants in. Black's brother Blue was the first lieutenant voted in at the meeting.

One week after that Frank called a commission meeting in New York City without the Christopher Larkin family. He said they were a little hot and he just wanted to iron out a few things. At the meeting Charles Cores was recognized as head of the Philadelphia family and Frank was recognized as head of the Manhattan family. Now Manhattan had two bosses - Shawn Coles and Frank Jones.

If Christopher was convicted Frank was going to hold an official commission meeting. After this first meeting that he headed, he rented a hotel where the five New York organizations named him "Boss of all Bosses," and fitted his head with a solid gold crown made by Blue's Jewelry in Harlem. Franklin loved it. He wished he had made the move a long time ago.

Chapter Forty Center City, Philadelphia

Shall We Dance Again

It took the United States government six months to prepare for trail and prepare their case against the defendants. Everyone was denied bail because of their influence over the streets and positions of being head over organized crime.

Michael Kennedy, the head prosecutor for the government stood up. He was wearing a navy blue suit, a navy blue tie and navy blue shirt. He was 6'3", slim with thick black hair, piercing blue eyes and chiseled features. He was extremely handsome.

"Ladies and gentlemen of the jury. First I want to thank you for taking time out of your hectic schedules to participate in this jury, because I know serving jury duty isn't always easy, but as law abiding American citizens it's your honor and duty to serve jury duty. It's your responsibility to make sure that these men are stopped and put away for the crimes that they've committed. The United States government has proof that these men sitting in this court room here today oversee one of the most organized and complex narcotics distribution networks that America has ever seen."

Kennedy walked over to the jury stand and rested before he continued. "They distribute cocaine, heroin, marijuana, anything illegal. They highjack trucks and over see gambling and other criminal enterprises, which they are willing to protect by murder and other terrorist acts like car bombings and house bombing. Ladies and gentlemen, they have no regard for human life and they will do anything to protect their illegal interests. It's the responsibility of the ladies and gentlemen in this jury to make sure that justice is served, so that American citizens can live back in a society that it once lived. If these men are convicted, some of the crack houses that litter the streets of Philadelphia and other cities in Pennsylvania will disappear. Some of the senseless murders that are being committed will disappear. Ladies and gentlemen of the jury, it's your responsibility to do the right thing because the streets have gone insane, and drug addiction, the very thing that supplies these men their wealth, is the cause of it. While they build successful legal businesses other families suffer physical and mental abuse because of drug addiction. Other families have once civilized members of their families commit heinous acts. If you know somebody suffering from drug addiction it's because of men like this," Kennedy said and he pointed towards the defense table.

"Ladies and gentlemen of the jury you have to help America got rid of its drug addiction and the senseless men that control it. Ladies and gentlemen, the decision that you make today gravely affects crime of the streets of Pennsylvania today and other cities for that fact. These men have major distribution outlets in New Jersey, Maryland, Virginia and other major cities in Pennsylvania. I'm going to bring you the evidence to prove this and it's going to be your responsibility to accept this information and convict these men so that we can work towards bringing Pennsylvania back to it's former glory. Thank you." Kennedy sat down with the rest of his colleagues and they patted him on his back congratulating him.

As soon as Michael Kennedy took his seat Mr. Johnson's attorney Leonard Lehman stood up to address the jury, the defendants had chosen Mr. Lehman to head the defense team, which wasn't a problem because Lehman had the guts and experience. Lenny Lehman was one of the most respected criminal lawyers in the tri-state area. He was a partner in the law firm of Lehman, Rubenstein and Kratz - some of the most powerful Jewish attorney's practicing law in Pennsylvania. They were a prosecutor's worst nightmare. They were connected tightly with almost every prosecutor and judge in Pennsylvania and they had one of the most impressive victory records in existence. The firm consisted of more then twenty-five high-powered attorneys and a twenty-man private investigating firm. They had defended some of Pennsylvania's largest cases in the last twenty years and they had thirty years experience between them.

The other defense attorneys were Christopher's lawyer Daniel Kraft from Kraft, Jones and Blakely - one of the only racially diversified law firms in the South Jersey area. Michael Donaldson wanted to represent Christopher in the case but Christopher thought that it would be better if a Jew represented him. So the law firm of Donaldson, Harris and Davis along with their investigators was hired to assist Mr. Kraft along with his investigators and law team. Christopher was going to have twenty to thirty people working on his case and it was going to cost him at least a million dollars to defend himself. Black had an attorney. Tommy Can's hired an attorney working with the Lehman law firm, so did Ray Guns, Andrew Stewart and Albert Wagner.

Mr. Lehman walked towards the jury box. "Ladies and gentleman of the jury, thank you for taking your time to participate in this trial. A trial that lacks evidence, a trial that you're going to find was a waste of taxpayer's money. A selfish trial were you're gonna witness a young man with political ambitions misuse justice for his own egotism. A trial where there is no evidence but some shaky, barely audible audiotapes, which possess anger and old men ranting about legal business. The prosecutor claims these men control a vast narcotic empire, but there wasn't one single gram of heroin, cocaine or marijuana found on any of the defendants. Oh, the government might bring in witnesses who have already been convicted in federal and state court to testify that they worked for these men, but no concrete evidence. What's really terrifying is that these gentlemen own legitimate businesses and pay taxes. Is this the government's way of destroying African- American morale? Is America trying to say that every successful African- American businessman is somehow involved in the distribution of narcotics, gambling or some other illegal enterprise? That's what I think this is - a witch-hunt. You have guys having shootouts on the streets of Philadelphia everyday and usually the victims of these attacks are innocent bystanders. Do you think these seven gentlemen are the cause of that? Ladies and gentlemen of the jury, will you honestly believe that seven men control organize crime in Philadelphia? Doesn't this somewhat remind you of the case against the Nicodemo Scarfino? What happened to him? If I recall he was the reason that the streets of Philadelphia were so unsafe and dangerous. Are you telling me in five years that these men have replaced him? They're going to show you pictures of these men attending weddings, funeral and sometimes conversing outside of their businesses, or on their properties. Does that mean that they're criminals? Does that mean that they control this criminal entity? I believe that Mr. Kennedy is young and impressionable. I believe that he's been watching too many gangster movies and reading to many Godfather books. I want you to convince him, ladies and gentlemen of this jury, that you can't believe everything you read in the paper and that you can't sleep at night an imagine a conspiracy. It's not going to work. You'll be sending innocent people away just like J. Edgar Hoover did in the forties and sixties. He imagined this invisible force of communism in Hollywood and a lot of actors and innocent lives were destroyed. Well, I'm telling you, ladies and gentlemen, today that the government is at it again. In the forties fifties and sixties it was communism now it's drug conspiracies. None of these men own property in Colombia, Afghanistan or Jamaica. So how can they control this vast distribution entity? Ladies and gentlemen of the jury, the defendants want justice and to return to their families and businesses that they pay taxes on just like me and you."

Lehman walked back over to his seat and took his chair. The defendants, their attorneys and the prosecutors started scribbling things on their
note pads.

The next day after opening arguments the prosecution

called its first witness. Special Agent Charles Strop was called to the stand. Agent Strop was a short, fat white man with greasy hair and pinkish skin. He was raised in the mountains of Virginia and taught to look at Blacks as the enemy. His father was in law enforcement, so was his grandfather. He thought he had broken the circle by entering college, but as soon as he graduated he went over to Vietnam and when he came out he got a job working for the F.B.I. The beautiful thing was he went to Vietnam after the work ended for the military's information sources. It was think kind of work that brought him back into the opening arms of this glorious government.

"Can you state your name for the records?" Kennedy asked when he stood up and walked over to the witness stand.

"Yes Special Agent Charles Bartholomew Strop the third."

"And Special Agent Strop what is your job? What do you do for a living?"

"I'm a F.B.I. agent sir."

"And what do you do for the F.B.I?" Kennedy asked.

"I work for the surveillance and drug intelligence agency."

"If you don't mind me asking, how long have you been doing this?"

"Oh, for the last ten years."

"Mr. Strop, what are some of your responsibilities?"

"Mainly surveillance and intelligence gathering."

"Which consist of?" Kennedy asked.

"Sometimes I tail suspects or monitor their telephones."

"Mr. Strop, are you familiar with any of the men sitting at the table across from me?"

"Yes I am."

"And from your surveillance what information can you convey that you have on them?"

"Well, I believe that they'r all members of a criminal organization that participates it several different kind of criminal activities."

"Can you name any of these criminal activities?" Kennedy asked.

"Well, from wire taps and surveillance the government has surmised that they run a major narcotic entity and information from informants in the past state they control gambling, loan sharking."

"How long have you been investigating this organization?"

"For at least fifteen years," the agent said and Kennedy could see the interest in some of the faces of the jury. Some of them were jotting things down on paper along with Kennedy's colleagues and the defense team.

"Do you have any physical evidence?"

"Yes, we do wire taps and some informants."

"That brings us to exhibit A. Ladies and gentlemen of the jury, we ask you to please listen intently."

A microphone was set up next to the tape recorder and a bailiff was standing next to the player. "Mr. Kennedy are you ready?"

"Yes, I am. You can press play."

"Bill, what's up?" It was Andrew Stewart's voice on the tape.

"Nothing much. I need you to handle Aaron for me," Mr. Johnson was saying.

"Why? WHAT'S going on? What's the matter?" Andrew Stewart was saying. Hearing the tape made both of them sick to their stomachs. It was evidence like this that could send them away for the rest of their lives. The F.B.I. had broken into Mr. Johnson's office at his house and wired the entire place.

"He's acting up saying if we don't handle Christopher he's going to the police?"

"Why don't you let Christopher handle him?" Andrew asked.

"I was going to but since he's my lieutenant I figured I would do it?"

"Okay, Jeremiah's down there?"

"Yeah, but I want to use explosives and Jeremiah's not capable of that. I need you to handle it. You and Albert are the only one who know how to do that."

"Damn," Andrew said pissed. "I thought we weren't using explosives anymore. They draw to much attention?"

"Yeah, they do, but I'm trying to make an example."

"Why don't you use Albert? He taught me how to use them."

"Because he's gonna handle Black for me. I figured you blow one to smithereens and he'd blow the other." There was laughter in the background.

Mr. Kennedy signaled for the bailiff to stop the tape. There was more, but that was enough. "Agent Strop can you identify the men on that tape?"

"Yes I can. It was Mr. William Johnson, the head of the

organization and Andrew Stewart, a man our intelligence has listed as his lieutenant."

"How can you be one hundred percent sure that that was them?"

"Because we have experts that worked for the agency that specializes in identifying voices from previous phone conversations. We have all of the defendants telephones tapped and then we have computers that match their voice patterns on other materials."

"I heard both of the defendants talking about using explosives. Do you have an idea of what they were talking about?"

"Well, two men who would have been co-defendants were killed in explosions, we believe the defendants were referring to those gentlemen."

"Who are the people killed in explosions?" Kennedy asked.

"One was Mr. Aaron Gaston and another James Lockport a.k.a. Jubbie Love."

"Agent Strop, is this recording from a telephone tape?"

"No it is not. It's from a listening device that we placed in William Johnson's business office."

"Agent Strop, how long had that device been placed in Mr. Johnson's business office?"

"At least twelve months?" the agent said. The F.B.I. had broke into Mr. Johnson's house the year that he was in the hospital when the house wasn't being frequented. They didn't activate it until after Mr. Johnson's release. A day after the family meeting where Ray Guns was voted in underboss and Thomas McCant was made counselor.

"Okay, thank you Agent Strop. That will be it for now."

Agent Strop's testimony was damaging, but the thing that was more damaging than anything was the fact that Mr. Johnson's house was wired. A lot of meetings were held there. Any information or minutes presented in trial Christopher immediately sent home. The F.B.I. could have broken into all of there houses, and cars.

The day after court Andrew Stewart, his wife, his daughter and his attorney were sitting in the visiting room going over family business. Mr. Stewart owned a successful flower shop, several buildings and a small construction company.

"Andrew, you alright?" his wife asked. She was 5'5" brown-skinned with a nice blemish- free face, very nice looking for a woman in her mid-fifties.

"No, this shit is driving me crazy. They've got me pent baby," Andrew said. "William fucked up big time running his fucking mouth in that office and I don't know what I'm gonna do. If they pin that homicide on me because it was explosives I'm gonna get life."

Mrs. Stewart gasped. She couldn't imagine life without Mr. Stewart. They had been married at eighteen and she had never been with another man since. "What's your lawyer saying baby?"

"If I plead guilty they're not gonna give me a deal unless I cooperate and tell them everything I know and baby I can't do that."

"How much time would you get if you cooperate, daddy?" Janine asked. She was brown- skinned with the same round, pleasant- looking face as her mother's but she took her thickness from her father's side. She had the butt and breast to match.

"Something like five or ten years."

"Five or ten years after cooperating? That's a lot for you to tell everything," Mrs. Stewart said.

"Not when murders involved Mommy," Janine said. She was so smart but recently she had fell out with her family over the fact that she was dating a Caucasian. "They could send daddy away for the rest of his life."

Mrs. Stewart looked towards Andrew to see if her daughter was correct.

"She's right baby."

Mrs. Stewart burst out into tears and they all embraced. Everyone started crying once the reality of the situation hit them. They hadn't been this close since Janine was small.

Court resumed the following day and Leonard Lehman started his cross-examination, "Agent Strop, how long did you have the defendants under investigation?"

"For about ten to fifteen years."

"And it took you all this time to build enough information to make an arrest?"

"Well, to be honest with you we didn't know that this organization was as organized as this. We've had Mr. Johnson under investigation for years and we knew he was selling heroin and speed for the Italians. We knew he was running numbers and gambling houses for the Italians, but we didn't know he actually headed his own organization until all the killing started happening."

"Agent Strop, you said that experts at your labs identified the voice on the recorders as Mr. Johnson and Mr. Stewart is that correct?"

"Yes that's correct."

"And when you listened to these voices did you immediately understand what they were talking about?"

Agent Strop paused to get his thoughts together. "Yes, we did."

"So why didn't you warn the gentlemen that were harmed in the attack?"

"Well.... Actually we did. I immediately faxed the information to New Jersey and told the agents there and they informed my superiors and told me that Mr. Gaston was a new informant and that he had been warned but we couldn't find Mr. Lockport. He lived in various places. We did inform his parents that he needed to contact us because there might be a contract out of his life, but Mr. Johnson moved to fast. A week after the conversation both men were killed in explosions."

"So you failed to warn the victims?"

"To my knowledge we did not fail in warning them."

"Mr. Strop, if you knew that the defendants were planning to blow somebody up why didn't you arrest the defendants?"

"Because by law the evidence would have been considered a threat and not enough to make an arrest."

"Agent Strop, you had the defendants under investigation, but you couldn't stop them from setting up a bomb on two victims who you alleged you knew were gonna be attacked?"

"That's correct."

"What happened? How were these men attacked when you knew the defendants move?"

"I don't know. Maybe the information wasn't relayed in enough time."

"You said you relayed it immediately."

"I did."

"So obviously there's a flaw in your system."

"I doubt it."

"You should two men are dead that you could have prevented. I think the agency needs to go back and design a better system. Mr. Strop, did you find any narcotics when you conducted the raid?"

"No, we did not. We did find several unregistered guns," the agent replied.

"I'm finished with my questioning, your honor. That will be it. Thank you, Agent Strop."

Mr. Lehman walked back to the defense table. The jurors and the media were left with questions. The next morning it hit the papers.

Chapter Forty One Pennsylvania

The Miseducation of the FBI

Michael Kennedy and a group of his colleagues were sitting in Michael's office having a brief meeting eight o'clock in the morning right before court started.

Michael was resting against his desk sipping coffee.

"How's everything looking?" One of the F.B.I.'s investigating officers asked.

"Everything's looking good at this point but that doesn't mean anything exactly."

"What do you mean that doesn't mean anything?" the man asked pissed.

"Well, we've got three of the defendants by the balls, but the other defendants might slide if we don't get one of the other defendants to flip. Just having somebody say something on tape doesn't necessarily mean you can take a whole ship down. You've seen federal cases tried before. Yes, we have a high conviction rate, but most of our victories are based on the fact that somebody flipped. You do have cases where maybe the defendants don't go free but they're convicted on lesser charges, and this could happen unless we get somebody to flip."

Just as Michael was saying it a bailiff knocked on the door. "Excuse me, Mr. Kennedy, but the judge will be here in thirty minutes."

"Thank you Walter," Kennedy replied, then he and his colleagues started moving around, stuffing their brief cases with the information they needed for the trial that day.

Judge Ermino Scorros walked into the courthouse quietly without anyone noticing until the bailiff announced, "All rise. The honorable Judge Ermino Scorros."

The judge looked at everyone. "You may be seated." Judge Scorros was a thin, olive complexioned man with stringy salt and pepper hair that he let fall to his ears. His face and hands were covered by liver spots but he was still handsome. He had been a judge for the last twenty years and he was fair.

Kennedy stood up and called Agent Strop to the stand. The tape recorder was sitting on a table next to a microphone and a chart was set up on the side with all the family member's pictures and names listed under captions.

"Walter, can you hit the tape?" Kennedy asked.

"Yes, I can." The Bailiff walked over to the recorder and hit it.

"I talked to Christopher and we outlined the deal," Mr. Johnson's voice was saying.

"So what's going on? What do you want me to do?" Ray Gun's voice asked.

"I want you to get with Black and tell him we'll give him the peace if he gives us two of his men."

"Two of his men? Which two? You know he ain't giving up his brother?" Ray Guns said.

"His brother's a nobody. I want Frog and Jubbie," Mr. Johnson said.

"Frog's nobody," Ray Guns said

"Yeah, but he was a soldier in this family. If he wanted to report to anybody he should have reported to me, but you see what he did. We need to make him an example. That's the only way I'm gonna make peace. He gives us two of his men and he'll be a lieutenant again but if he sneezes the wrong way your gonna handle it. I swear to God, if it wasn't for you and Christopher, I would just hunt him down. We're two seconds off of his ass." Mr. Johnson paused and then he continued. "In a lot of ways I hope he doesn't go for the deal because I would love to get his ass just like I did his father. I would let Andy do it so it could be like when we got, his father then if his brother didn't move we'd get his ass."

Everyone was sitting at the defense table silent. They knew not to take anything personal. They were enemies at the time of the tape. Black sat at the table with a blank expression of his face.

"That was the hardest hit I ever did in my life," Ray Guns said on the tape. "I love Big Richard like he was my brother, but he had a terrible gambling problem."

"Yeah," Mr. Johnson said on the tape reflecting. "And he owed too many people money. He was a bum just like his son. Who did that hit, Andy and Albert together?" Mr. Johnson asked on tape.

"No, I think Andy did it with his crew by himself," Ray Guns said.

"When you meet with Black, if he acts like he doesn't want to meet, the next meeting is gonna be the set up and I don't want to here no excuses. He's got a hideout in York. I should just let Cottie handle it and be done with it," Mr. Johnson was saying.

Then there was a sound of water being poured.

Where and the fuck was that bug? Mr. Johnson was thinking as he listened to the tape.

"I'll handle it. I don't think he's going to refuse the offer if Christopher guarantees his safety," Ray Guns was saying on tape.

"He better not," Mr. Johnson said on the tape. "I wish I could put a bomb in Christopher's house and blow up his entire fucking family," Mr. Johnson said laughing after the statement. "I'm gonna get his ass one of these days. All this shit is indirectly because of his ass. He better not ever let me meet those Colombians. His ass is gravy then."

Mr. Johnson and Ray Guns could be heard laughing then.

Kennedy gave the bailiff the signal and he ended the tape. "Agent Strop, who was that speaking on the tape?"

"William Johnson and Raymond Jones."

"Do you see those men sitting in the court house today?"

"Yes, it's the defendants sitting right over there." The agent pointed to the two men.

"Agent Strop, what do you think the defendants were talking about when they said have a meeting with Black?"

"Well through intelligence we gathered information that Mr. Jones and Mr. Johnson were referring to the defendant Anthony Miller also known as Black. Through intelligence we learned that Anthony Miller had something to do with Mr. Johnson being shot at a restaurant where he and another associate were killed. The meeting they were referring to was a meeting that took place in Atlantic City, New Jersey at Christopher Larkin's residence. The codefendant was sitting next to the Mr. Jones, Mr. Miller, and Mr. Johnson. When the agents found out that a meeting might be taking place, we set up surveillance on both of the Joneses and have pictures of them meeting on the outskirts of Philadelphia. We believe this was the meeting where the defendant Anthony Miller was told of a peace meeting and obviously accepted."

"Did this meeting ever take place?" Kennedy asked.

"Yes it did. We believe it took place after Aaron Gaston's funeral in Pleasantville, New Jersey. We believe the meeting was in order to establish the peace between Mr. Johnson and Anthony Miller."

"That brings us to Exhibit B. Kennedy pointed to a chart, which showed pictures of the defendants talking outside of the gravesite in Pleasantville. Everyone knew the F.B.I was there but nobody paid any serious attention to it because they were so used to federal surveillance.

"Thank you that will be it for now." Kennedy walked back to the prosecutor's table.

"Mr. Lehman, will there be any cross examination?" the judge asked.

"Yes, there will be," Mr. Lehman replied jumping to his feet. "Good morning Mr. Strop. How are you doing today?"

"Fine and yourself?"

"Couldn't be better thank you. Agent Strop, why wasn't Clayton Goines or Anthony Miller warned by the F.B.I that their lives were in danger by the F.B.I.?"

"Well, basically because we couldn't catch Clayton Goines. He wasn't a prime target and Mr. Jones, I believe we were going to warn him, but didn't get around to it yet."

"Agent Strop, are you aware that Clayton Goines was killed in a nail bombing when he went to visit his parents house?"

"Yes, I'm aware of this."

"Do you think it could have been prevented if the F.B.I would have done their job and warned him?"

Agent Strop was stuck. "Mr. Lehman, the F.B.I. always does its job. It's the life that Mr. Goines lived that caused his death."

"So everyone that the F.B.I. believes is involved in an illegal activity should be blown to death?"

"No. I didn't say that."

"Objection. Your honor that question was irrelevant and misleading," Kennedy said jumping to his feet.

"Mr. Lehman I'm gonna have to ask you to be careful on how you direct your questions."

"Sorry your honor. Agent Strop, you have surveillance pictures of the defendants meeting at Aaron Gaston's funeral. do you have any audio recordings?"

"No, we do not."

"Why not?"

"Because, to my understanding Mr. Larkin's phones are tapped, but wires haven't been placed in his house yet."

"So how do you know what was being said in the house while they were having this alleged meeting if you have no recordings?"

Strop was stuck. "Well I don't know exactly what was being said, but I know they were having a meeting because a previous recording said they were."

"No. The recording said that Mr. Larkin approved a meeting. That's different from participating in one. Is that correct?"

"Yes it is, I guess. I would say that's correct."

"No, I'm telling you it is. Agent Strop, have you ever been to a funeral where the deceased's friends or family prepare a meal for him?"

"Yes, I have."

"So is it possible that these men merely ate dinner and left?"

"It's possible, but I doubt it."

"Agent Strop, I'm not asking for your opinions I'm asking for facts. Do you have evidence that a meeting between Christopher Larkin and the rest of the defendants took place?"

"Yes, I do."

Mr. Lehman looked shocked. "Where is it?"

"Those pictures," Agent Strop said.

"Can those pictures talk? I just see people embracing each other. Agent Strop, I want to remind you this is a court of law and what you say here is extremely important. Please don't assume anything when talking here. It might confuse the jury. I repeat: do you have audio proof that William Johnson, Christopher Larkin, Anthony Miller, Raymond Jones, Thomas McCant, Andrew Stewart or Albert Wagner held a meeting at Mr. Larkin's house and discussed anything about Anthony Miller or anything else illegal?"

"No, I do not."

"Thank you. That will be it for right now." The most important thing established for the defendants at the court date was that the only place that the F.B.I. had bugged was Mr. Johnson's place.

Everyone had spies following the trial and everyone was afraid, but everything seemed to get extremely quiet now that the trial was in session, proving that the F.B.I. didn't actually know anything.

Charles Cores, the new boss, Blue, Frog and Cottie, Mr. Core's right hand man were walking together in a small park in West Philadelphia. One thing they had learned was that there should be no talking in the house. Everything had to be taken to the streets for brief little street walks.

Charles Cores was brown -skinned, with a nice grade of hair. He wasn't bad looking, but he had an obnoxious personality. A lot of the older members couldn't believe he was voted in as boss and the vote was that he wouldn't be around long.

"Blue, I called you over because you're a lieutenant now and I want you to know one thing; I'm not Mr. Johnson. You can trust me. As long as you're not doing side business and you cut me in you can sleep around me. I'm not trying to double cross anybody. I know Frog had a contract on his life but I'm lifting it right now. Most likely none of our people are coming home. They're history and we have to move on. I want to me with you once a week and I don't want anybody doing side business with Corey Taylor. I mean he's cool but he's nothing without us. If we keep our unity and cut this bullshit fighting out we can all make millions quietly," Charlie said.

"Mr. Cores, I'm young I don't really know everything, but I

do have common sense and I know how to be loyal. I stuck with my brother and we were fighting a losing battle. As long as my crew is safe you have our loyalty. As far as dealing with Corey, I heard they're not doing anything and I won't ever contact them as long as you take care of me. My brother said everything was so sweet before the war and I want it that way again."

"Oh, and there's one other thing," Cottie, the second or third in command said. "Don't hold meetings in the house, in your cars, or over the telephones. The feds will bug anything."

"That's right," Mr. Cores added in, "And don't discuss family business with your brother until after the case, even on visits because the feds are trying to get us like crazy." By the time he said that they were back in front of the bar that rested at the head of the park. Mr. Cores had purchased a house in the heart of Philadelphia so that he could be closer to the lieutenants.

Animal was sitting in the car with several chicks. Blue and Frog jumped in a separate car and pulled off.

Janine and Brad, her fiancé were lying in the bed reading the paper. They were both naked. "Baby, I didn't even know no black mafia existed. You fucking father could have had me killed. I didn't know I was fucking with the black Al Capone's daughter." They laughed. "You sure I'm safe?" He continued.

"You're safe," Janine replied. Then she grabbed his pale penis and put it in her mouth. Slowly she started sucking on him. If you gave a white boy head, you had to do it right. They were getting sucked off by the seventh grade, the same grade that the average black teenager started experimenting with kissing and stuff like that.

Brad grabbed Janine's head. "Okay, Al Capona do ya thing." He pushed her head into his privates with one motion. Janine kept sucking him off until he came in her mouth. Once he started coming he pushed her head down more. She had to swallow it like all the white girls did if she wanted to keep him.

While Janine was having oral sex with her boyfriend her father was in a meeting room having a meeting with the feds deciding whether he would cooperate or not.

Fat Albert and Andrew were walking in the prison yard. "Albert, you done lost your mind. They've got us on several killings."

Albert just stared at him.

Andrew continued. "They got us for blowing up Jubbie and Big Aaron. Now, because of Ray's big ass mouth, they know we killed Richard." Black father. "And other shit's gonna pop up. I don't think Christopher's lawyer is gonna let him go down on a murder he knew nothing about. They don't have no murders on Tommy or Ray, just conspiracy. I'm letting you know right now: the day you come to court and don't see me, you know I made my move to take care of myself and I'm offering you the same thing. We blow tria,l life; we cooperate, five to ten years."

"How you know they're gonna give us five or ten? Have you talked with them?" Albert asked.

"Listen, man," Andrew said later. "Just remember what I said. If you don't see me in court, don't take it personal."

"Yo, why don't you talk with your attorney and accept a plea? It's better than telling."

"From what I understand, our only plea is telling. The mother fucking F.B.I. don't play. This is the United States Government. You either cooperate or you don't. I'll talk with you later." Andrew jogged away. He was trying to lose weight so he would be light on his feet. He might have to stay light on his feet and watch his back for the rest of his life if he made it out of here, but it was sounding better and better everyday. Thinking of life with a release date made his bid a whole lot better.

Chapter Forty two Federal Courthouse Pennsylvania

Diarrhea and an Upset Stomach

The next Monday after the family's last court date, Christopher and the rest of the defendants were sitting in a holding cell adjacent to the court like they did every single day. The bailiff didn't usually escort them out of the holding cell until after the judge arrived and told him he'd be ready in five minutes.

Christopher and the others sat silently amongst themselves until Christopher looked at his watch. "It's nine o'clock. We should have been out of here."

Mr. Johnson looked at his watch. "You're right. They never leave us back here this late." They could hear the lawyers and the prosecutors talking amongst themselves. It sounded like they were arguing.

"Yo, where and the fuck is Andy?" Charles McCant said. If he made it out of this case he was going to be elected boss. There was no way anybody was ever gonna let Mr. Johnson continue to operate the family. He already had all of the lieutenants coming to visit him on different weeks and the F.B.I. was monitoring everything. Christopher didn't find out yet, but when he did he was going to put a stop to it. It was too risky.

"He's probably sick," Mr. Johnson said. The last thing any of them would have thought was that he had turned government witness on them.

Albert was sitting in the corner sweating. His stomach hadn't been right since the arrest. He thought he might be able to get his nerves together when the trial started but after hearing his voice on the tape he had diarrhea and an upset stomach. Every night he cried in his cell. He was too old to be going through this.

Five minutes after their discussion, Christopher's lawyer Daniel Kraft walked into the back of the holding cell. "Good news or bad news? Which one first?" He asked.

Ray flipped. "Listen coward don't fuck with me. You think this is a game my life's in jeopardy. Don't play fucking games with me. What's going on?"

"Ray, please calm down," Tommy Cans said.

"Andrew Stewart flipped over the weekend. He's going to testify against you guys."

"What?" Mr. Johnson was shocked. "I can't believe that shit. That fucking coward. Damn it." Mr. Johnson stood up and lightly pounded his hands against the wall.

"And the good news?" Ray guns asked.

"You guys can go back and rest. Court is recessed for at least a week until we go over the evidence."

Ray jumped up and slammed the attorney against the wall. "You stupid, white mother fucker." The others had to jump up and pull Ray off the attorney. "Don't ever play with me like that again. I'll have you killed. I'll split your fucking scull."

The bailiffs heard the screaming and rushed to the back. "Is everything okay? What's going on back here?"

"Nothing. Everyone's a little upset over bad news." The lawyer said brushing his clothes off.

The bailiff walked away.

"Mr. Jones, I apologize." He said extending his hand.

Raymond ignored him.

The day that they agreed to flip and turn government witnesses, the feds showed up to their houses. Janine, her mother, and her brothers and sisters were sitting in the living room to the house that they grew up in." Janine was the baby. She was born in the projects, but she was raised in the house after she turned one. The other kids were little when they moved into the house and it still held the warmth and power it held when her father was home. It just lacked the invisible security that her father provided.

All her life, the only thing that Janine knew was that her father owned a famous flower shop in Center City, Philadelphia. That flower shop turned into a successful construction company, a bar and real estate property. It wasn't until the seventies, when a man was killed in Atlantic City at a club named club Harlem, did her father pop up in the papers. The articles stated that he was a lieutenant under her Uncle William Johnson, the head of the Philadelphia Black Mafia and that the man killed at the bar was her father's best friend. Janine never heard of the man but after they arrested her father for questioning, Janine went to her mother who denied everything. She wasn't satisfied with her mother's answers so she went to her brother, Andrew Junior, who was a cop who never got along with her father and he told her everything.

Surprisingly, Junior had even showed up to the house to give support, but he did, and they had been close every since. Her father was released after the incident and never charged for anything.

"What we usually do in a case of this magnitude is ask who feels there lives are in danger and who wants to move?" the white agent was saying to the family as everyone sat quietly listening.

"Actually, none of us are leaving. I would feel better if my mother was provided a place," Andy Junior was saying.

"Andy, I can't leave your father, He needs me. I have to talk with him and see what he says."

"Mrs. Stewart, during the trial we would hide you close that way you could handle all legal business like selling your house, selling the businesses or transferring them over to your children. You would be here until the end of the trial if needed and then you would be relocated along with your husband."

"Relocated where?" she asked.

"The government has hiding spots all over America. We would ask you to choose a predominately white area or a small town. Crime in small towns flourish, but there's never a true criminal presence there," the agent said.

"Oh yeah, Atlantic City's small and you're telling us all this bullshit started there."

"Yeah but even in Atlantic City none of the real business is handled there. Most of your father's associates conduct business out of town. It's just a coincidence that they live there. They do more business here then they do anywhere."

"I like Ocean City, Maryland," Mrs. Stewart said.

"Ocean City, Maryland would be nice if your case was based in California. We're thinking more California, northern area. Montana, Idaho, places like that."

"I can't live there. We're would I shop?" It wasn't a joke but her children laughed.

"Mom, this is the wrong time to think about shopping."

'Mr. Stewart, that's later on. You can handle where you want to live after you discuss it with your husband. Right now, we're gonna put you in a hotel and move you once a week until the trial's over. After the trial is over you'll be situated near your husband's facility until his release, which will be in a year or two and then you guys can move to a new location or completely disappear if you've got the money."

"How am I going to move my stuff?" Mrs. Stewart asked.

"Mrs. Stewart, your children are gonna have to handle everything. It's going to be like you and your husband died. This is material stuff. None of it is important. What is important is that we get you to a safe place. That's what your husband wants."

"Has anybody made threats on my Mom's life?" Andy Junior, the cop asked.

"There have been no threats as of yet, but you can never be too safe."

"My father and all those guys have been friends for years I don't think they would hurt any of us. They're businessmen. None of us knew what was going on with our father until we read the papers," Janine said.

"You father said the same thing," The quiet agent said who hadn't spoken the entire time. "Better safe then sorry. Mr. Johnson had somebody blown up with bombs and that's devious. You can't underestimate people like that," the agent said.

The children remembered reading about the bombing. It would have killed them if they knew that their father had something to do with it.

"That's terrible," Mrs. Stewart said.

"So you'll move?"

"Yes, but when can I talk to my husband?"

"Right now we're moving him to another facility to protective custody. We don't want you to visit until you move out of here. We don't want anyone to follow you."

"Okay. When would I leave?" Mrs. Stewart asked.

"Tonight an agent will pick you up from one of your children's houses." He passed her a card, shook everyone's hand and left.

Condezza Wagner and several agents were sitting in her family's restaurant in West Philadelphia. "I'm not going no where. My mother and William Johnson's mother were second cousins. William is my family. I love my husband and I support my husband and I'm not going anywhere. I don't care what he says and I don't care what you say. I've known almost every one of those guys all my life and one thing I know about them is they don't kill women and children. If William and my husband have a beef, then that's between them."

"Well, will you at least go and visit your husband and listen to what he has to say?" one of the agents asked. Black women could be so dumb and difficult was what he was thinking. That's why their husbands could never accumulate anything. Their wives hindered their businesses.

"I'll listen to what he has to say when I see him on a visit like I do every week. Now if you gentlemen will excuse me, I have breakfast to tend to. The restaurant opens in twenty minutes." Mrs. Wagner wiped her hands on her napkin and fled to the back.

Four weeks after the recess court resumed. The F.B.I. had approached the other defendants and offered them plea agreements where they could plead guilty and testify against the other. They all refused except Albert.

Because Albert had done the most recent murder, Jubbie's house bombing, the prosecutors decided to use him first. Christopher and the others were shocked when their lawyers informed them a week after court recessed that Albert had decided to flip also and become an informant.

Albert walked to the witness stand. He was no longer

housed in the same facility and he never traveled with the defendants anymore. He had lost over seventy-five pounds since his incarceration.

The bailiff walked over to Albert and swore him in. "Raise your right hand and place your other hand on the bible. Do you swear to tell the honest to God truth as you know it in this court of law?"

"I do." It was official. Albert was an informant now.

Kennedy jumped up from his seat. He loved prosecuting serious trials. His name was in the paper and he was becoming an instant celebrity.

"Please state your full name for the record."

Albert leaned towards to the microphone that was set up on the podium. "Albert Wagner, the third."

"Mr. Wagner where do you work?" Kennedy asked.

"Wel,l I own Albert's Jazz Club and Grill, several pieces of commercial and residential property throughout Philadelphia and New York." Impressive.

"Do you have another job?" Kennedy asked.

"No." Albert had told Kennedy be direct. He was turning on his friends to play games.

"Were you a member of a organized crime group?" Kennedy asked.

"Yes, I was." And who was the head of that organization?" Kennedy asked.

"At what time?" Albert asked finally comfortable in his chair.

"When you joined."

"Michael Donaldson was the head of the family when I joined."

"Is he alive?"

"No, he passed away a couple of years ago from Alzheimer's."

"Who's the head of that organization now?" Kennedy asked.

"William Johnson is."

"Do you see him seated in the courthouse today?"

"Yes, I do."

"Can you identify him?"

"Yes, I can. He's the older gentlemen sitting at the defense table with the bandage on his head and the small blood stain."

"Let the record state that the witness, Albert Wagner,

identified one Mr. William Johnson, the defendant sitting at the defense table."

"What year did you join the family?" Kennedy asked.

"Probably 1950, maybe a little later."

"And what position did you hold in the family?"

"In the beginning I was a lieutenant. In the early fifties my father ran a successful gambling house and a numbers racket. When he got older he turned everything over to me and my younger brother and cousin who all turned out to be junkies. Somewhere in the early fifties, Mr. Donaldson stepped to me, told me he loved my business and that he wanted me to join his organization. At first I was hesitant but in the fifties Mr. Donaldson was a legend and it was every hustler's dream to deal with him. So I talked it over with my father and he told I could do what I want. He said he liked Mr. Donaldson and maybe we could expand."

"Did you?" Kennedy asked.

"Yes, we did. Mr. Donaldson had a fifty maybe sixty man crew and he told me to step to every gambling house and number, runner in the area and inform them they had to pay a street tax if they wanted to continue to operate."

"Did you do it?"

"Yes, I did."

"Did it work?" Kennedy asked.

"Yes, it did. Mr. Donaldson said only step to the gambling houses and numbers runners that were making serious money and that's what I did. Usually they agreed because when Mr. Donaldson became your partner he would invest in your business and make partnership with him a wise move. A lot of the guys we didn't have to say anything to because they were small time nickel and dimmers. They weren't really competition and as long as they operated on a small scale we had no problems."

Kennedy loved it. "Did you guys have to harm anybody who refused to pay?"

"Every once in a blue we would come across a knucklehead that we had to kill but the organization became so big that eventually everyone was just waiting for us to approach them. They wanted to work with us. If you were part of our families we handled all of your problems and I mean all. We had police officers, murderers, everything. It was nice and beautiful."

"When did you meet Mr. Johnson?" Kennedy asked.

"In the early fifties there was a guy in Lancaster, Pennsylvania that was running a large gambling house and he didn't want to pay. Me, Mr. Johnson and a group of my friends busted his place up. After that, he didn't learn, so we killed him. Made peace with the guy that took over and the rest was history."

"Was that the killing that officially made you a lieutenant?" Kennedy asked.

"I don't know, but a couple of weeks after that Mr. Donaldson called a meeting. There were about twenty or thirty people there. At that meeting Mr. Donaldson asked me to pledge my loyalty to the family and named me a lieutenant. He told me to form a crew of soldiers, which I already had. He introduced me to his counselor and underboss who were both real old men at the time. They died."

"What were the counselor and underboss's names?" Kennedy asked.

"The second in command was named Lloyd Miller and the underboss was named Jason Sales. They were in their late sixties when I met them. They died a couple of years later. I think in the early sixties."

"Who replaced them?" Kennedy asked.

"William Johnson and Thomas McCant, Mr. Donaldson's two most powerful lieutenants. William and Tommy were always rivals because they had the most successful businesses. I don't know how true it was, but both of them were supposed to be making about a million dollars a month from gambling houses, prostitution, number, running and extortion?"

"What about drugs?" Kennedy asked.

"In the early sixties you had guys using heroin, marijuana and people using hallucinogens but it wasn't like it is now. Back then, you had lieutenants dealing in drugs, but nothing major. Everyone was making a fortune off of gambling and number running. There was no real need to deal with drugs."

"Mr. Wagner, how did Mr. Donaldson get paid?"

"The lieutenants are supposed to give him half of everything they make profit-wise."

"Do you think the lieutenants did it?" Kennedy asked.

"I don't know if they gave half but you better had turned

over something that's why you were a lieutenant and let into the family, but I don't think anybody turned in half. They were too greedy. In the early fifties and sixties I was making about a hundred grand a week profit sometimes I turned in probably twenty thousand maybe thirty thousand a week."

"That's a lot of money." Kennedy replied trying to get jurors to recognize the wealth and power of these mne.

"Now, say if fifteen lieutenants turn in thirty thousand a week. That's about what two, three hundred thousand a week. Which translate, into about three to four million dollars a year profit. Sometime like New Year's Eve and special holidays you had to turn in more because the gambling houses would rake in, especially the nice ones. That's what Mr. Donaldson was famous for. He would definitely invest heavily in your business."

"When did business change?" Kennedy asked.

"In the late sixties. A group of men calling themselves the "Black Extortion Army started running around extorting drug dealers and businessmen."

"When did the drug business get big?"

"In the mid sixties. By the early seventies the heroin business had exploded just like crack cocaine dominates today."

"Was your organization involved in it?"

"Mr. Donaldson and the head of the Italian Mafia were good friends, so when heroin got big our family entered it in a strong way. For a minute we were supplying people in New York, then the guineas got smart and start dealing directly with the young blacks like the Italians in Philadelphia were doing."

"When did Mr. Johnson become head of the family?" Kennedy asked.

"In the early seventies Mr. Donaldson was in his early seventies and he started knocking off extortion army members and one of them came into his office and shot him in the chest with a sawed off shot gun. He was never the same. He semi-retired named William Johnson boss and Ernest Clark counselor to keep the peace between William and Thomas. He named Thomas underboss but everybody knew Clark was just a gofer. William and Tommy held the real power."

All of this information was shocking and amazing. The jurors loved it.

"Mr. Wagner when's the last time you killed under the orders of Mr. Johnson?" Kennedy asked.

"A couple of months ago I had a meeting with him and he told me to kill Clayton Goines."

"And is this same Clayton Goines this man right here on the chart?"

"Yes, it is."

"Let the record state that the witness identified one Mr. Clayton Goines also known as Jubbie."

"How'd you kill Mr. Goines?" Kennedy asked.

"I broke into his house, tied his mother up with my crew and set up explosives on his door. Then we forced his mother to page him and he came."

"Were you in the house when he came?"

"No, I left, but my crew parked outside and one stayed inside with his mother in case she came a loose."

"What happened?" Kennedy asked.

"Jubbie came, the nail bomb exploded and he was history, just like we planned it."

"Did you make it to the funeral?" Kennedy asked.

"I was right there," Wagner said.

"That will be it for now, No further questions." Kennedy said walking over to his colleagues with the biggest smile on his face.

"Mr. Lehman will there be cross examination?" The judge asked.

"There sure will." He jumped to his feet.

A couple of days after the court hearing Frank, Corey, John Martin and several of Frank's bodyguards from New York City were having a business meeting in Sylvia's restaurant in Harlem on 126th St and Lenox Avenue. Sylvia's was a Harlem landmark. Corey hated the food. He thought it was overrated, but everybody else loved it.

"Frank, Christopher wants his money," Corey said.

"Core what you mean Christopher wants his money? Christopher said I could work with the money until he came home." They were the only ones sitting at their table. Frank's bodyguards were sitting at another table conversing amongst themselves.

"That's not what he told me," John Martin added. "He said collect his money just in case he didn't make it home and that's what we're suppose to do."

Franklin was pissed. He couldn't believe these cowards had the authority to tell him what to do. "Well I'll go and talk to him."

"Christopher said he doesn't want any visits because it might be too dangerous for everybody. That's why John's the only one that can go and see him," Corey added.

"I can't believe this shit. All the money I made for this family and he's pressuring me over a measly four million dollars? I put in too much blood, sweat and tears for this bullshit."

The real problem wasn't the debt that Franklin owed but he was causing a lot of confusion because he had broken off and started supplying a lot of the guys that dealt with the family.

"Frank, it wouldn't have been so bad if you weren't running around supplying everybody."

"Oh, so that's what this is about? I'm making to much fucking money?" Frank said.

"No, it's not even that, but you're supplying our customers and they owe us. They're taking our money and spending it with you," Corey said.

"Well, that's not my problem. You should have a beef with them," Franklin said.

"It doesn't matter. Just make sure Christopher gets his money, It's been a couple of months now."

Frank was pissed because it was sort of embarrassing. Even the fact that they knew he owed Christopher money. "Listen, this is what I'm going to do. I'll give you guy a quarter million dollars a month and if the trials over before the debt is paid off I'll hit you off with the balance. Is that okay with you big shot?" Franklin asked. He was trying to be sarcastic.

"Of course it's okay with me," Corey said. "I'm just following orders."

"You guys better be careful having those meetings with Christopher. The entire place is bugged. I hope no federal indictments pop up over those meetings. You know the fed's don't play. Look how they've got Christopher by the balls." He chuckled after he said it. Franklin didn't care about anybody and his sentiments showed it. If it weren't for Christopher he would have been dead for owing that kind of money. It wasn't even the money. It was the fact that he was doing side business with the other families and that was causing a lot of commotion.

Franklin looked at his watch. "Oh shit. We better get out of here. I told Cores and them to meet us up the block at Lenox Lounge."

"Okay, let's move," Corey said standing up to exit the restaurant.

The Lenox Lounge bar and café was located three blocks down on 124th St. and Lenox Avenue. It was small but it was famous for it's historic jazz history.

When Franklin, John Martin and Corey walked into the bar followed by their security team Charles Cores and his second in command was already sitting there having drinks. They had brought along two nice looking girls so they could spend the weekend in the city and catch The Whispers musical group singing in some Brooklyn Café.

"Corey, what's up?" The gentlemen embraced.

"Mr. Cores, what's going on?" Corey asked.

"Everything's okay," Mr. Cores responded. "Frank baby, how are you? Long time no see," He said.

"I'm excellent, and you?" Franklin asked.

"I'm fine, just trying to stay out here baby." They were doing side business and thought that nobody knew it. Frank didn't know that Charles Cores was telling Corey everything. He had to stay close to Corey. It was the only reason that he was alive. He knew the younger lieutenants wanted to kill him. Everyone thought of him more as a pimp because, before drugs, most of his money came from running whorehouses. Now he was one of the biggest strip clubs owners in the entire Philadelphia area. He owned more than fifteen strip clubs.

"Let's take a walk, me, you and Frank. The bodyguards can follow us," Corey said.

Frank walked over to his bodyguards and said something. When they left the lounge they made sure they stayed a couple feet behind. Even John Martin had to walk behind with them.

"Mr. Cores, what's going on in Philly?" Corey asked.

"Everything's cool just watching out for the feds."

"I talked with Christopher and he said you guys have to pick one person who's gonna be your contact with Mr. Johnson because all the lieutenants visiting is too dangerous. How's Blue acting?" Corey said.

"He's acting cool right now, but I've got my eye on him."

"If his brother acts up he has to go. Remember the only reason he's alive is because his brother's doing the right thing"

"What are we going to do about Al Wagner and Andy Stewart?"

"I don't know, but when I find out I'll have a meeting with you. Don't forget to tell your lieutenants no talking in the house and to watch what they say in their cars. The feds are fucking with people's cars also."

"No problem." Before he knew it they had walked all the way to Lenox Hospital. They turned around and started walking back.

Chapter Forty Three Pennsylvania

Just a Small Matter of Extortion

Daniel Kraft, the defendants and the rest of the defense team were sitting at a table when Leonard Lehman started cross-examination on Albert Wagner.

"Good afternoon, Mr. Wagner. How are you doing?"

"Excellent and you?"

"I'm fine, thank you. Mr. Wagner, how many people do you think you've killed in your life time?"

"About fifteen, maybe twenty-five."

"Whoa, that's a lot. How many murders have you ordered?"

"About the same amount."

"How many murders have you conspired with associates?" Lehman asked.

"Hundreds." The jurors sat in their seats in shock.

"Did Mr. Johnson order some of these murders?"

"Most of them, but not all of them." Albert had nothing to fear because when you made a deal with the feds you were supposed to tell everything and get immunity for these crimes.

"Mr. Wagner, did you ever control an illegal numbers businesses in Philadelphia?"

"Yes, I did."

"Gambling?"

"Yes, I did."

"Were the businesses lucrative?"

"Excuse me?"

"Were the businesses profitable? Successful, Mr. Wagner."

"Yes, they were."

"Excellent. Did you control narcotics? Illicit drugs, Mr. Wagner."

"Yes, I did."

"Were there any narcotics confiscated during this raid?"

"Not to my knowledge."

"Mr. Wagner, in 1970 a man named Arturo Samuels was blown up in a car bomb. Did you have anything to do with it?"

"Yes, I did."

"Why was this man killed?"

"Because he was extorting my business associates."

"So it would be right for me to say that you were using explosives before Mr. Johnson so called became the man who gave you orders?"

Wagner paused for a second. "You can say that."

"Okay then. No further questions." Lehman walked back over to the defense desk and sat down. The defendants started having their own private meetings after Albert and Andrew decided to testify. Something had to be done, something serious.

Blue, Frog and Animal were sitting in a small apartment with one of their associates counting money. They had five kilograms of cocaine sitting on the table.

"You want some of this?" the associate said, holding up a joint of marijuana.

"What's that, weed? It stinks," Blue said.

"Yeah, and it's got a little bit of coke in it," the associate said.

"Give me some," Animal said coming out of his heroin-induced daze.

The guy passed Animal the joint and he inhaled half of it. "You got anymore?" Animal asked reaching in his pocket pulling out a wad of money.

"I don't have no weed but if you want to buy a piece of this coke you can," The associate said.

"Yeah, give me a twenty."

Blue and Frog looked over at each other. They were gonna have to straighten Animal out later. While in the apartment they didn't say anything. They just continued counting the money. After the money was rubber banded Blue counted the stacks. He placed the money in a bag.

"Let's get the fuck out of here. Kelly walk us to the steps," Blue said.

Kelly walked them down to the bottom of steps. He was wearing a stocking cap, pajamas and a robe.

"Kelly, all this money you making, I think its time you move buddy."

"Then how am I gonna get all this money?" Kelly asked carrying his gun in his waistband.

"You don't have to get money where you live. In fact you don't want to get money where you live. I'm gonna kick it with you one of these days. I like your style," Blue said.

"Okay then, partner." They shook hands.

Blue and his crew walked to the car. Frog opened the trunk and Blue dropped the bag in the trunk they hopped in the car and pulled off. When they pulled away they noticed a cop sitting at the corner conducting surveillance on the guys hustling at the other end of the block.

As soon as Blue and his crew drove past the cop he pulled out and threw on his siren.

"I told you we shouldn't come around here to pick up this money. You should make that mother fucker come to you," Frog said.

When Andrew Stewart walked out of the back of the holding cell he looked extremely happy and well rested. He smirked at the others as he walked past the table and Black couldn't help it. He made the shape of a gun and pointed it at him.

When Andrew turned around and saw him, Black pulled out a gun and snapped his finger. That was the shot.

For one second Andrew was thrown off and he wanted to yell. "Did anybody see that?" But he remained silent. He wasn't a sissy. Andrew took his seat and the bailiff walked over.

"Raise your right hand and repeat after me. I swear to tell

the truth and nothing but the truth, so help me God."

Andrew repeated the words and then took his seat. "Do you mind if I have a glass of water?"

Kennedy walked over to the small table that sat next to the witness stand and poured Andrew a glass.

"Good morning, Mr. Stewart," Kennedy said after passing the man a drink.

"Would you please state your full name for the record?"

"Yes, I will. Andrew Clarence Stewart, Senior."

"Mr. Stewart, do you own any businesses?"

"Yes, I do. I own Philadelphia Rose Company and Flower Shop."

"And how is business going?"

"Excellent, so far."

"Do you have any other business interests?"

"Yes, I own a few pieces of property, a small construction company and a Laundromat."

"And these businesses, do they provide for you well?"

"Last year, among my companies, I've grossed three million dollars. Business has been growing ever since the mid-seventies."

"Do you have business associates or partners in these businesses?"

"I was a partner with Mr. Donaldson in the flower shop. When he died I bought his family out. I own the Laundromat with William Johnson, and the construction business and properties are solely owned by me."

"The William Johnson that you're referring to who owns the Laundromat with you, is he in this court room?"

"Yes, that's him sitting there with the beige suit on." Mr. Johnson was sitting in the last chair with the rest of the defendants. He was still wearing the bandage on his head to protect his injury from bleeding. Even though the wound had closed, sometimes it still bled from a tiny crack in his flesh that didn't completely close or heal. Mr. Johnson couldn't believe that Andrew or Albert were really testifying. It hurt him that they made the cowardly move. He had an ace up his sleeves. He was meeting with his lawyers and his codefendants and they were strategizing their last moves everyday.

"Mr. Stewart, did you belong to a criminal organization that was involved in murder, gambling, extortion and drug trafficking?"

"Yes, I was."

"And what position did you hold in that organization?"

"In the early fifties I was a soldier and voted in as a lieutenant by early 1960. For a little while I was voted in as acting underboss because Mr. Johnson was almost killed in an assassination attempt."

"Mr. Stewart, I want you to take this pointer stick and Identify Mr. Johnson on this F.B.I. chart." Kennedy passed Andrew the stick and he pointed to Mr. Johnson's picture.

"Mr. Stewart, to your knowledge, what year did Mr. Johnson become the head or lead of this organization?"

"In 1970, to my knowledge, he became the leader. Then, about seventy-two our old boss officially retired making Mr. Johnson the official leader."

"And as leader of this organization what kind of illegal activities did Mr. Johnson oversee?"

"As the boss he was in control of everything."

"Such as?"

"Narcotics..."

"What kind of narcotics?" Kennedy interrupted.

"Cocaine and crack right now. Heroin and speed in the seventies."

"Who were his sources?" Kennedy asked.

"Mr. Johnson had thousands of sources. I believe that Christopher Larkin supplied our family with the cocaine, our heroin came from New York or the Italian Mafia, and so did our speed."

"Were there any other businesses?" Kennedy asked.

"We controlled gambling houses all over Philadelphia before the casinos came to Atlantic City. Whorehouses, numbers spots everything."

"Were you directly involved in these activities?"

"Yes, I was."

"And did you profit from them?"

"Yes, I did."

"Did you share these proceeds with Mr. Johnson?"

"Every single dime. I wasn't like Albert. Everything I made I split it right down the middle." He was exaggerating but the jurors would never know that.

"Mr. Stewart, can you identify this man for the record?"

"Yes, his name is Ernest Clark."

"And is he in this room?"

"No, he was killed by Anthony Miller and his associate Animal."

Is Anthony Miller in the court house right now?"

"Yes."

"Can you point to him for the record?"

"Yes, the man sitting there in the bright blue three piece suit."

"Let the record state that the witnesses identified the defendant Mr. Anthony Miller."

"What about Animal?"

"You guys didn't get him yet."

"Do you see him in the court room?"

"No, I do not. He might be back there with the other spectators."

"Mr. Stewart, what position did Anthony Miller hold in your organization?"

"He was a lieutenant."

"And Mr. Johnson was the boss."

"Yes, that is correct."

"Why would Anthony Miller, a lieutenant, try and have his boss killed?"

"They were having a disagreement over the drug business, and while we they were having a meeting Animal came up and shot Clark and Mr. Johnson in the face. Mr. Johnson lived and Clark died."

"Mr. Stewart, can you identify this man?" Kennedy asked.

"Yes, his name is Thomas McCant"

"And what position did he hold in the organization?"

"Second in command. He was the underboss."

"I thought the counselor was second in command?" Kennedy said.

"The Counselor holds the title of second in command because he's usually close to the boss but it's usually the underboss who's truly second in command."

"And this man?"

"Raymond Jones became underboss but he was a lieutenant until recently."

"And this man?"

"Charles Cores. He wasn't arrested in this raid. He's still out there. He's a nobody lieutenant out of Scranton or Pittsburgh, Pennsylvania."

"And this man?"

"His name is Aaron Gaston. He was killed in a bombing done by me from the orders of Mr. Johnson."

"Why?"

"It's a long story."

"Go on, we've got time." The jurors laughed.

"Mr. Johnson was mad at Christopher Larkin because he wouldn't join our family. So a couple of years ago, we put a hit on him and we weren't successful. That started a war where Aaron Gaston's son little Aaron was killed. Mr. Larkin was supposed to kill him but for some reason he was taking a long time. So our family and their family got together and formulated a peace agreement. Aaron Gaston kept saying he was going to break that peace, so Mr. Johnson ordered him killed and I set it up with a lieutenant name Jeremiah Lewis and his little brother Michael or something."

"Is Jeremiah in this court room right now?" Kennedy asked.

"If he is he's probably ducking." The jurors laughed.

The entire defense table were sitting silently, staring, and jotting things down on small pieces of paper.

"Identify this man for the records, please."

"His name is Clifford Jones and he's a lieutenant by now. He's Mr. Johnson's go between to the streets as we speak. He used to visit us and pass messages between us during this trial."

"Is he present today?"

"He's got to be sitting in the spectators stand," Stewart said.

Big Cliff had walked out as soon as Michael Kennedy had started pointing to the chart that morning. He wasn't a dummy.

"And this man?"

"Morris Oliver. He disappeared nobody knows what happened to him."

"And this man?"

"Edward Gordon. He's dead. It was in the papers. I don't know the details."

"And this man."

"Michael Williams. Christopher Larkin killed him, but I don't know how."

"And this man?"

"Andre Harrington. Christopher Larkin killed him, but I don't know how. He was shot with a woman in an Atlantic City motel or something. I don't know the details. He was a nobody."

And this man right here?"

"That's Christopher Larkin. He was a lieutenant but he broke off and formed his own family. So we tried to kill him, but he survived and formed his own family."

"So, he's a boss?"

"Yes, he is."

"What sections does he control?"

"The entire state of New Jersey," Andrew Stewart said.

"Thank you, Mr. Stewart. There will be no further questioning." Michael Kennedy said.

The judge looked at the defense table. "Does the defense wish to cross examine?"

"Yes, we do, your honor."

"Okay, we'll recess today and cross examination first thing tomorrow morning." The papers ate it up.

Christopher was pissed. The thing that upset him the most was that he knew he would never snitch in his life. Why get involved in a business if you can't handle the consequences.

That weekend Christopher made his first move. Stewart Rose Company was located in Jewelers Row, the diamond district. When Mr. Stewart was alive it was his headquarters. Now that he was incarcerated and testifying against the family it was completely legitimate.

Sandra Connelly Stewart, Andrew Stewart Jr.'s wife was sitting behind the counter of the flower shop watching soap operas on television when the phone rang.

This job had to be done by a lieutenant. It was too important and serious.

Big Al, the newest lieutenant in the family walked into the flower shop pushing a handcart with empty boxes. He was wearing a brown uniform that resembled UPS. Mrs. Stewart looked up smiling. They received deliveries several times a day.

"Good morning," She said, and Alex reached into the box sitting on the top of the cart. He pulled out two Glock handguns and opened fire.

Mrs. Stewart was pregnant so when she started running it seemed like she was moving in slow motion. Alex shot behind her. He wasn't ordered to kill a woman; that was a no-no. He just wanted to scare who ever was working there.

Sandra started screaming her husband's name as she ran to the back, barely being missed by the shots. By instinct, he pushed the door close when he heard the shots and she exploded through it. He pushed the doors closed again and reached for his guns.

He waited a couple of seconds and ran out but he was met with a barrage of gunfire. He dove behind the counter and tried to wait until the shooting stopped.

Alex walked backwards while he was shooting at the counter and exited the store. A stolen getaway van was outside waiting for him. He jumped in it and sped away.

When Andrew Stewart got the news he went crazy. the F.B.I. had made a mistake and told him it was his wife but they were wrong. It was his son and daughter in-law. Fortunately nobody was hurt.

Chapter Forty Four Pennsylvania

Weekends Can Kill You

Two weeks after the shooting, pictures of several members of the Philadelphia family popped up in the paper as possible suspects in the attempted murder of Andrew Stewart's daughter in-law. Everyone wanted to know how could it be attempted murder when nobody was shot?

Animal, Blue and Animal's lawyer were standing at city jail bailing Animal on the gun charges they had received a couple of weeks earlier. Blue would have bailed him earlier but he wanted to let Animal detoxify. They needed him more than ever.

Andrew Stewart took his seat in the witness stand on Monday. He was pissed because one of the guys sitting across from that table had ordered somebody to shoot his shop up. He knew the message they were trying to send. The message was that they had other ways to get to him besides his wife, but he had come too far now and there was no turning back. Even if he wanted to withdraw his guilty plea it was virtually impossible. He would lose everything and still be running for his life when he came home. His son had gone crazy searching for suspects even when he was on duty.

Andrew told them just sell the shop, it was going to be sold anyway. The house was up for sale and they still had property, which Janine was collecting the rent on.

The bailiff swore Andrew in. This time he didn't look as relaxed. The event from the weekend had worn him down. This time when he took the stand the defendants were smiling at him and he wanted to jump from his stand and attack them.

"Mr. Stewart, have you ever murdered anyone before?" Leonard Lehman asked.

"Yes."

"What position did you hold in this organization, Mr. Stewart?"

"I was a lieutenant."

"Were you involved in drugs?" Lehman asked.

"Not really, the soldiers handled all of that."

"You stated previously that Mr. Larkin supplied your family, excuse me, organization with cocaine. Is that correct?"

"Yes, that's what I said."

"How could a lieutenant supply a boss? I don't understand. I thought a boss controlled everything?"

"He does, but Christopher Larkin's not a part of our family."

"That's not what this F.B.I. chart says."

"That F.B.I. chart's not correct."

"So you're saying that the feds made a mistake?"

"Basically."

"Mr. Stewart, can I get a yes or no? Did the F.B.I. make a mistake?"

"Yes."

"Mr. Stewart, you testified that Mr. Johnson was shot by a guy named Animal. Did you attend that meeting?"

"No."

"Did you witness the shooting?"

"No."

"So how can you testify about the shooting when you weren't even present?"

"Because Mr. Johnson told me personally who did it."

"Mr. Stewart, isn't it true that you tried to have Mr. Johnson killed because he headed your gambling operations and told you he would support you or Mrs. Stewart's drug business?"

"No, I never tried to have Mr. Johnson killed."

"You sure?"

"Yeah, why would I…"

"Thank you there'll be no further questioning."

"Objection, your honor, the witness did not complete his answer."

The judge looked over to Andrew. "Mr. Stewart, would you like to continue?"

"Yes, I didn't try to kill Mr. Johnson."

"Okay thank you Mr. Stewart," Mr. Lehman said.

Blue, Frog and Animal were driving around in Blue's brand new BMW. Besides that bullshit gun charge they had things were running extremely smoothly. As long as they didn't talk on the phone, in their cars or at their residences they were cool.

"So how you feeling boy?" Blue asked.

"Blue, that heroin was kicking my ass in there. Detoxing was a bitch. I'm gonna have to disappear and go to a drug program. I want to get my shit together. Your brother's gonna need me."

"You're right. What did your lawyer say?"

"I might have a federal indictment if they believe that bullshit that Black Rose is saying. I can't believe he's snitching."

"Why don't you fly down to Mexico to one of those six month drug rehabs on us. Come back clean and if the feds want to question you they can talk to your lawyer."

"I need to go to my wife's house."

Frog was driving. "You need to stay away from there until the heat fades."

"Well give me some money," Animal said.

"How much you need?" Blue asked.

"At least a grand."

Blue reached in his pocket and pulled out a stack. "This is five grand. Hold on to it; make sure you make it last for a week. I'm going to take you to my old apartment. You can hide there until we get that Mexico information."

"Cool," Animal said while taking the money.

Michael Kennedy and the rest of his colleagues were sitting in his office holding a meeting. "We have to find out who this Animal character is, arrest him and then convince him to cooperate."

Just as he was saying it, Robert Moby, a short African American agent walked into the door. "What's going on gentlemen? I have good news and bad news. Which one you want to hear first?"

One person said good news and one person said bad.

"Ah, fuck it. Here's the good news. I have a confidential informant who can identify Animal."

"So where is he?" Kennedy asked excited. This case was making him famous and he didn't want to lose it. He wanted to work the system like Rudolph Giuliani.

"The informant's in a drug program right now, but that don't matter. He gave me a party picture of Animal at a club, we ran it through our files and we came up with a name."

"What's the name?" Kennedy asked.

"George Grouse."

Kennedy snatched the picture. "Let's get this guy's information."

"Too late, I already did it. He was incarcerated but he got bailed yesterday."

"Do you have his address?"

"I sure do. It's right here." The agent passed Kennedy Animal's address.

After Blue and Frog dropped Animal off at the apartment he went over to the local drug block and bought a half ounce of crack cocaine, a half ounce of powdered cocaine, a quarter pound of skunk weed, and three bundles of dope. He was going to have a going away party to celebrate his getting clean. After he copped his drugs he caught a cab to the Pink Pussy and paid a couple of the girls to come back to his apartment to celebrate.

Animal and four shapely women were laying naked in the bed. Some of the girls smoked crack but only if it was in weed and nobody sniffed heroin until that day.

Animal had unprotected sex with all of them and the craziest thing about heroin was that it was supposed to keep your penis hard when you used it.

The phone rang and Animal reached over to get it.

When Lea realized he was up she grabbed his penis and placed it in her mouth. She started sucking on him while he talked on the phone.

"Hello. Blue what's up? Yeah I'll be ready.... What am I doing? Getting head by this bad ass light-skinned freak." He laughed after he said it. Maybe he wasn't going to go to rehab just yet. He was having too much fun.

"Yo, Blue hold on, listen to this." Animal put the phone down. "Sexy, chill for a minute." He grabbed the girl's hair and lifted her off of him. The other girls were still lying down.

"Get on your knees." he commanded. Animal lifted the phone. "Blue listen to this," he said, and then he grabbed himself and entered the girl from behind. She moaned out loud because of Animal's size, he was pretty big. Plus she wanted to impress him by making noise because she knew Animal wanted his friend to hear.

Animal placed the phone near her vagina and started pounding away. Her vagina made noise from him entering her. He slapped her on the ass.

"Yo, Blue, you hear that?"

Blue started crackling up. "You're crazy."

"No, you're crazy," Animal responded. "You need to come up here and get some of this free pussy. I got those bitches from the Pink Pussy Strip Club."

"Nah, I'm with my girl. I'll pick you up at eight, be ready. We've got work to do."

"Okay," Animal said hanging up the phone and returning to business.

Eight o'clock that night Blue and Frog picked Animal up at the apartment building. Blue's old apartment was one of the apartments Black left and the building was nice. There was a doorman and everything.

Animal walked out of the building dressed in one of the sets he had bought from Boyd's, a famous clothing store in Philadelphia.

They embraced. "What's going on?" Animal asked.

"I have to pick up this money from this clown that owes me," Blue said. He passed Animal a small caliber handgun. "Hold this and I'll get you something bigger in a couple of weeks. The dude didn't call us back about the rehab in Mexico."

"Thank God," Animal thought. Frog jumped in the driving seat, Blue got in the front passenger seat and Animal sat in the back seat. They drove all the way to Germantown outskirts, a quiet residential block that the guy that owed Blue lived on.

"Frog, park over there," Blue said. "Behind that car." Because it was winter and the area was quiet hardly anybody was out.

"Animal you alright?" Blue asked when they pulled over. Blue looked in the back, lifted his gun with the silencer on it and hit Animal in the chest twice. Animal's body shook from impact of the hit.

"Do it," Blue said. They both jumped out of the car. Frog opened the back door pulled the yellow canary out of his pocket and pried Animal's mouth open. He stuffed the bird inside and then started walking to the getaway car.

Blue opened the other and shot Animal in his head one more time. Then he walked to the get away car. They jumped in and sped away.

Chapter Forty five *Federal Courthouse Pennsylvania*

The Table Turns Again

After the prosecutors called their first and last witness defense called its one and only witness. When Leonard Lehman called Mr. Johnson to the witness stand the entire courtroom was shocked except the defendants. Andrew Stewart's and Albert Wagner's testimonies were extremely damaging and they were gonna have to do something serious to counteract it.

Mr. Johnson took the stand wearing a dark-colored suit with a plaid shirt and a conservative tie. If it wasn't for the bandage on his head he could have easily been mistaken for a distinguished lawyer working with the rest of the attorneys.

Mr. Johnson entered the witness stand and the bailiff swore him in. "Do you swear to tell the truth and the whole truth, so help you God?"

"I do."

Michael Kennedy was shocked. He was going to destroy Mr. Johnson as a witness.

"State your full name for the record please."

"William Marshall Johnson the third."

"Mr. Johnson, if you don't mind would you tell how old you are?"

"Seventy-one, seventy-two, no just kidding. I'm sixty-seven, but I'll be sixty-eight this November."

"Do you own any businesses?" Lehman asked. He was dressed in a nice three-piece suit. He bought most of his clothes from Boyds or Bloomindales in New York City.

"Yes, I do. I own a small construction company, real estate and various other businesses."

"Mr. Stewart and Mr. Wagner testified that you're the head of a criminal organization is that true?"

"Yes, it is," Mr. Johnson responded pouring himself a glass of water from the pitcher that was sitting on top of the witness stand.

Kennedy was shocked. The prosecuting team immediately started jotting things down.

Even some of the jurors began writing things down on the small note pads, the court had provided them.

"Mr. Johnson, what kind of activities did this organization participate in?"

"Gambling houses, numbers running, and whorehouses."

"Were you involved with narcotics?"

"Never. A lot of the younger guys wanted me to support them in the drug business, but I refused. I never wanted anything to do with drug trafficking."

"Were any of the older lieutenants involved in narcotics?"

"A couple of lieutenants were involved, but I had forbidden it. We were making too much money from gambling, prostitution and loan sharking."

Kennedy was sitting there shocked, but he knew what was going on.

"At the meeting where your were shot, can you fill us in on what happened?"

"Well, we were at this restaurant eating, waiting on Andrew Stewart and Albert Wagner to come in, (they were partners) when this man came in and shot me and Ernest Clark in the head."

"Do you see the man that shot you in the courtroom today?"

"No, I do not, but I know who it was."

"Who was it?" Lehman asked.

"Albert Wagner, Jr." Mr. Johnson responded and Kennedy jumped to his feet.

"Objection, your honor, the defendant is lying."

"Your honor, the witness is testifying under oath. Mr. Kennedy cannot interrupt that testimony because he is upset. When his witness was up here lying, even though I wanted to, I didn't interrupt."

The judge looked at them both. "Mr. Kennedy, do you have evidence to substantial that accusation?"

"No, I do not." Kennedy sat back down in his seat.

"Mr. Kennedy, you'll be afforded the opportunity to cross examine. You may continue ask questions at that time."

"Thank you, your honor."

"Mr. Lehman you may continue."

"Thank you, your honor. Mr. Johnson, why did Albert Wagner Jr., shoot you?"

"Because I had given his father a loan to finance his gambling business, but later I found out he was involved in drugs and I informed him that I wanted him to stop. He said he would but he never did."

"So he shot you because you wouldn't continue to finance his drug business?"

"Yes. I believe that was the reason."

"Mr. Johnson the F.B.I. has you on tape asking Mr. Wagner and Mr. Stewart to blow somebody up. Is that true?"

"Yes, it is, but I didn't mean literally. On the streets blow somebody up meant beat the shit out of them."

The judge used his mallet to hit his bench. "Mr. Johnson, I'm gonna ask you to refrain from using obscenities."

"I'm sorry, your honor."

"Thank you, Mr. Johnson there will be no further questioning," Mr. Lehman said. He had done the one thing he wanted to achieve and that was place doubt in the juror's minds. If one person doubted the prosecutor's case, they could win a mistrial or a hung jury.

Six o'clock that morning several F.B.I., D.E.A. and A.T.F. agents surrounded Animal's girlfriend's row house in north Philadelphia. They were dressed in black with skullcaps and black clothing that identified their agencies on the back.

Ralph Crane, the head agent, was on the walkie-talkie. "How we looking in the back?" he asked.

"Two seconds," was the radio response.

"Let's start the count off in one minute." One minute later he was counting in his walkie-talkie and they exploded into the door.

Animal's seventy-year old mother was walking around her living room drinking from a cup of coffee. When the agents burst through, she collapsed and had to be rushed to the hospital.

Two days after the last court-date Mr. Johnson was back in the witness stand being cross-examined by Michael Kennedy.

"Mr. Johnson, how are you doing?"

"I'm fine," Mr. Johnson replied.

"Two men testified you were the head of your own criminal organization is that true?"

"Yes and no."

"Yes or no will be fine, Mr. Johnson."

"Yes, I headed an organization that controlled gambling, prostitution and loan sharking but I've never committed murder and I've never sold drugs," Mr. Johnson responded upset.

"So the F.B.I. tape recorders are lying?"

"Mr. Kennedy the F.B.I. makes mistakes. They have Christopher Larkin listed as working for me and we have never conduct any kind of illegal business. He's only my friend, so yes, they make mistakes." A murmur went through the juror's stand.

"Mr. Johnson, after you found out that Mr. Lockport and Mr. Gaston were killed in bombings, why weren't you heard reprimanding them?"

"Because I was afraid that they might try to attack me again."

"If you were so afraid of them attacking you, why did you continue to do business with them?"

"Mr. Wagner and Mr. Stewart are not the kind of gentlemen that you stop doing business with if you want to live. Don't you see my head?" Mr. Johnson asked and the defense table laughed. Not because Mr. Johnson was funny but that he was reversing everything, and Kennedy was foolish enough to continue.

Kennedy turned around and glanced towards his table and he could tell by their faces they wanted him to stop before he ruined himself.

"Thank you, Mr. Johnson. There will be no more questions." Kennedy walked back over to the prosecution table pissed.

He glanced over at Lehman and Kraft. They were smiling. He wanted to spit up, that's how upset he was.

Chapter Forty Six New Jersey & Pennsylvania

Hit Him Again, Sam

Taylor Construction and Labor Co, was located in Corey's house on his property in Galloway Township, New Jersey. The area was recently developed and extremely nice. Corey lived a couple of houses away from a record executive and his brother in a quiet Cul de sac, they were the only African Americans in the entire area.

"Frank when do you want to set up the next commission meeting?" Corey asked. They were sitting in his kitchen having breakfast before they went to Christopher's last court date. Mr. Johnson's testimony had strongly damaged the prosecutor's case and the others had a possibility of being released.

"If Christopher doesn't come home I want to do it next week." Franklin said.

"Did you bring the rest of Christopher's money?" Corey asked. He hoped the kitchen wasn't bugged and if they did talk about anything they never discussed anything incriminating.

"I bought a hundred grand. I'll give him the balance this week."

"Okay," Corey responded.

Azmar one of the soldiers in Mark's crew walked into the kitchen while they were meeting. "Mr. Taylor it's eight o'clock we should be leaving?"

"Frank I want you to drive with me and Mark." Corey said.

"What about my bodyguard?" Frank asked. He drove down with Frank Frets a lieutenant that ran several projects for him in Harlem. Frank was fucking his sister and they had become close. Everyone called Frank Frets "Beanie," so that they didn't confuse the too because they were always together.

"He can drive with me," the bodyguard said.

Just as they were saying it Mark appeared carrying a coat. "You guys ready? Which car we driving in?"

"Were driving the Frank's Lexus it's parked in my garage."

Frank walked to the living room where his lieutenant from New York was sitting. "Beanie let me talk to you for a second."

The bodyguard jumped up and walked over to him. "What's up?"

"You're driving with the bodyguards and I'm driving with Corey and them."

"You gone be okay?" Frank asked cautious.

"Of course homey."

Frank walked back into the kitchen and grabbed his jacket. Corey's garage was enormous. His Mercedes Benz and Frank's Lexus was parked side by side.

Frank reached in his pockets and removed his keys. When he looked at the reflection in his passenger side window, he saw Mark raise his hand. He couldn't believe it, they were going to kill him.

Mark pulled the trigger and let out two shots. Both of them hit Frank in the back of his head. His body slid to the ground.

"Hit him again." Corey commanded jumping into his car and turning on the engine.

Mark stood over Franklin and shot him four more times.

"Mark step back for me." Corey hit the button on his garage door and the door slide open. He drove the Mercedes out while the door quietly closed.

Mark was a professional, he was going to wrap Franklin's body in plastic and drop it off at the grocery store in Atlantic City. The same grocery store that they had robbed ten years earlier.

While all of this was going on Michael Kennedy the prosecutor for the federal case was addressing the jury. "Ladies and gentleman of the jury the defense is going to make the defendants out to be angels that have been falsely accused. The defense is going to make you think that the prosecution made a mistake. These men are innocent, that they were just running a little numbers. Ah they were running gambling houses and a little prostitution but these crimes within themselves are horrendous. If you believe that these men could do these crimes and not switch over to drug distribution and murder then you're crazy, and you've been tricked by high price lawyers. Mouthpieces that don't care about anything but getting their defendants free, even when they know they've done it. Well the government is asking you to put a stop to it right now. To show these men even though they think they're invincible they're not. When you leave this place and you read the papers you'll realize that you've done the right thing. Thank you." Kennedy walked over to the prosecutor's table and took his seat. He was proud of his achievement regardless of how the trial turned out.

The trial lasted from December 1989 until March 1990. Janine was outside washing her birthday present. Her father had told her to buy herself anything she wanted for her birthday because she had done so good with helping her mother handle her real estate business. She had truly made him proud. She refused to get the truck she really wanted but it popped up in front of her driveway on her birthday anyway.

Janine couldn't understand why her father was still involved with the crime business. After going over his records and everything she realized that her father was ten times wealthier then she originally believed. He owned property all over Pennsylvania. The only good thing about the trial was that her family had become closer. They were acting like they might even accept her boyfriend. They were gonna have to accept him now because him and Janine had recently gotten engaged and even though it didn't show she was three months pregnant.

Janine was outside in the driveway washing the truck. For the last couple of days it had been hot and she was outside washing the car with short shorts on. Her boyfriend was upstairs laying in the bed enjoying his Saturday off.

The commercial van pulled up a few yards away from Janine's driveway. Four men jumped out carrying automatic assault weapons. Janine glanced back when she heard the van come to a halt. "Oh shit." She attempted to run but they opened fire riddling Janine's body in the process. They didn't know she was pregnant, it wouldn't have mattered anyway.

While Janine was being murdered Mr. Lehman stood up in the middle of the courtroom. "Ladies and gentlemen of the jury I hope that you were able to see as clearly as I saw it. The prosecution is over zealousness presented a terrible case. They have a man here charged with being a lieutenant that even their witnesses testified that he was not a lieutenant and I hope you recognize their other mistakes. There were no drugs found. If you believe the witnesses these men are major drug traffickers but not a gram of heroin or cocaine was found, incredible. Yes there were two bombings and the defendant stated that men who were going to murder him earlier did it themselves. The gambling business is a tricky business but what happens is you promise two defendants charged with murder their freedom and they will come in and give you a show. They will exaggerate just like children because they're fighting for their freedom. Every man sitting at the defense table tried to acquire a plea agreement but the difference between them and the informants was they were not willing to lie. Ladies and gentlemen I'm not asking you to lie or for a favor. I'm asking you to make your decision based on the truth thank you very much." Lehman walked over to the table and took his seat.

Every single morning the restaurant Mrs. Wagner opened up the restaurant at seven o'clock every morning. When Andrew's shop was shot up police set up surveillance on the restaurant but once nothing else happened the police disappeared.

Mrs. Wagner pulled up to the restaurant in her brand new Lincoln Continental. When Albert was home they traded their car in every two years and nothing was going to stop her from living her life. She had agreed to sell the restaurant to her children because the Feds were moving her husband to Nevada on his release but everything else stayed the same. The same house, the same everything.

As soon as Mrs. Wagner parked and exited her car the van

pulled up. Four men jumped out wearing mask, they were carrying small lead pipes. Mrs. Wagner tried to run but they easily surrounded her and started beating up on her. Most of the blows were to the head. One of the men pulled out a gun while she was on the ground and pumped two bullets into the back of her head. She was dead before they jumped into the getaway car.

Chapter Forty Seven Atlantic City, New Jersey

As Time Goes By

It took the jury two days to deliberate, but when they came back their verdict surprised the prosecution. Nobody was found guilty of drug trafficking. Mr. Johnson was convicted on conspiracy to murder on both counts. Thomas McCant was convicted on gambling, along with Raymond Jones and Black. The gambling charges dropped their time from twenty years to ten and they were happy. Christopher was found not guilty of all charges. When the reporters asked the one juror that was interviewed why wasn't Christopher Larkin convicted on any of the crimes, she stated that there were no recordings of him on the tape. Plus, the witnesses stated that he didn't even belong to the organization, but the prosecution had charged him with the opposite.

Christopher and Tahwan were in their bedroom dressing for Franklin's funeral. A couple of days after the trial ended Franklin's body was found parked at the grocery store in the trunk of his car. One of the customers shopping at the store reported the horrendous smell to management and they called the police.

Beanie's body was also found in the trunk of a stolen car right outside of the Manhattanville projects in Harlem. His family had walked past the car plenty of times and didn't even know that he was lying inside. The housing police discovered his body while they were having it towed. Somebody noticed the smell.

"Who's picking me up to go to the funeral?" Tahwan asked. She knew the ritual. It was too unsafe for her to drive to the funeral with him especially since her cousin was found murder. There was about to be another war.

"Nobody's picking you up. You're riding with me." Christopher said fixing his tie. It felt good to be home. An hour later their car was there.

When Christopher and Tahwan exited the car followed by two bodyguards. Franklin's wife and children were sitting up front. Tahwan sat in the vacant seat that was left for her and Christopher.

Christopher sat. As soon as the priest finishing saying his words, Christopher stood up. It must have been a signal because John Bules, the Boss of Staten Island; Sean Carver, the head of Brooklyn; Peter Terrence, the head of the Bronx; Jean Dupree, the head of Queens; and Shawn Coles, the boss of Manhattan stood up. They walked over to Christopher.

Christopher walked over to Corty's tombstone. He was carrying three-dozen roses in different bundles. He laid the bouquets on Corty's grave, and the other two on Mr. Gaston's and his son Little Aaron's. "I miss you guys," Christopher said realizing how fortunate he was.

The other men surrounded him. "No talking on the phones, no talking in your houses and no talking in your cars. Next month we'll have a commission meeting if I think it's safe. Until then, everyone be safe. I guess my release can prove that this thing can be done. We've still got work to do. I don't want to hear about nobody going crazy buying cars and houses or none of that until we set up the next move. I'll try to visit you guys individually, but I think I'm gonna disappear for a couple of weeks," Christopher said.

"Welcome home baby," Crazy the head of Brooklyn said. Then they embraced. There had been peace in New York for the last three years now, but before that, it was hell. Christopher had smoothly and quietly put things in order.

Flashback 1976

You think I'm bullshitting? This boy gon' be just like his father," Smash said. He was a car thief and ex-heroin addict that terrorized the South Jersey streets with Christopher's father. They were first cousins.

"Well, you see what happened to his dad. He married that broad and went straight. If that ain't some sissy shit. I've never seen any," David the owner of the pool hall said.

They were speaking in front Christopher like he wasn't even there.

"Yeah, but his father was the smartest mother fucker in the world. All he needed was a couple of jobs and he had enough to quit."

"I can quit right now if I want to," David said insulted that his friend wasn't recognizing his success.

"Yeah, but you know what I'm talking about Dee. Some people just got it. If we can train this kid he's gonna be a bad mother fucker."

"We'll see when we reach this rest area," David said.

"You saw my nephew's work when we were in Club Harlem.

The entire club was under tables when the shooting started and this mother fucker was sitting there like nothing happened. I didn't even see him flinch," Smash said. He was in the passenger's seat fixing himself a needle. He was short and dark-skinned with enormous eyes, the eyes that were a trademark in his family. Smash took a lighter and heated the spoon with the heroin in it. Then he drew the heroin up with a needle. Five seconds later he was shooting it and moaning like he was having a orgasm.

David looked at him and then at Christopher. "You might be sharp like your father, but if you shoot heroin like your uncle you'll be nothing but a junkie." David and Smash laughed after David made the comment.

Ten minutes later they were on the highway. It was five o'clock in the morning. It hadn't got light out yet because it was winter. David pulled his car next to the truck. "That one, that one right there."

Franklin, John Martin and another group of guys were sitting in another car. They had followed them.

Christopher and his uncle Smash jumped out of the car. They were wearing grey uniforms. Smash walked over to the driver's side of the freight carrier. He snatched the door opened. "Get the fuck out the car."

It was one of those trucks that transported brand new cars to dealerships. The car tires had never even set foot on the ground before. None of the cars had more than factory test driven mileage on them.

Smash and the driver started wrestling. The driver was one of those southern, alcohol drinking hill billy that did nothing but drive trucks, fuck trucker girls and drink all night, and he was also strong as an ox from working with shipments and labor jobs all his life.

Christopher quietly walked around the corner and yelled, "Get off of him?"

The white boy looked back, turned around and decked his uncle with another solid punch.

Christopher raised his gun and shot the driver right in the ass. "Ah!" the driver screamed. He jumped up and tried to run but Christopher shot him four more times in the buttocks and he collapsed.

"Christopher no! What and the fuck's wrong with you?" His

uncle was on his feet and jumping in the cabin of the truck. Christopher jumped in on the same side, then climbed over his uncle to the passenger's seat. His uncle revved the truck up and they sped away. They drove the truck all the way to the inlet and parked it in a garage that George Crouch owned. Once they were there they placed fake license plates on the cars and drove all twelve of the cars to Philadelphia where Christopher's uncle Smash. operated a chop shop with his partners. Christopher's take was three thousand dollars.

When he came back, he got his uncle to purchase nine thousand dollars worth of scrambled heroin from his Philadelphia contacts. Three weeks later Christopher and his partners had turned the nine thousand-dollar investment in heroin into twenty-five grand.

That evening when Christopher went home he was arrested and charged with highjacking. Some informants on the street and told the police that Christopher's uncle was involved with a highjacking and shooting. They arrested Smash and Christopher to shoot that guy that was Christopher's stupidity.

Christopher left his share of the money with Franklin and John Martin, his girlfriend's cousin. He wasn't there when his girl graduated or lost their first baby from stress, and he wasn't there to see her off to college. He was incarcerated for the next three and a half years.

Flashback 1982

Christopher, John Martin, Mark, Lynn and Lawrence Timberlake, the family's Pleasantville lieutenant, were driving in Christopher's brand new Lincoln Continental. Shawn was a short nice looking light-skinned dude who controlled all the bars in Pleasantville for the family. Even though he was only eighteen he had been working with Mr. Gaston for years and he was a loyalist.

"How's everything going in Pleasantville," Christopher asked.

"Everything's cool." Larry was a hot head that Christopher was trying to teach to control his anger. Just a couple of days earlier he nearly beat a guy to death for owing a couple hundred dollars. He had a strong crew, a massive dude name Jamil and another pretty boy named Brian.

"You watching your temper."

"I'm trying to," Timberlake replied.

"Well the next time somebody agitates you let us handle it," Christopher said. He knew the Timberlake boy had a lot of potential. He knew how to get the money he just needed to learn to control his anger. "Everyone deserves a second chance," was Timberlake's favorite saying.

"Chris, I can handle my own problems."

"I know that but I want you to lay back. We're making a lot of fucking money, ain't we?"

Timberlake smiled on that one. "Yeah we killing them."

"I have to make it back to the city," Christopher said and everyone shook hands.

Christopher jumped on the Atlantic City expressway and they were in the city before he knew it.

"Go past the bar. I have to pick up this money," John Martin said.

"You know I don't like taking the car past the bar." Timbuktu was hot and the police were crazy around there. Nobody knew that Christopher had a brand new 82' Lincoln Continental and he wanted to keep it that way.

"Okay, then just drop me off."

Christopher pulled the car on Adriatic Avenue and John Martin spotted him. "There he goes." He couldn't believe his eyes.

"Who?"

"Mr. Joe, the mother fucker I told you was molesting my little sister. The mother fucker that was fucking my Mom and when they locked him up, she wouldn't testify against him. That nigger gon' be living in my house tomorrow, mark my words."

"Not if we get him now," Lynn said. This was his first time hearing the story.

They looked at each other. "Christopher, you packing?" Mark asked.

"I sure is," Christopher responded in slave talk. Everyone's adrenaline started racing.

"Let's get him then, for Joanna," Mark responded.

"John you gonna do it?" Christopher asked.

"Yeah."

"Let's hit him on the street then," Lynn said. This was gonna be his first killing.

"No, you crazy? This is a brand new car and I ain't getting rid of it. If we gon' hit him on the streets, let's follow him to a dark are," Christopher said and that's exactly what they did.

Joe, who had just copped a bag of dope from the spot Christopher controlled, walked all the way from Timbuktu to Ike's Corner on Center Street. When he got to Center Street he walked down the block and entered an abandoned building.

Christopher pulled the car next to the building and everyone jumped out. "Mark watch the car."

"Fuck! I want to see this shit."

"No, we need a look out. Lynn guard the door and make noise if somebody comes." Lynn stood near the door.

Christopher and John Martin walked up the creaky steps of the abandoned building. Chris and John removed their guns and held them by their sides.

They walked into what use to be a bedroom. It was small and musky smelling from years of abandonment and neglect.

"Johnny Boy, is that you?" Mr. Joe asked. He was sitting on a wooded crate with a heroin needle sticking from his arm. "What you doing with that gun? Boy, you better get over here and suck my dick." He laughed after he said it.

John raised his gun, but his hands were shaking uncontrollably. Christopher was waiting for him to pull the trigger.

"Hit him Jay. Let's get out of here."

"Did you tell your friends I was fucking the shit out of you and your mother." Mr. Joe stood up and he was enormous. He had obviously been in jail working out. He was six-three maybe two hundred and fifty pounds of muscle.

John wasn't saying anything he was just holding the gun shaking with tears running from his eyes.

Mr. Joe took one step closer. "What's wrong? I'm gon' fuck you and your Mom again or your little sister if she's old enough now. Hell, I've got principles," He said with a smirk on his face.

He started walking towards them and Christopher raised his gun and let off four shots. All of them hit Mr. Joe in his chest and he fell over a pile of trash or wood. Christopher couldn't tell because it was dark, but he was still alive because he was moaning.

"Finish him, John," Chris said.

They walked over to the lump on the ground. John was still shaking. Mr. Joe was looking up at him smiling. He blew John a kiss. "I love you. Tell everybody I broke your virginity," and then he smiled.

Christopher held his gun above Mr. Joe's face. Out of nowhere, Mr. Joe opened his eyes and grab Christopher's leg in an attempt to flip him over. Christopher jumped, but didn't move. He just emptied the rest of the clip in Mr. Joe's body.

Two seconds later the silence that they were in was broken and they came to. "John let's get out of here," Christopher said. He took John's gun and put it in his waist, and then they walked down the creaky steps. When they got outside Lynn and Mark were in the car with eyes as big as frying pans.

"Come on," Lynn yelled through a cracked window. "Did you get that mother fucker?"

"He's dead," Christopher said. "Take John home. John, throw your clothes away you probably got gun powder on them." John didn't even respond. He just sat in the back of the car quietly crying.

Christopher went home and took a shower. After that he threw his clothes in his neighbor's trash. Killing somebody felt weird, but in away the killing was justified. So much had changed since he came home in 79'. He didn't know the course that his life was going to take, but he knew it would never be the same. One of his friends had been molested by another man, he was gonna have to protect his children. Little Christopher was three and Tahwan was pregnant with twins. He was hoping it was boys. He never wanted to have a daughter. All boys, that's all he ever wanted.

FBI CHART Christopher Larkin Crime Family

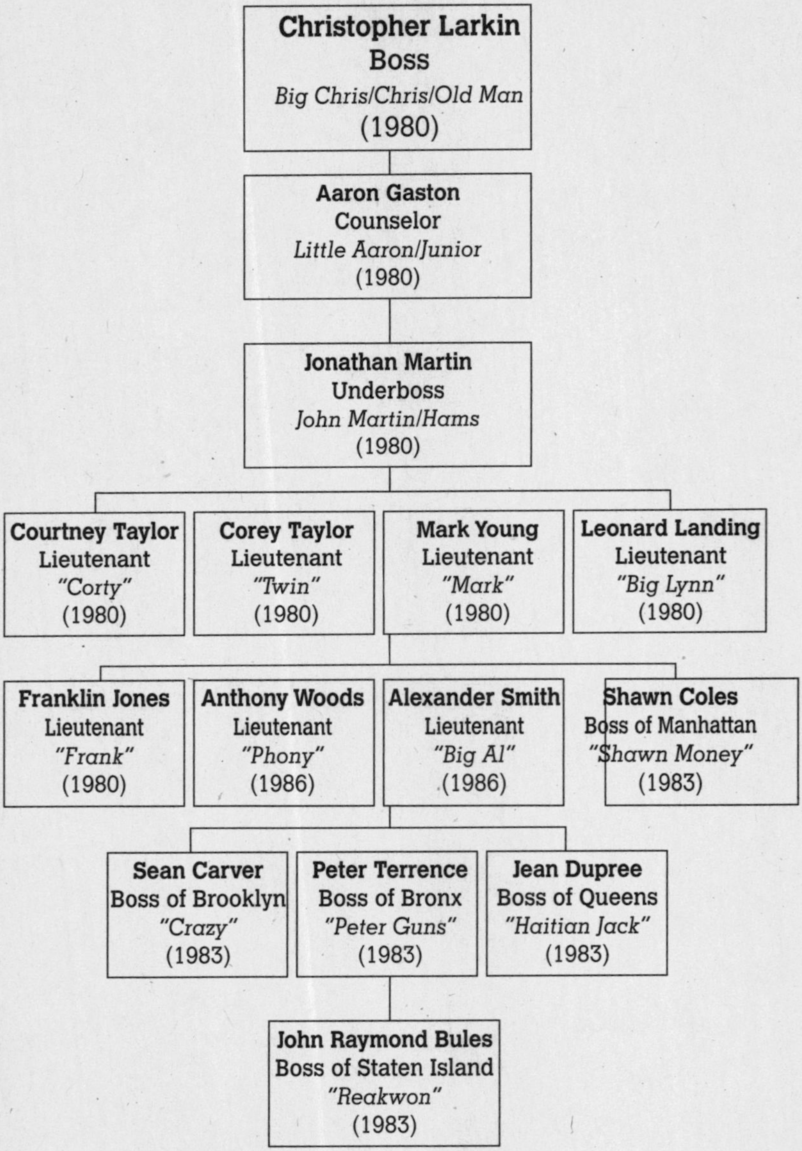

New York Organization included because of Christopher's influence over them.
Year states time brought into organization

FBI CHART William Johnson Crime Family

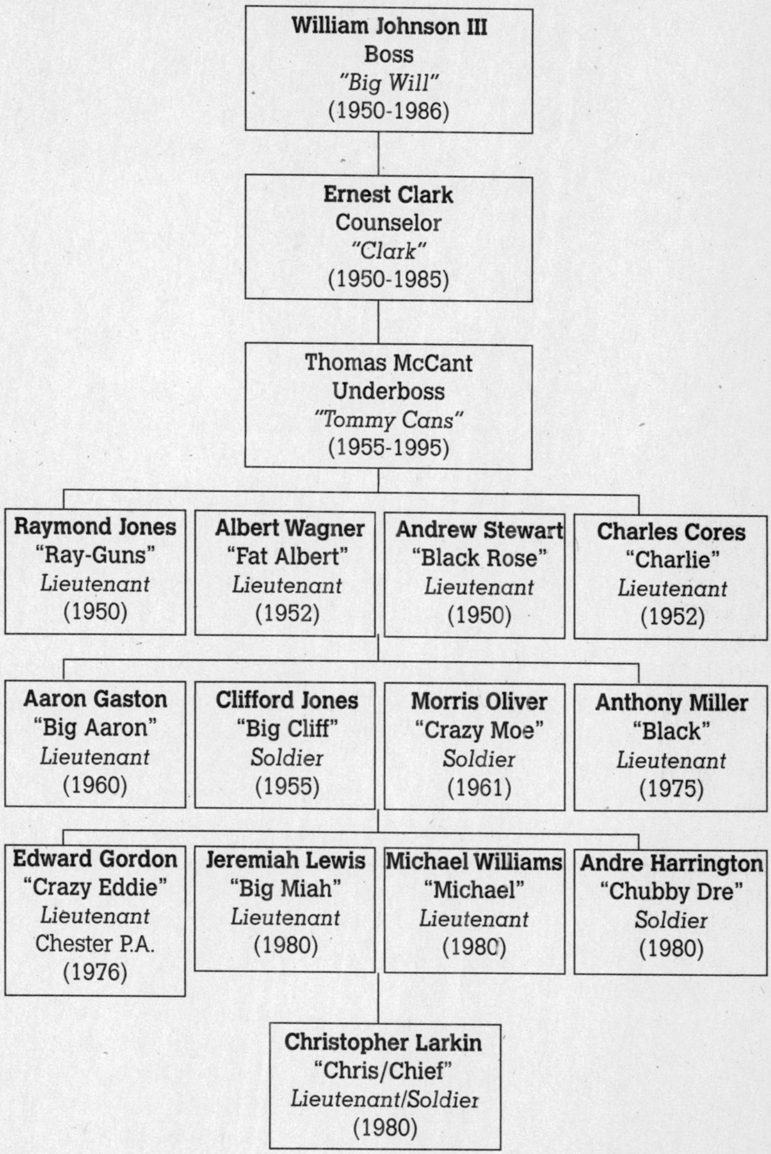

not listed: Scranton Pennsylvania Lieutenant or Pittsburgh Lieutenant because incarcerated.

Acknowledgements

Meet The Mob

Al Humdulillah, Animal, A&B books, Azmal my street brother, Bilal, Babette, Bubba big daddy Kane, Big Boo, Beanie, Beck, Bookmasters, Carmen, Aunt Cynthia, Cavario Don-Diva Magazine, Dexter Culture Plus, Caprice (Conflict), Choppy, Aunt Connie, Aunt Evelyn, Uncle Coty, Dupree & family, Curly hair Dana, Dawn, Jahna, and Inayah (my baby). Derek Brock, Mutual Cab Co., Duke, Daryl, Victor, Wendy, Bobby Levy, Diaab, Khadijah, D.X., Teeky, Danita, Mrs. Ernestine, E-love rest in peace, E.B. Lee, Arty Feds Mag, Fahiym, Farad, Gwen, Garland, Charmaine, Robin, Little Jay, Gabriel | 42nd&3rd , AVD Graphics I love you guys, Mr. Price | 125th& Lennox, Hawkins | Smith St Brooklyn, Mrs. Mimi, A Hope Austin, my sisters Hope, Indra, Kim, my brothers Diaab, Kareem and Juice. Hasan Salaam, Shannon Holmes, "Be more Careful," Omar Tyree, Terri Woods, Michael Presley | "Black Funk Publishing," one of the realist people in the industry. Vicky Stringer, "let this be the reason," Bro. Jay, Jayrock, Steven Biko aka Khaiym, Corey Smallwood **for holding his head**, Jayel **for holding his head**, Jacque and the barbershop crew, Vic the barber King, Omar, Abdul, Reece, and Jay-Love. There's only one Jay-love baby. Jamal Bro-**Jay's brother**, Kia, my Muslim brother Rashad aka Tom McCant, NY Kev, Mike Ses, Kemba, Kristy, Connecticut Kev, Mr. Kilcoyne, my heart O'dume (beautiful person), Lemmie, Phony, Alex and Dashuan (I'm so proud of you four), Black Malcolm my Atlanta people, Muhammed, Mike Lee, Merv, Black Rock, Wenny, Nadir Muhammed, Polite, Patrice, Rah-soul, Mr. Perry, Anthony Pitts, Pooh Ananda, Big Rell, Rahiym Sallahuddin, Rob Brutus white plains road the Bronx, Reg white, Reg Barnes, Rahman, Raheem Cherry, Simeon, Ras Dan, Mrs. Asher, Big Sean Timberlake, Ms. Tracy, Tknowa, Tyrsa, Titico, Chandra Sparks Taylor, Tahwan and Najwa (my baby), Vicky Dehart printing, Mark McCollough, Tibah, Vic, Wallerby for the computer, Sadiiq B. Jetter, Wali, Carl Webber, Wykil, Zambiek.

Mikell is currently working on his next two books: "Conflict of Interest" arriving September 2003; and "Black Mafia II & III: Conspriracy" arriving 2005-2006.

Order a great book

Please send me ___ copies of Black Mafia. I have enclosed $13.95 US for each book plus shipping ($4.00 for each book).

Name ____
Address ____
City ______________________ State ________ Zip __________
E-mail ____
Phone ______________________ Fax ____________________

ITEM	QUANTITY	AMOUNT

Subtotal ________
Tax ____________
Shipping ________
Total ___________

Mail your payment and this form to: Stepping Stone Publishing, PO Box 567 Atlantic City, NJ 08404. Please make all checks or money orders out to Stepping Stone Publishing.

Please put me on your mailing list to receive information about other Stepping Stone Publishing products.